SUSPICION

Also by Julia Grice

Jagged Light
Suspicion
Tender Prey

JULIA GRICE

SUSPICION

TOR®

A TOM DOHERTY ASSOCIATES BOOK
NEW YORK

A Tor Book
Published by Tom Doherty Associates, Inc.
175 Fifth Avenue
New York, N.Y. 10010

Tor® is a registered trademark of Tom Doherty Associates, Inc.

Library of Congress Cataloging-in-Publication Data

Grice, Julia.
 Suspicion / Julia Grice.
   p.   cm.
 "A Tom Doherty Associates book."
 ISBN 0-312-85185-5
 I. Title.
PS3557.R4873S8   1992
813'.54—dc20   92-23030
                                                    CIP

First edition: October 1992

Printed in the United States of America

0 9 8 7 6 5 4 3 2 1

All of the characters in this book are fictional. If any one resembles a real person, either in name or in physical characteristics, it was only accidental, not intended in any way. The town of Clyattville is fictional.

I would like to thank my wonderful editor, Melissa Ann Singer, for her enthusiasm and good advice.

An additional thanks to the Detroit Women Writers, a group of professional women writers which celebrated its 90th birthday in 1990. These women became my friends, mentors, and teachers. Most especially would I like to thank the late Vera Henry, who believed in my talent and was a gifted teacher.

SUSPICION

PROLOGUE

The working-class neighborhood was a tapestry of sound. Dogs barking, kids yelling, a TV set, someone revving up a Harley-Davidson. Traffic from Woodward Avenue created a constant, low-level roar. An ambulance whined toward William Beaumont Hospital, only blocks away.

For eleven-year-old Stacey Orchitt, whose lavender Kmart bike was flung down in her aunt's driveway, this was the familiar background of life, too normal to be noticed.

The immediate question was the whereabouts of her Aunt Abby. Stacey's mother had recently bought her an embroidery kit and the girl was anxious to show it off to her favorite aunt, who was twenty-six years old and worked as a medical transcriptionist at the hospital.

She stood on the back stoop of Abby Tighe's modest yellow aluminum-sided bungalow, pounding and rapping at the screen door with increasing persistence. She was a thin girl, with wide blue eyes that looked too big for her. In her hand she clutched a small embroidery hoop, from which dangled a white cloth and several colored threads.

"Aunt Abby!" she shouted. "Aunt Abby! I got some more 'mbroidery! My ma got me all the colors, she got me two cats to do! At Kmart's!"

Although the screen door was slightly open—in fact, there was a large, tricornered tear in it that Stacey had not seen before—no response came from within the house.

"Aunt Abby!" Stacey shouted, her face against the screen. "Can I come in? I gotta—I wanta show you . . ."

Still there was no response from inside the house.

Now that the screen was open Stacey noticed a funny smell. Like the wrapper from a package of meat, left out too long, the girl decided. Not really ucky, but not nice either.

Maybe Aunt Abby had to go into work today.

But it was Saturday morning. Her aunt didn't work on Saturdays.

The eleven-year-old took a tentative step across the threshold. When she was home, Abby usually played the stereo—she liked the Stones and Aerosmith. But Stacey didn't hear any music now. Or any sounds, really, except for a couple of buzzing flies.

"Aunt Abby?" she called. She took one step further into the back hallway, the embroidery hoop trailing from her right hand. Her eyes traveled downward to the linoleum block floor, and that was when she saw the first piece of broken glass.

It came from one of Abby's new, blue-rippled drink glasses. A jagged half-circle of blue, rimmed with blood around its edge.

Stacey stared at the piece of glass. Had Aunt Abby dropped a glass and cut herself? Maybe Abby needed a bandage.

"Auntie?" she called again tentatively, and stepped into the back hallway. The enclosure was cluttered with jackets hanging on plastic hooks, folded laundry, a paper bag full of returnable pop bottles, and a stack of old newspapers. The top newspaper had a picture from last week, Stacey noticed.

A reluctance came over her.

The house felt . . . funny. Like her aunt wasn't here and hadn't been here in months. Which was silly because they had baked chocolate-chip cookies only four days ago. She began taking tiny, baby steps that led her into the kitchen. The kitchen was small and the cabinet doors were freshly painted in light blue, Abby's favorite color. But the room no longer smelled deliciously of chocolate. In fact, Stacey saw, the cookie sheets were still on the table, greasy circles showing where the cookies had been. One metal sheet lay on the floor, dented and twisted. It looked as if Hulk Hogan had bent it in his two enormous ham hands. There was a spatter of blood on it, and a dab of dark-red, fleshy matter.

"Oh," the girl mumbled, stricken.

Stacey's reluctant gaze traveled across the floor, which was a welter of smashed glasses, plates, sugars and creamers, a blue ceramic candlestick. A bare path through the mess looked as if something had been dragged through it. The blue doors hung open, some smashed halfway off their hinges. Others were splintered and broken.

Something had hit them.

Something big and terrible.

Stacey caught her breath, too frightened to scream. Rolling her eyes to the right, she saw a smudged red handprint on the edge of the door that led to the dining room.

"Aunt . . . Abby?"

Pushing back her terror, Stacey walked across the demolished kitchen into the tiny dining room. This room, too, had been destroyed, as if by a madman with a hammer—the table smashed in upon itself, splinters remaining of what had once been prettily polished oak. Great holes had been whacked into the wallboard. Blood was sprayed on the walls in wild droplets; there were bloody handprints and long streaks that looked as if they'd been made by terrified, scrabbling fingers.

"AUNT ABBY! AUNT ABBY!"

Crying, Stacey raced through the eerie, damaged room to the living room. It was empty, still intact.

She hurried down the short hallway that led to the bedrooms. The little TV room was as she had seen it last, neatly arranged with needlepointed pillows. Abby's bedroom, too, was untouched—the plain, neat room of a woman who expects nothing to happen. Her aunt's teal-colored chenille bathrobe, hanging from a hook, seemed to mock her. Abby loved that robe, and wore it every day, even in hot summer.

"AUNT ABBY!"

Panic overtaking her, the child ran out the way she had come in. In the kitchen she tripped on a broken plate and cut her knee. Blood ran down her leg as she exploded out the screen door.

"MA! MA!" she screamed into the September morning.

Inside the house, a fly had found the crumpled cookie sheet and was crawling onto the largest hunk of human skin, its proboscis and front legs working feverishly. There was no other sound inside the bungalow.

It was empty.

Abby Tighe was somewhere else.

"Boy," said the voice in his head. *"Boy, you are stupid."*

"I'm not, Pa," he said back.

"You are. You're a stupid little shit who is an affront, an insult to God."

"I'm not. I'm not."

"Sin," said Pa. *"They are all sinners, those sluts, sinful and wicked."*

Shut up, he tried to tell him, but the words congealed in his thoughts.

"They have to be punished before God can cure them," Pa grated in his ear, the voice familiar, part of his heartbeat. *"A sign! A sign! God creates sin! You know that, boy, you know how I taught you, you know the truth, you know it don't you, boy? Don't you know it?"*

"Yes," he said.

"You know it because I taught you! God makes, God takes. Yes, yes, Lord. GOD IS EVERYTHING, BOY, GOD IS WICKEDNESS AND GOD IS STRENGTH. GOD'S HAMMER BEATS DOWN ON THE SINNER AND OPENS HIM TO HIS EVERLASTING LOVE. GOD'S HAMMER IS HOLY, BOY! DO YOU HEAR? HOLY! HOLY!"

"Yes, Pa," he said, blinking the tears out of his eyes.

ONE

Cici Davis hated quarrels that hung in the air and weren't resolved. Maybe that was why she'd done the impulsive thing and decided to walk down the four blocks to Bryan's.

It was a brisk September night that already tasted of rain and Halloween. A huge moon hung over the tree-lined suburban street, its champagne-colored light creating sharp contrasts in light and shadow. Bryan's Colonial stood on a cul-de-sac with two others, all different versions of the same basic floor plan.

Still wearing her blue DanceFit sweatshirt from aerobics class, Cici paused at the curb on the opposite side of the street, startled to see her fiancé, Bryan Wyatt, unloading something heavy from the back of his Aerostar van, which had been backed up to his garage.

It looked like Bryan was hauling a rolled-up rug out of the back of the vehicle. It thumped to the ground and he dragged it toward the opened door of the garage. But the cylinder of rug seemed oddly shaped, too fat in the center, and too heavy.

Cici had been about to cross the street, but something

made her pause in the concealment of a shadow cast by a triple planting of medium-sized pines. Maybe it was the alert way that Bryan kept looking around, his eyes scanning the street. Or maybe it was the eight-foot-long, cigar-shaped bundle, which was folded in a way that made her think of something else . . . a person, bending at the waist.

A person, wrapped up in the rug.

Oh, come on, she ordered herself, jamming her hands into the pockets of her sweatshirt. *It's just a silly trick of the light. Harvest moons always do funny things.*

"Bryan!" she called, waving. "Bry!"

But he had finished hauling the rug through the two and a half car garage to the back door of the house, and the automatic garage door was already rumbling down.

Cici stepped out of the shadows and started across the street, formatting her apology in her mind. She and her fiancé had had a little tiff the previous day—nothing serious. But since Bry only lived four blocks away, she'd decided to walk over and clear the air with him.

She padded up the front walk, her Reeboks noiseless. The window set in Bryan's front door was of Victorian etched glass, carved in a swans-and-curlicue pattern. Below it, affixed to the door and somewhat spoiling the effect, was a security service sticker.

ARMED RESPONSE, read the notice.

Cici rang the bell and waited impatiently for Bryan to answer. She could see her reflection in the window glass, her blond hair still rumpled by aerobics, her high cheekbones and full mouth sculpted by shadow. She was frowning slightly, she saw, and carefully straightened her face.

Several minutes passed before she finally heard sounds in the hall and saw him through the glass. A tall, handsome man of thirty-four, Bryan looked like one of the models in the Hudson's/Dayton catalog, with that same square-jawed, clean look, and full, blondish hair excellently cut. He looked startled to see her, perhaps even annoyed.

"Hon? Cici?" She noticed he was slightly breathless from carrying the rug. "It's nearly ten-thirty."

She probably should have called instead.

She gave him a swift hug, anxious to get the apology over with. "I just got back from aerobics," she explained in a rush. "I couldn't let it wait until morning to call you—I had to talk. I'm so sorry about what Aaron said last night. He was terribly rude."

Aaron was her fourteen-year-old son. A good kid, bright and warm and sweet and funny. But he was having trouble accepting Bryan—a good deal of trouble, if the truth were known, far more than Cici had ever envisioned when she accepted Bryan's engagement ring four months ago.

"He called me dickhead," Bryan remarked dryly. "Or was it dickface?"

Cici flushed. Aaron's brightness and sweetness had certainly not been in evidence last night. "Oh, God! Please, Bry . . . I really *am* sorry. Please accept my apology. I don't know what else to say. I love you so much. I'll talk to him tonight, I promise. He won't do it again."

Bryan's frown faded and after a pause of several seconds he finally enfolded her in an embrace. They stood leaning into each other, Cici's 5'7" frame fitting against Bryan's 6'2" height as if made for it. She wrapped her arms around him hungrily. God . . . she had known him for five months and she still couldn't get enough of him. His lean, health-club muscles and spicy aftershave mingled with the spice of his own skin and a faintly sharp odor of perspiration.

"Oh, I love you," she murmured into his shoulder.

He seemed preoccupied as he answered, "I love you, too, honey."

"Forever?"

"Always, Cic."

Behind them one of Bryan's grandfather clocks was ticking, providing a counterpoint to their breathing. In the other room, other clocks could be heard, each with a different, rhythmic tick-tock. In a few minutes they would chime the hour, a cacophonous sound she would always associate with lovemaking.

"He's going to settle down," Cici promised finally, pulling back a little. "It's just that he's still angry about the divorce. It's only temporary, Bry."

Bryan nodded. "I hope so."

"He will, he will. Aaron is a good person, he really is, deep inside. But you know how boys try to hide all of that. Don't you remember how it felt to be fourteen? Wasn't it just a crazy age? You loved, you hated, you worried about things, you were afraid to grow up?"

But Bryan began to kiss her neck, cutting off their conversation. He had a way of doing that sometimes, when she started talking to him about feelings. A self-help book Cici had read called him a "closed" type of man. It was a part of him that Cici was working on. She felt sure that as their intimacy developed, Bryan would open up more. Marriage, she believed, would unlock a lot for both of them.

A few minutes later, they walked through to Bryan's large kitchen, which was newly decorated and immaculate. Even the stainless-steel sink had no watermarks or stains on its shiny surface. As Cici's sister, Jocelyn, said, any man who could keep a kitchen that clean had to be a good catch.

"Coffee?" Bryan offered.

She glanced at her watch. "Oh, good grief, it's nearly eleven! I can't. I told Aaron to be home at eleven on the dot. Did you buy a new rug?" she added as an afterthought. "I saw you unloading one from the van. I called to you, but you didn't hear me, I guess."

"Oh . . . yes, a very nice Kurdistan rug. I was in Northville today; we had a lunch meeting over there with the people from Ford. Afterward I saw this antique shop I hadn't tried so I stopped in. They had a very nice steeple clock by Chauncey Boardman, too. I bought it. It runs perfectly—a real find."

Cici relaxed a little. Bryan's collections included clocks, silver, cast-iron mechanical banks, music boxes, and four or five other items. He also owned several very expensive Oriental rugs.

"Honey," he added, tipping her chin up and planting a butterfly kiss on the end of her nose, "I didn't forget you either. They had a couple of nice pins. I got you one."

He pulled a tissue-wrapped object out of his pants pocket and carefully peeled away the paper. It nestled against the flesh of his palm, a springing puma done in onyx and silver, with

amethysts for eyes. Authentic Art Deco, she felt sure. It loo.
as if it had been plucked from the Duchess of Windsor's jewel,
box.

Cici gasped with pleasure. "Oh, Bryan! It's just lovely! It
looks so real!"

He smiled. "It is real."

"I mean—" She laughed.

The support staff at the agency where she worked were
openly envious of Bryan's gifts to her. The jewelry, the flowers
three or four times a week. His presents were always romantically
perfect, as if he was using them to say something he could not
put into words.

"It reminded me of you," Bryan added now, softly. "Pumas
are very beautiful, Cici, just like you."

Just then the clocks began to chime the hour. Large and
small mechanical *bongbongbongs* created a variegated cacophony
that sounded like special effects at Walt Disney World—a sound
that always charmed Cici. She loved the way two or three smaller
clocks trailed the bigger ones with tinier *bongs* as if hurrying to
catch up. Bryan's house was always alive with their clicks and
ticks.

She laughed again, happy that they'd made up, that there
wasn't going to be any tension between them. "I really do have
to go home, though," she added. "I set a curfew for Aaron and
I've got to make sure he's home. You know kids."

"Sure," he said.

"Bry?" She flung herself into his arms again, burrowing
close for one more kiss. She stood on tiptoe and gave herself up
to it, thinking that she was really so lucky, wasn't she? Out there
in the singles world, how many men like Bryan were there?

Damn few.

Meeting Bryan Wyatt had been massive good luck. It had
come at the lowest time in her life, a time when she didn't think
she'd ever have another man again.

Eighteen months ago, Cici had found a lump in her right
breast. The doctor said the tumor was in the nipple duct. To her
shock, this meant she couldn't have the humane lumpectomy

recommended by the women's magazines, but needed more radical surgery. Thank God, she'd arranged right away to have a good plastic surgeon operate along with the other surgeon.

Three operations later, she now possessed a reconstructed breast that looked amazingly smooth, rounded, high, and taut. She could even undress in the locker room at Vic Tanny among all those gorgeous twenty-two-year-old bodies and no one stared.

But that had meant nothing to Tom. Her husband of fifteen years had walked out on her while she was still in the hospital.

"It's too depressing" had been his weak apology. "I can't face it, babes. I know I'm a shit but I can't help it. It just seems too repulsive to me."

Deserted. Because of a cancer she had never asked for.

For months, struggling to get her life in order, Cici had swum helplessly in the anger, the rejection, the desertion, the fear. She was thirty-seven years old, and had had a mastectomy. It was a reality that terrified many men. Was she ever going to find another partner? Or would her surgery scare them all off, as Tom had been scared off?

Her sister, Jocelyn, felt that the surgery would be a good test for future men. "If he accepts the surgery, then he's a decent prospect . . . more than decent," she insisted.

It was a concept that terrified Cici. She felt paralyzed, incapable of trying again.

"Dammit, Cici," her best friend, Ann Trevanian, exploded one April evening, five months ago. Ann was tall, brunette, vibrant, and happily single. "You're turning into a major couch potato. I mean, we're talking *major* here. Watching 'Roseanne' is for rejects, not for you. You're a very, very pretty woman; you're still very desirable. You know you've got to get out and face it again."

It—as both knew—meant men. Dating again. Risking rejection.

Cici had felt a tightening in her stomach. "You mean like falling off a horse and getting on again? I can't. Ann, I'm really

not ready. I thought I'd wait another year before I even thou~~g~~
about—"

"Waiting a year is only an excuse," Ann scoffed. "Anyway,
I'm not asking you to *find* someone. I'm only asking you to go
to a meeting with me. You should socialize, mingle a little. You
haven't mingled in seventeen years, Cic."

"On the contrary, I mingle all the time at work. People are
my job, Ann." Cici was a job developer for an outplacement firm
that helped corporate executives get new jobs.

"Okay, so that means you're not shy. One night, Cici. Just
talk to a few people and then go home again. You don't have to
get laid."

"Ann!"

Ann grinned. "Good news, honey—nobody has to get laid
anymore unless they want to. AIDS has taken care of that, and
it's the one blessing to come from it. The men don't dare harass
us for sex anymore."

"I'm not . . . I mean, Ann . . . sex? I don't want sex. I don't
even really want a man."

"It won't hurt just to look."

"I don't want to look."

"*One* night," Ann insisted. "One harmless night."

The Friday Nighters, a local singles club, met at a banquet
hall called Vanelli's. There were more than fifteen hundred
members, Ann said. At various times, she had served on its
board of directors, and she still had a wide circle of friends there.

Tonight's speaker was an astrologer who talked about
cusps, moons, and planets. Cici sat at a table near the back of
the room, eyeing the others around her. Slim women in their
thirties. Heavy women in overblouses. Short men with mus-
taches. Amazingly handsome men with cool expressions. Some
of the men tried to make eye contact, but Cici quickly glanced
away. This was terrifying!

At about ten a disc jockey stationed at his equipment
turned on his speakers, and Tina Turner began to sing "Steamy
Windows." Within minutes, the dance floor was crowded with

gyrating couples. How had they even found partners that quickly?

The sight overwhelmed Cici. At work she was competent, considered top-notch in her field. Not only did she interact with hundreds of clients, executive-search firms, and companies, but she also taught classes in job search and did counseling. There wasn't anyone she couldn't talk to on an equal basis—in the safety of the workplace.

But here . . . what did you *say* to these milling people? Prospective lovers, if one wanted to be blunt. How to talk without advertising your vulnerability? Were there special "lines" you need to use, and if so, what were they? Would your choice turn away, rejecting you?

Even as she watched, a pretty woman of forty-eight or forty-nine did walk up to a gray-haired man and say a few words to him. The man shook his head, looking apologetic. Smiling, the woman walked away. Or was there a tightness about her face now, a shininess to her eyes?

God, she *had* been rejected.

What kind of jerk would reject a nice woman like that? The men here were dweebs. Her case of nerves rapidly developing into panic, Cici turned and started toward the door. She wasn't ready for this. She was totally out of place here.

"Quite a zoo, isn't it?" a male voice said to her left. "All the mingling and the posturing."

She turned nervously.

He was in his thirties, one of the better-looking ones, and tall. His appearance reminded her of a star she had seen in a movie recently. He had crisp, wavy blond hair that fell over his forehead, blue eyes, straight eyebrows, a patrician nose. A cuteness about his mouth.

Oh, definitely, *very definitely* attractive. Her hand went to her own blond hair, adjusting the curls that had been carefully moussed to look casual.

"I'm Bryan Wyatt," he said. "I don't like name tags so I never wear one. And you're . . ." He leaned closer to peer at her name tag. The woman at the door who had written it with a felt pen had atrocious printing and the name was nearly illegible. "Cici Davin?"

"Davis," she corrected. "And my first name's short for Cecilia. This is my first time here, as if you couldn't tell. I'm not sure I'm quite ready for single mingling yet. Actually I was just leaving."

"Leaving?" He looked regretful. "Could I at least buy you a drink before you go?"

She felt a delicious, nervous shiver overtake her body, racing from her groin up to her throat, where a pulse seemed to be jumping madly. William Hurt, that's who he looked like. "I . . . I like wine spritzers."

"Good. I'll be right back with it."

Later, in the ladies' room, she encountered Ann. Groups of women were clustered by the towel rack or preening in front of the mirrors. The enclosed space held the scent of hair spray, perfume, hope, and fear.

"Well, Cic," her friend said in the tones of one who wasn't the least surprised. "It looks as if *you* found a live one." Ann, who always found live ones, inspected her creamy complexion in the mirror, adding more blush with a sable brush.

Cici was torn between stage fright and her exhilaration that she had been noticed by a man like Bryan. He was actually interested. It was a terrifying idea.

"Yes. Oh, Ann . . . he's so good-looking . . . He wants me to have lunch with him on Monday at the Cooper's Arms."

"So go. You need to get out. And lunch is very safe. You'll meet him there, I hope. I've seen him here before. What's his name?"

"Bryan Wyatt. He's some kind of automotive engineer. His company makes passive seat restraints. He helps them open new plants; apparently it's a very good job. Ann . . ." Cici clutched at her friend's arm. "Ann, I don't know if I want to do this! I mean, my stomach is getting in a knot just thinking about it. What if . . . I mean, how . . . how do I tell him?"

About her mastectomy, she meant.

"You don't tell him anything, hon, not right now. You

don't have any obligation to talk about your personal things with someone you've just met. Maybe it'll be just one date anyway. Maybe it'll never come to that."

"Oh," Cici said, feeling dashed.

"Cic, just go and enjoy it. When you talk to him, really, really listen, though. Men say all kinds of revealing things, and you want to pick up on everything."

Cici laughed nervously. "You mean, in case he's a psycho or something?"

Ann's eyes glinted with a spark of her offbeat humor. "Maybe he's a guy that needs six different women a week, or he's a lingerie freak, or maybe he keeps whips and chains in his closet, or maybe—"

Cici giggled and threw a scrap of damp paper toweling at her friend, hitting Ann in the lapel of her teal-blue silk blouse. "I promise you, if his middle name is Norman Bates, I won't go out with him more than once." Then her mood grew more sober. "Seriously, Ann . . . I can't believe he really likes me."

TWO

Cici walked back home. The huge moon had risen further and hung overhead, the face of the "man in the moon" eerily clear.

The suburban neighborhood had settled down for a September night, TV sets flickering blue behind windows. A lone man walked a dog, calling to it. A jogger puffed past, wearing reflective tape on her jacket.

Cici smiled, her hand in her pocket closed around the onyx pin, which would look wonderful with the new suit she had bought last week. Bryan's taste was exquisite.

Five minutes later she had reached her own house, a trilevel shielded behind a mini-woods of young birches and a few pines and oaks. The little stand of trees looked dark and the leaves picked up a sudden night wind, giving a papery rustle.

Approaching, Cici could see by the sparsity of lamps switched on in the house, the same two she'd left burning, that her son, Aaron, was not yet back from his junior high football game. She'd have to talk to him, a prospect she dreaded. They'd already fought about Bryan several times, and she was afraid of driving her son even further from her.

She sighed and let herself in, putting the panther pin on the hall table next to a bouquet of deep red roses, sent by Bryan two days previously.

The phone rang, and she snatched it up, thinking it might be her son.

"Hello? Aaron? Where are—?"

"It's me, babe," said her ex-husband, Tom.

As always when she talked to the man who had abandoned her, Cici felt her heartbeat speed up uncomfortably and a swirl of nausea in the pit of her stomach.

He went on, in an aggrieved tone, "I tried five times and you didn't answer."

Did she have to explain her schedule to him? "I was at my aerobics class."

"Aerobics. You're always doing aerobics," Tom accused. "Are you trying to look like Jane Fonda?"

She didn't respond to the crass comment.

"Hey, I hope you do, Cic. Fonda looks wonderful and we don't want the wedding to fall through, right? Hey, just kidding," he added. "Just because I don't want to pay alimony for the rest of my life—"

"Tom—" she began angrily.

"Look," he interrupted. "I had something come up at work, we're crashing on a big project, and that's why I've called tonight."

"Why?" But she already knew the answer.

"Look, Cici, I know it's tough on Aaron, but he's a big kid, for Christ's sakes. He's almost fifteen."

She felt tears sting her eyes at the injustice of her son's treatment by his father, who couldn't even remember his age. "He had his birthday in May, Tom. That's four months ago. That makes him fourteen, not fifteen. You're not coming tomorrow, are you? You've got work again. Or is it your new twenty-two-year-old girlfriend? Is that what this is all about? You prefer to spend your time with her rather than with your son."

"Hey, enough guilt trip," Tom drawled.

But Cici, fueled by a year of divorce acrimony, couldn't stop. "I went up to parent-teacher conferences last week, and Aaron's teachers told me he's underachieving, that he's angry and defiant, that he acts out in class."

" 'Acts out'?"

"You know what I mean! It's not Aaron's fault we're like this. He didn't cause anything, but he's paying the price, isn't he? He's got a father who cancels half of—"

"Okay, okay, okay," Tom said. "I get your point, Cici. You don't have to dump all over me on behalf of Aaron. Do you want to know why I can't see him sometimes, why I have trouble? Because it's too depressing, that's why. Because I'm depressed the whole week before I see him, and the whole week after."

She held on to the phone, her words stopped in her throat.

You started it all! she wanted to shriek. *I tried to hold us together, but you couldn't stand being married to a woman who had a mastectomy. That "depressed" you, too.*

"So you're not picking up Aaron tomorrow, then?" was what came out of her mouth.

"No. I can't. Cici, have a heart, will you? I have a life to lead, we've got this huge push at work, I've been working six days a week—and that's no lie."

"Fine," she responded sarcastically. "I'll tell Aaron."

"Would you? Look, tell the kid I'll call him sometime next week. I'll get tickets to something—we'll go over to the Silverdome. Don't they have wrestling matches over there? I'll have my secretary call Ticketmaster this morning."

His secretary. She thought of a dozen replies, then bit down on her lip.

"Cici?" her ex-husband said.

"If you can't be a good father, at least be a mediocre one," she snapped. "And if you can't be a mediocre one, then don't hurt Aaron. It's all I ask."

She hung up in Tom's ear, banging the phone into the cradle with a crisp, plastic slam.

Still angry, she settled down at the kitchen desk to revise a report for her boss, Quint Flannery.

Over fifty percent of the agency's clients were getting jobs through the nationwide computerized job bank, Cici's own project. She frowned as she rewrote a section explaining this, her thoughts of Tom intruding again. No more feeling sorry for herself, she had vowed. She had Bryan now. Someone who accepted her surgery and still thought she was sexy.

As for Aaron, somehow she would get her son to accept her fiancé, and they'd try family life again. God . . . she wanted it to work so badly.

The phone rang again. Cici jumped for it.

"Cici? Your voice sounds positively snappish," her best friend said. Ann's rich voice laughed down the telephone line.

"I was just talking to Tom," Cici admitted.

"Tom Turkey, the major jerk of the western world."

"Jerk of the entire universe," Cici said, pushing away the report and letting herself relax. "Can you believe, he's cancelled on Aaron again? I can't believe that bastard. How could he be so callous to his own child?"

They settled into one of their gossipy, sometimes raunchy sessions, mostly about men and their foibles. Ann's love life was complex, full of phone calls, invitations, and intrigue. Cici found herself laughing at Ann's dry witticisms, which were so on target. In a world that often seemed like a "Cathy" cartoon turned sour, Ann was a devoted curmudgeon.

"So, what about Bryan?" Ann said after twenty minutes or so. "Tell me what's happening with the lovebirds lately. Anything exciting?"

Cici almost told Ann about the odd trick of the moonlight tonight with the rug, but then decided it was too trivial to mention. "Oh, we had a small tiff about Aaron. My son called Bryan a dickhead. I can't believe he did that."

Ann laughed. "Dickhead? My, but your son's vocabulary has grown. I remember when he used to run around with a couple of squirt guns yelling 'bam, bam, dummy!' "

"Yes," Cici sighed. "He was so cute then."

"He's cute now. Fourteen-year-olds are adorable, if you can just get past the peach fuzz and the cracking voice."

She told Ann about their fight, embellishing the conversation a little, describing Bryan's expression of shock and disgust when the word had popped out of Aaron's mouth.

"He's kinda conservative," she told Ann. "I mean, I've never even heard him curse."

"He doesn't swear?"

"No . . . I haven't heard him. He's always pretty much in control."

"I see." Then Ann gave a little sigh. "I don't know, Cic. A man who doesn't say shit and fuck and damn? Everybody says those words now. I guess I'm not as sympathetic as I ought to be about your little quarrel with Bryan, and I don't really know why. I just wish you hadn't set the wedding date. December twenty-six. That isn't so far away, just a couple of months. I wish you'd held your options open for a while longer."

"Ann," Cici said, hurt. This was the first negative thing Ann had said about Bryan.

"He's too good to be true, Cici. Doesn't he ever fart or anything? I've been thinking about this. He's just too perfect."

"Ann!"

"Does he ever give you a gift that doesn't fit, or some jewelry you hate, forget to bring you flowers some night? I mean, if he didn't send so many flowers, maybe I could like him, but, Cic, what man really does all that once the first week of dating is past? Don't you think it's a little mechanical? All he has to do is make a note to have his secretary call the florist once every couple of days."

The way Tom had his secretary order tickets to the Silverdome.

Cici glanced at the three fragrant and expensive bouquets lined up on her kitchen counter, in stages ranging from buds to full-blown blossoms, and felt an odd twinge of unease.

"I'm sure Bryan does it himself, Ann. He's never mentioned having his secretary do it."

"Okay. Look, I'm sorry." Ann seemed uncomfortable. "Anyway, are we still on for Chaplin's on Saturday?" Chaplin's was a comedy club in Fraser. Four of them, Cici and Bryan, Ann and her current boyfriend, Larry Watts, planned to attend.

"We're still on," Cici said.

"Bryan *does* laugh, doesn't he? And won't object to a few off-color jokes and 'F' words? I mean, we don't want to offend the guy."

"Bryan is going to be fine, Ann. What on earth is wrong with you tonight?"

"Oh, nothing," Ann said. "Hey, really. I'm a brat, Cic. I just want what's best for you."

Cici decided to let it go, changing the subject to work instead. She'd known Ann since college, and they'd enjoyed one of the fine friendships that women often have with each other. They'd been each other's support network, and she treasured that.

After she hung up, Cici began fussing with the roses, sweeping up a few fallen petals and adding water to one of the vases, a job she usually enjoyed. Tonight the pleasure palled a little.

Ann possessed a streetwise wisdom. Cici had always respected her opinion. Now her conversation with her best friend bothered her. Ann had expressed reservations about Bryan, but wasn't it Ann who had forced her out of the house to meet Bryan in the first place?

At 11:55 she heard a blast of rock music in front of the house, accompanied by a rackety car muffler and the sounds of teenagers' shrieks and laughter. The car pulling up was the rusty, scrofulous old Mercury Bobcat belonging to sixteen-year-old Heather Pickard, who often drove Aaron and his friends around.

Which meant that her son was home.

When Aaron didn't appear after ten minutes, Cici went to the front door and flicked the porch lights pointedly on and off. Finally her son slouched into the house.

"Didn't I tell you eleven o'clock?" she began in annoyance.

"You said twelve," Aaron protested, tossing his jacket toward a chair back. It missed and fell on the floor.

Cici looked at her son. He was a young-looking fourteen, with an innocent face that had not yet seen the humiliation of acne or the use of a razor. Aaron's eyelashes were incredibly long and sweeping, as glossy as the shock of brown hair that hung over his forehead. His face was square, the jawline firm. In a few years, when he grew into his body, Aaron would be considered a "hunk."

"Pick your jacket up, please. It belongs in the closet," Cici said automatically.

"Sure." Aaron scooped the jacket up with the toe of his shoe, managing to kick it so that it flopped across the chair again. He regarded his feat with the pride of Isiah Thomas sinking a basket. "Hey," he exclaimed. "How do you like that, man? Am I good or am I good?"

Despite her resolve, Cici felt a smile tug at her lips. She quickly erased it. "In the closet, Aaron. And let's talk about what you said to Bryan yesterday. You used a word to him that I won't permit in my house under any circumstances—to any guest here, whether it's Bryan Wyatt or anyone else."

Aaron winced. "Oh, Mom—"

"Don't 'oh, Mom' me, please. Aaron, Bryan isn't trying to hurt you or threaten you. He just wants to know you better. Is that so wrong? He loves me and he wants to like you if you'd just let him try."

Aaron looked down at the floor, a gamut of emotions crossing his face. Sullenness, replaced by hurt, then doubt, embarrassment, and hurt again.

"Aaron." She said it gently. "Why don't you like him? Is there any special reason?"

"Nothing."

How many other divorced mothers had had this exact same conversation with a child? "Nothing? It sounds like a lot more than nothing."

Aaron lifted his eyes to hers. She saw the faint sheen of moisture in them. "Look, Mom, I'm sorry, I really am. I . . . I let you down, but I *don't* like him. I just think he . . . stinks."

The word was so childish it startled her. "Stinks? Oh, Aaron—"

"Hey, I told you, I'm *sorry*. Hey, did you buy any more grapes today? Are they seedless? You know how I hate seeds. They get down in your stomach and start trees."

Aaron loped over to the refrigerator, hauling out a bowl of

seedless red grapes and preparing to take it into his bedroom. Cici sighed, realizing that he considered the conversation over and was about to slip off to his room again.

"Take a dish with you for the stems," she told him automatically. "I don't want to see any more stems or garbage in your room, Aar. And Aaron—"

But, cramming three or four grapes in his mouth at once, her son skidded across the kitchen floor in the direction of his first-floor bedroom. Within seconds she heard the loud blast of Guns 'N Roses coming from her son's stereo—his way of walling out what he didn't want to deal with or hear.

Cici returned to her report, a heaviness sitting like a leaden lump in the center of her stomach. The only flaw on the horizon of her life with Bryan was Aaron . . . and now, Ann's questioning of him, too.

That day of her first lunch with Bryan, even the waitress had responded to him, taking their order with a flirty, feminine switch of her hips.

However, Bryan barely glanced at the perky young woman with her order pad. He had a flattering way of devoting his entire attention to Cici, gazing into her eyes as if she were the only woman in the room.

Flattered and nervous, she found his scrutiny even a bit alarming. But, oh, yes, a pleasant kind of alarming. It made her sense all kinds of potential deep feelings.

"Have you lived in the Rochester area all your life?" Bryan wanted to know.

Cici gave him a capsulized version of her life, thinking that her typical suburban background sounded pretty dull.

"And you?" she finally said.

Bryan seemed to hesitate for a brief second. "Oh, I was born in northern Michigan in a little town that's barely on the map."

She was intrigued. "Oh, where? I've traveled over most of Michigan, and maybe I've been there."

"Near Houghton Lake," he said vaguely. "Has anyone ever

told you that you have eyes like a cat? With beautiful gold specks in them?"

"Cat eyes?" She laughed. "No one's ever told me that before. You're a first."

She found herself confiding in Bryan about a dream she had to open her own job agency sometime. "When I win the Lotto, or raise the money to start it," she specified. "But I'm sure I could make the company pay. Detroit is a wonderful town for executive outplacement since the Big Three are always cutting back somewhere, and they have hundreds of thousands of employees."

They discovered so many things they had in common. A love of antiques, though hers was only casual. Dancing. Both belonged to Vic Tanny. Both had even attended the University of Michigan, although Bryan's tenure in Ann Arbor came four years after hers. But to crown it all, she discovered that Bryan lived only four short blocks away from her.

"You don't mean you live in my *same subdivision*?" She felt foolishly, inordinately delighted with this discovery, as if it were a cosmic sign of some kind.

"You know where Poplar Way is?"

"Oh, absolutely. I jog there all the time."

"Well, Poplar Circle is right off that. We're a little cul-de-sac with only three houses. All of our lots are pie-shaped and Paint Creek runs in back of us."

"Wonderful," she said, then felt the blush rise, because she was being foolish thinking the accident of their living close to each other had anything to do with anything. And yet it did seem to put a kind of seal on their relationship.

They talked about some of the antique clocks Bryan had bought over the years. "My house is full of them," he confessed. "I buy and sell them, and I've taught myself how to repair them, too—very exacting work. It's getting to be a dying art."

The hour and a half sped by.

"Will I see you again?" Bryan asked as she reluctantly said she had to go back to work, pleading an afternoon meeting.

She laughed in delight that he really wanted to call. Then became nervous again. "Yes, but I have to warn you, I haven't dated. Not in the last sixteen years, anyway. This is pretty new to me and I'm not sure I even know all the rules anymore.''

"I'll be in touch, Cici. That is, if you'll write down your phone number for me.''

Flustered, she found one of her business cards and scribbled her home number on it. She double-checked the digits before she handed it over, to be sure she'd written down the right numbers. This felt so bizarre, a thirty-seven-year-old woman trying to get with it again.

"Thank you.'' He pocketed it carefully. "You're very, very pretty,'' he added, smiling.

She floated through the afternoon at the Job Center, Bryan's last words drumming in her thoughts.

Very, very pretty.

Could this be for real? But what would he say if he ever saw her naked? Would he think she was very pretty then? Or would he be turned off by her reconstructed breast, which, although adequate, still didn't quite resemble a normal one?

She arrived home from work that night to find a delivery girl standing at her front door, holding a huge, green-wrapped package from Holland Florist, the arrangement so tall it concealed half the girl's face.

"Those aren't for *me*?'' Cici cried, unable to stop the wide smile from breaking across her face.

"If you're Mrs. Cici Davis.''

"Oh, I definitely am. Oh . . . flowers! Would you believe I haven't had any flowers in ten years?''

"Well, these more than make up for it,'' said the girl, sharing her delight. "Enjoy.''

Cici carried the package into the house. Setting it on the dining room table, she carefully stripped away the green florist paper. Inside was an extravagance of perfect white roses, contained in an exquisite, pink-swirled milk-glass vase that looked to her like a genuine antique.

Breathlessly she counted. *Four dozen.* And the vase alone had to have been expensive. Why had he spent so much money on a woman he had barely met?

My God, she had thought in a delicious agony. He had liked her, more than liked her.

It was getting late, nearly one-thirty A.M. A wind had come up, rattling the window casings with a chilly, hollow sound.

Cici put her report back in her briefcase, then went around the house switching off lights and checked her son's room. Aaron had fallen asleep across his bed, still in his clothes, but he was a heavy sleeper and she knew it would be difficult to wake him, so she didn't try. It would not hurt him to sleep one night in jeans and a T-shirt.

She locked all the doors and dead bolts. When she'd been married to Tom, this had always been his job. Now the chore belonged to her, and there were times when, sliding the bolt shut, she wondered just how safe dead bolts really were, and indeed how safe doors were. Couldn't an intruder just take the door off its pins or something? Or was that possible only from the inside?

Being single upset that delicate balance, the feeling of safety you had about the world. It made you feel vulnerable. Even Aaron's presence wasn't really a deterrent. He was still a baby, after all, too young to protect her. A boy who still kept a gerbil in his room.

She finished locking and went upstairs to her bedroom.

She'd redecorated after Tom left, desperately wanting to erase all traces of his presence here. Gone were the heavy book-cases Tom had insisted on, the TV sitting on the dresser that sometimes ran until three A.M. Now there were chintz country roses on all the walls, with a matching border around the ceiling. A mauve comforter was piled high with lacy pillows, embroidered with more rosebuds. Her rose bower, her safe place now.

As she entered the room, a branch knocked against the window, making an unpleasant rapping sound.

Cici jumped a little. A large birch grew too close to the house, and had several branches that needed trimming. She reminded herself to have Aaron do it tomorrow.

She began to undress, pulling off her jeans, then the leo-tard and tights she still wore underneath. Something moved, and she realized it was her own reflection in the dressing-table mirror.

She'd been so terrified of the moment when Bryan would first see her breast. She'd spent days barely able to eat or sleep, worrying about his reaction. One man had already found her disgusting. Would another share the same reaction?

They'd been necking on the couch one night when she'd finally gathered her courage. "I . . . I have something to tell you, Bryan. I've had some surgery, serious surgery."

Tears had rolled down her cheeks as she forced the words out, explaining about the reconstruction. Bryan said little, just letting her talk. She couldn't even read a reaction on his face . . . God! She was turning him off. This had all been a terrible mistake.

"They shouldn't have touched you," he finally said in a hoarse voice. "It wasn't right."

She stared at him despairingly. Did he think she should have refused surgery? "I *had* to, Bryan," she blurted. "I have a son, and I'm only thirty-seven years old—I wanted to live. I'm glad I did it, and I'd do it again, too. Being alive is the most important thing there is."

Another silence while they just stared at each other, and she felt the despair of knowing it hadn't worked. If only he could *see* that her breast looked all right. Maybe it was just the idea that was scaring him off . . . the unknown.

Desperately she took his hand and brought it toward her, placing it on her right breast. Then, pushing his fingers, she encouraged him to knead her flesh through the sweater she wore. The silicone implant had a fleshy, bouncy texture that was nearly identical to natural.

"There," she said. "Feel it. Feel me."

His hand moved, experiencing her. "You wiggle," he said in wonderment.

"Yes, although not quite as much as the other side."

He kneaded her again, his expression incredulous. "I can't believe it, you're actually . . . kind of jiggly."

"Yes."

"Does it hurt?"

"No, not at all. I don't even notice it."

"Do you have any sensation on that side?"

"Only on the top half of the breast," she told him. "And there's no sensation in that nipple. But . . ." She faltered at last. Her courage, stretched taut, had finally wavered. "It doesn't really matter . . . Bry?"

Finally he pulled her toward him. "It's okay, Cici. This was not your fault. Your breast is new, the skin all new now. To me, the body is holy. And I still find you so beautiful."

Strung tight with unbearable tension, she had started to cry. Her sobs had begun with slow, choked gulps and proceeded to shake her entire body. Bryan held her, stroked her back, murmured to her. Something about God's will, she didn't really hear him clearly, but it didn't matter anyway what he said. Only that he accepted her, as she was. Accepted her scarring.

Now she turned away from the mirror, put on a sleep T-shirt, and got into bed.

As she was switching off the light, the phone rang.

"Cici?" It was Bryan. "Are you still up?"

"Just turning the light off. Hi, honey," she said into the phone, feeling pleased that he'd remembered. The moonlit illusion she'd seen tonight briefly came into her mind. A man hauling a rug that obeyed the laws of physics and bent like a person's waist at the center.

"I love you, honey," Bryan said in a deep, husky voice. "Don't you ever forget that."

She didn't think about the rug again.

THREE

When Cici woke on Saturday morning, a gray, misty rain was falling.

She left a note for Aaron, who was still sleeping, pulled on her sweats, and went running. Fog saturated the neighborhood like a cloud that had sunk all the way to the ground. It could almost be tasted on the tongue, faintly metallic.

A neighborhood collie followed her for a while, its collar jingling in the hush, the sound of its toe-clicks muffled on the pavement.

She turned down Poplar Way, stepping around the remains of a smashed pumpkin someone had left on the pavement. This part of the subdivision was fed by Paint Creek and the fog was thicker here, rising off the water in a misty blur. She narrowed her eyes, trying to catch a glimpse of Bryan's house, but the poor visibility revealed only his roofline and a suggestion of trees.

Only nine hours until she would see him. Bryan had consented to the evening at Chaplin's with surprisingly little fuss. He had even suggested that all four gather at his house tonight for drinks and hors d'oeuvres beforehand. He would order the appetizers from Max 'n Erma's, a local restaurant.

On her way back, Cici had to pass the subdivision entrance off Walton Boulevard, where some vending machines sold issues of various newspapers. She fished in the pocket of her sweatpants for a quarter, and bought the *News and Free Press,* now combined on weekends courtesy of the Joint Operating Agreement.

Starting out at a run again, she held up the paper for a quick scan. There had been another freeway shooting on I-94 near Romulus, the forty-two-year-old victim in serious condition. Cici had driven past that very exit only last week, on her way to a meeting in Ann Arbor.

She switched to another column, a smaller headline catching her eye. ROYAL OAK WOMAN DISAPPEARS AFTER BATTLE IN HOME.

Her eyes scanned the article.

> When Abby Tighe, 26, a medical transcriptionist, didn't answer her door, her 11-year-old niece went inside and discovered evidence of a pitched, bloody battle.
>
> "It was ferocious," said Diane Orchitt, mother of Stacey Orchitt, a student at Parker Elementary School in Royal Oak. "It looked like someone had taken a baseball bat and smashed everything. There was broken glass all over, and even the furniture was broken."
>
> Orchitt said her daughter ran home and begged her to come to her sister's house. She said she searched the house but could not find Tighe, and then phoned the police.
>
> "This is such a shock. Abby was a nice, quiet girl who had no enemies, and was not involved in anything like drugs. I can't imagine why anyone would do this to her," Orchitt said.
>
> Police say that there are no suspects. According to Detective Andrew—

Cici shivered and stopped reading. She hated news stories like that. They gave her the uncomfortable feeling of being too vulnerable.

Holding the paper awkwardly, she ran on through the fog, suddenly anxious to be home.

As she was jogging up her driveway she spotted John Pickard, her next-door neighbor, out in his driveway working on one of the four cars the family owned. Pickard, in his early sixties, was the father of Aaron's best friend, Dustin. He was a huge man, 6'3", with an old football player's build and blond hair aging to white. A model-maker for General Motors, he had custody of three teenagers, and was an outdoor tinkerer. This year alone he had already installed thousands of dollars' worth of shrubs.

"Yo, Cici." He waved to her now and, putting a tool down on the hood, started across the space of lawn toward her.

"Hi, John," she said without enthusiasm.

"Hey," he said, coming over to her, a spray of dew flying off his well-worn size twelve Reeboks. "Got a second to talk? Say, you look pretty good in that running outfit," he added, giving her a look that was barely short of a leer.

"I was just going inside to change," she responded coolly.

"I wanted to, you know, talk about the kids," he said. "Dustin . . . well, you know how boys are. You know the kind of trouble they can get in. They don't mean anything by it but it happens."

"Trouble?" Cici felt a spurt of alarm. The two boys, along with several others, saw each other daily. If Dustin Pickard was in trouble, could Aaron be far behind? "What kind of trouble?"

John Pickard cleared his throat. "I don't know for a fact. But I think they've been out riding around doing mailboxes. Throwing pumpkins. That kind of thing."

She felt a chill. "Doing mailboxes?"

"Running them over with the car. My daughter's Bobcat, that's what I'm working on now. She's dented the front bumper to hell. I told Dustin I'd knock him upside the head if I caught him doing it again."

The boys were only fourteen; they couldn't even drive unless Dustin's sister, Heather, who was sixteen, offered her car. The picture of her son being destructive surprised and revolted Cici. Instinctively she denied it. "Oh, no! Not Aaron. Aaron wouldn't be involved in something like that."

Pickard's eyes gleamed. "Lady, boys that age, they are involved in anything and everything. Look, I thought maybe you and me, we could get together and talk about it sometime. Decide how we want to handle it, you know. Since, hey, we live next door and our kids are like, best friends."

Was he coming on to her? Somehow he had moved, and now stood there wide-legged, blocking her way to her own yard.

"I don't think so," she demurred. "I'll talk to Aaron myself."

He took a casual step that seemed to block her again—the kind of man who used his body language to dominate women, a habit Cici loathed.

She excused herself and went into her house, snapping the dead bolt behind her. She couldn't believe a man like Pickard would use his own son's problems as an excuse to put the make on a woman. Did she really expect her to join the procession of over-made-up blondes who parked in his driveway overnight?

In the kitchen she found Aaron sprawled at the dinette table, staring at a half-full bowl of cereal. A red sleep crease decorated his left cheek.

"I slept in my clothes," he told her. "I've got blue-jean marks all over me."

"On your face?" She suppressed a smile. With his hair stuck up in back in two sleep tufts, Aaron looked cute to her, unutterably lovable.

"Well, not there." Aaron dipped his spoon idly in the cereal, then allowed it to drop against the bowl. "Why can't we have pizza for breakfast? Pizza's good for you. Cheese is full of vitamins and stuff."

"Because it has such a high fat content, Aaron." Cici hesitated, then decided not to tell Aaron what John Pickard had said—not now, anyway. She had already scolded him last night. She had to let things heal a little. If she was constantly on his case, she'd destroy the fragile lines of communication that still existed between them.

"How about a little help this morning?" she suggested, keeping her voice light. "The kitchen floor needs one of your expert jobs of mopping."

Aaron looked up with interest. There were times when he actually seemed to enjoy housework, she had noticed, especially if she praised him fulsomely for the work he did.

"You mean with the sponge mop and that Mop and Glo stuff?"

"The very same."

"Okay," her son agreed cheerfully. "I like those crazy mops, man, with that snapper at the end, the squeezer for the water. I like to snap them."

"Whatever turns you on." She smiled.

Bryan's clocks struck the hour, bonging and repeat-bonging, like an explosion in a Swiss watch factory. It was six P.M. and they were having cocktails before leaving for Chaplin's.

"Incredible!" exclaimed Ann when the noise was over. This was the first time she had been in Bryan's house.

"How many clocks have you got, anyway?" Ann's date, Larry, asked Bryan.

"Only eight in the living room and five more upstairs, and six or seven I'm repairing in the basement," Bryan explained. "I repair and sell a lot of what I buy—it helps finance the things I really want."

Larry, a systems analyst for Ford Motor Credit, reached out and touched one of the clocks. "What does it take you, Bryan, an hour to wind all of these things? And what's this one? It looks like a damn keyhole."

"Only fifteen minutes to wind them. And that's a spring-driven banjo timepiece," Bryan explained. "I bought it in Bristol, Connecticut, where it was originally made in 1850."

Ann and Larry were walking around Bryan's living room touching this, and exclaiming at that, just as Cici had on the first occasion she had come here. Bryan's house *was* overwhelming, reminding one of a crowded but elegant London shop. Shelves gleamed with Bryan's impressive collection of silver tankards and tea services, each piece polished to a high glow. There were music boxes of all varieties, and cast-iron toy banks that performed mechanical tricks with coins. On the walls, Bryan's pen-and-ink drawings vied for space.

"Interesting," remarked Ann, standing in front of a drawing Bryan had done of two clocks. "Have you ever had art lessons, Bryan?"

The drawing depicted the clocks standing apart from each other. The background, done in painstaking crosshatch strokes, was full of amorphous swirls and darker areas.

"No," Bryan said. "I just dabble. I like pen and ink because it can be so precise."

"But this picture isn't precise at all. Actually, it's almost Daliesque. Here you have the two clocks, and they are technically accurate, but you've almost turned them into human representations—facing each other, yet apart, like two people who can't communicate."

"Ann . . ." Cici said it warningly. Although Ann worked as an executive recruiter, her degree was in psychology. She could hear the analyst in Ann beginning to surface.

"And some have rather interesting human faces suggested on the clocks, almost biblical in emphasis. I've had a little art myself. It must have taken you hours. What were you thinking of when you drew these?"

Bryan began to look uncomfortable. "I don't think about anything when I draw."

"You don't? I find when I paint my mind ranges over everything, my entire life. It's very freeing."

"Ann," Cici interjected hastily. "Let's go and have some of that seafood dip Bryan's put out. It looks delicious."

But Ann wasn't going to be distracted. "Bryan, I can't believe how many *things* you have," she remarked, turning away from the picture and walking to a shelf that held Bryan's collection of Massachusetts tankards. "How many collections do you have, anyway?"

"Not that many, actually," Bryan said modestly. "Of course, if you have a broad category, like silver, and break it down, I do collect subcategories within the main category. For instance, those tankards—I've been buying those for about six years. But as I said, I sell most of them. And I do repair some of the things I buy, too. Not just the clocks but the mechanical banks and music boxes."

"Where?"

"I have a big basement hobby room, very well equipped."

"Oh, I'd *love* to see it! I love hobby rooms. I always make people show me theirs because I think that shows so much about the inner character, don't you?" Ann took a step toward Bryan, giving him her best smile. "You wouldn't mind giving us a peek, would you? I'd love to see what you're working on down there."

Bryan didn't look particularly glad to reveal his innermost character through his hobby room, but he nodded, telling them to follow him.

Beyond the kitchen was a mudroom area, which Cici felt sure had never seen dirt, much less any mud. Cupboards held a full array of cleaning supplies that apparently Bryan used himself, since he had no maid service.

The stairwell was a cavern of black, quickly dispelled when Bryan flicked on the light. They tramped down, Bryan first, followed by Ann, then Cici and Larry.

"Over there, the furnace room and some storage," Bryan said, briefly pushing open a door to reveal two modern-looking furnaces, each with a dehumidifier. "And this other door's the hobby area. Actually, I don't bring guests down here very often. It's a room where I go to get away from things, not have company."

Was that a note of ungraciousness? Bryan was probably annoyed at Ann for being in her questioning mode. Ann could be nosy sometimes, and occasionally people felt antagonized by her.

He pushed open the door, flipped another light, and they walked into a huge room that took up nearly the entire basement, ticking and humming with more clock noise.

"Wow." Ann whistled and Larry echoed her. They stood looking around at golden parquet floors, walls paneled in expensive, warm oak. One entire long wall was devoted to deep, floor-to-ceiling cabinets. The other walls held rows of Formica-topped worktables, with bracketed shelves overhead displaying rows of banks, clocks, and other collectibles. There was a sink, a small lathe, a drafting table set up with Bryan's drawing equipment. Only the high, narrow windows, filled in with security glass bricks against break-ins, betrayed the fact this was someone's basement.

"Oh, fantastic!" Ann enthused, striding in. "I love it! You have everything you need here. And even the lighting—you've got it on tracks, I notice."

"I need plenty of light for my clock repair."

"What's in that cabinet over there?" Ann said, pointing.

"That's for tools," Bryan explained. "Some of my watchmaker's tools are antiques in themselves, and they are so small and fragile I like to keep them put away. Also, I do worry about break-ins. Where I lived before I had several burglaries, which was pretty traumatic, and even now, my house is being vandalized."

"Oh?" Ann said.

"What?" Cici echoed. This was the first she'd heard of it.

"Didn't I tell you, Cici? Some of the neighborhood kids have apparently decided I'm a good one to play tricks on. I've found raw eggs all over my front siding, and on my front windows. Not just once, but five or six times. Also a candy bar smeared on my front door. I hate vandals!" Bryan exclaimed.

Cici froze, remembering what John Pickard had said about the pumpkins and mailboxes.

"Halloween is coming up in another month, so what can you expect?" Ann said, shrugging. "Some of the kids think Halloween lasts for two months."

Bryan led the way back to the door, and they all trudged up the stairs again. "Well, I think I might know who these kids are."

"Who?" Ann questioned.

"Oh, kids in the neighborhood. Just kids," Bryan said vaguely.

Cici felt another chill. Bryan was being polite and not saying who these "kids" were, but she had a very good idea that he was refraining from naming her son, Aaron.

They drove to Fraser in the fog, which had let up a little but still maintained its miasmal grip on the Detroit area. Inside the huge room at Chaplin's was another kind of fog, that created by cigarette smoke and the bodies of two or three hundred laughing and drinking people. Because they had not purchased dinner, they were given seats on an upper level toward the back.

Tonight's headliner was Richard Jeni, "The Boy from New York City." A small man dressed in a Charlie Chaplin costume came out and mimed for the crowd, which greeted the club mascot with jovial good humor. "Charlie" wandered through the audience, making animals and other figures out of colored balloons.

"Look, Bryan," Cici said during the applause for the MC, now coming up to take the mike, "about the eggs and things, about the vandalism on your house. You weren't referring to Aaron, were you? You don't blame him?"

"I don't know."

She shook her head, distressed. "How long have you thought this, Bryan? Are you sure? You didn't *see* who did it, did you?"

"No, I didn't see anyone. I didn't have to. Ever since I met you, Cici, it's been going on. Kids driving past my house in old cars, yelling things, throwing things at the house. I didn't want to say anything, but who else could it be but Aaron? You know he doesn't like me."

"He does like you," Cici protested automatically, but then she shook her head. Who was she kidding? When you liked someone you didn't call them a *dickhead.* End of argument.

The MC was wrapped around the mike now, telling a joke about burying a row of lawyers in the ground with only their heads showing. Everyone laughed at the punch line, which Cici didn't catch because she was trying to listen to Bryan.

"You'd better talk to him," her fiancé said.

"All right."

"I think he should treat me with some respect. It isn't right."

"Oh, Bryan . . . he will, I promise. You just have to be patient, that's all. Boys can be difficult. Fourteen is a rough year. You know that . . . you were a boy once."

"I was never like that," Bryan said. "I had strict parents. I was taught to follow the right way and I followed it, too." He added something else, but she couldn't hear it because the crowd was roaring again, warming up to the MC's rapid-fire jokes.

After the two-hour show they drove to the Sixpence, where they had decided to stop for a late supper. At the restaurant, Cici and Ann excused themselves for the ladies' room.

"Whew," Ann said, heading for a stall. "All those drinks—I was floating. Well, I was surprised to see that Bryan is such a collector," she added over the sounds of fabric rustling, paper rattling, then urination.

Seated in her own stall, Cici frowned, wondering if Ann had offended Bryan with all the questions she had asked him, both at his house and in the car. Ann had grilled him on his background, everything from his college major to his political views. She had even pried out of him the name of his hometown, Clyattville, which he had not given Cici.

Cici called to the adjoining booth. "Yes, don't you think it's great? Tom didn't have any hobbies. I think hobbies broaden a man, don't you?"

"Cic. Those aren't hobbies."

"What are they, then?" Cici heard her voice rise. "Jesus, Ann, I can't believe you tonight. Why didn't you just bring a portable couch with you, get it out and make him lie down on it? You did everything but analyze his handwriting."

From the other booth, Ann sounded touchy. "And I would have done that, too, if he'd given me a sample."

"I can get one for you," Cici said sarcastically.

"Cici . . . I haven't got any hard evidence, and you know I don't. But he makes me uneasy. All those clocks, for God's sake, tick-tick-ticking. And the tankards, and the silver teapots. I mean, they were beautiful, but what man really collects crap like that? And fob watches. And cast-iron banks. And this. And that. Don't you know what collecting means in the terms of psycho-analysis?"

They both emerged at the same time, and Ann headed toward the sinks. Cici followed her. "No, I guess I don't."

"Anal retentiveness."

"What?"

Ann grimaced. "It means he's still holding back his caca, Cic. You know? He doesn't want to give it up, he wants to keep it."

"Oh, give me a break," Cici exclaimed crossly, scrubbing her hands.

"All those collections are a sure sign of a tightass. And another thing, his pictures. Everything is almost obsessively drawn, did you notice? Every damn detail, gone over and over and over. He draws inanimate objects and gives them a flavor of being human. But isolated humans. Angry humans. I'll bet anything that Bryan is a very angry man inside."

Cici had had enough. "Okay, Ann. I guess that's the way you see it. But I don't see it that way. I don't think Bryan has terrific drawing talent, but he can draw okay, and he enjoys doing it, and what more is there to it? He's a good man, he's good to me, and I don't see why you're acting like this."

A couple of women trooped into the rest room, chattering about someone's new perm.

"He gives me the willies, that's all," Ann said, lowering her voice. "And I just wish you'd wait a while before marrying the man."

"I love him," Cici said firmly. "We set the date for the day after Christmas and I'm going to keep it, Ann. I'm not going to mess this up."

It was after one when they reached Bryan's. Ann and Larry left, promising they would do it again "sometime soon," and Cici waited on the front steps with Bryan while he unlocked the front door and dead bolt, and disarmed the security system. She couldn't help noticing the code he punched: 2887, the number of the house she had grown up in.

As soon as they stepped inside, a loud barking started up that sounded exactly like a junkyard dog in full, rabid fury.

"God," Cici said, covering her ears. "The decibel level of that thing, Bryan. Turn it off."

Bryan walked over to a black metal box that sat on the floor by an electrical outlet, and toggled a switch. Instantly the barking stopped. The box was an Electronic Dog, which contained a microchip with the sound of the barking on it, and was noise-activated—a little security extra Bryan had recently added.

"Your friend Ann is quite a woman," he said now, turning to her.

Cici sensed criticism in his remark. "She *is* a little outspoken and she likes to ask questions, but that's how she learns about people. I hope you didn't mind."

Not answering, he slid his arm around her. "Let's go upstairs, shall we? Can you stay for a little while?"

Cici's heart gave a little jump. He meant could she stay and make love.

"A short while," she murmured, thinking of Aaron.

"Mmmmm." He nuzzled her neck, his breath warm on her skin. "I've missed you. We haven't made love in a week."

Bryan's bedroom was like the rest of the house, crowded with clocks, antiques, and more of the pen-and-ink drawings. The sound of old-fashioned ticking made Cici think of Victorian parlors.

"Your friend Ann doesn't like me," Bryan said, unbuttoning his shirt. They hadn't bothered to turn on the bedside lamps, and the glow of the hall light reflected off his smooth skin, his chest muscled from hours spent on the weight machines. Shadows played across his face, giving him for a brief second the look of a handsome stranger.

"Of course Ann likes you."

"No, I could tell. That's why she asked all those questions. She doesn't trust me."

Cici felt embarrassed and uncomfortable, especially since Bryan had read Ann accurately. "Oh, I'm sure it isn't that. . . .

It's just her way, Bryan. She does that to everybody. She grills people with questions."

"You mean every man. She's been through so many that she doesn't trust any of them anymore."

Cici, who had been unbuttoning her blouse, stopped. "Bryan!"

"Well, Cici, admit it, your friend Ann is a professional single. She's had, what, two marriages, and two live-ins, and how many lovers? Now she thinks that all men are out to get her and her friends, and the more she thinks along those lines, the more it happens. She creates it herself."

Cici busied herself with her cuff buttons, feeling redness flush her cheeks. "Ann is a good person," she began. "She's only trying to—"

"Anyway," Bryan interrupted. "Let's not talk about it. Let's get in bed. I've been thinking about you all day."

Bryan's lovemaking always had a greediness about it, a voraciousness, the one time in life when he really let go. His deep kisses devoured her, sweeping her off to a world composed only of skin and caresses and soft moans, both hers and Bryan's.

Afterwards, Bryan lay on his back with his arms folded behind his head, already drifting toward sleep. Cici cuddled up to his side, thinking that she really would have to talk to him about his attitude toward Aaron. But when? She certainly couldn't ruin the pleasant afterglow with a possible argument.

"Bryan?" she said, playfully touching his springy mat of chest hair, running her hand down his pectoral muscle. "Hey. Hi. Are you in there?"

She valued the after-love closeness and didn't want him to drift from her yet.

"Bry?"

He stirred and mumbled something, too close to the edge to come back, even for her.

"Wham bang, thank you, ma'am," she murmured softly, meaning it as a kind but pointed joke. He didn't respond, and the sound of his breathing deepened.

She gave up and lay holding him, gazing at his face so open before her, his mouth slightly open as he breathed. In sleep,

Bryan's face had a vulnerable look, the skin around his eyes relaxing. At work, she knew he was involved in intraoffice rivalry, jockeying for position as his company, R.E.L. Manufacturing, changed owners. For that he had to be hard-edged and competitive. But she preferred him like this. It felt as if she could get close to him now, as if he would finally open himself to her fully, and share his real self.

Beside her, Bryan suddenly stirred violently, as if someone had kicked him. He began struggling and thrashing, mumbling a string of garbled words.

The movements shook the bed.

"Bryan? Hey, relax," she murmured, attempting to stroke his forehead.

He pushed her hand away, struggling harder. His breathing had changed into deep, heavy gasps. *"No,"* she thought she heard. *"Ma? . . . Ma? . . ."* And then: *"Boy. Boy doesn't want it! PA! NO, PA!"*

"Bryan . . . Bryan . . ."

But he didn't hear her. His chest arched upwards, his throat contracting as he attempted to suck in huge gulps of air. The sheet had been knocked aside, and his naked body was tremoring like an epileptic in a seizure. Sweat poured down his forehead, neck, and chest.

"No! Please! I DON'T WANT TO! PA I DON'T WANT TO!"

This had happened several times before, nightmares so violent and graphic that they shook the entire bed. What were the dreams about? What horrible part of Bryan's past did they simulate? When she would question him the next morning, Bryan became uncommunicative, saying he didn't remember.

"Bryan," she repeated, patting him as she might have done for Aaron. "Wake up, honey, you're just having another bad dream."

"No! . . . No! Please, God! I'll pray! I'll pray! I'll pray!"

Cici shook him again, concerned. "Bryan, wake up!"

"God!" Bryan cried. *"I don'twantitIdon'twantit . . . Fury! Fury! God!"*

What on earth was he saying, all of his words chopped

together as if they had been run through a blender? Something about fury. It made no sense.

"Hammer!" Bryan suddenly shouted, the word perfectly clear. *"I don't want to do it, I don't want to DO IT! PA! PA!"*

There was more, but it had become gibberish again, the fractured words of nightmare. Bryan sank back on the pillow, his breathing slowing a little. He was wringing wet.

"Cici," he muttered, seeming to partially waken. "Is that you?"

"It's me," she said anxiously. "You just had another of those nightmares. Do you want to talk about it? Bryan, you can talk to me. About anything. I love you. I'll be a good listener—"

"No," he mumbled, turning over with his back to her.

Cici lay still beside her fiancé, listening as his breathing grew deep and even again. It was a curiously lonely feeling— herself awake, him sleeping, lost to her. Even in bed they weren't as close as she wanted to be. When was he going to let her into the deepest part of himself?

Or would he ever?

It was a thought she didn't particularly like. Her parents had had a very close and happy marriage and it was what Cici wanted too, for herself.

FOUR

Mom, what's this weird kind of red lettuce stuff? Do I really have to eat it?"

"That's radicchio, Aaron. I just wanted to try it. We always eat head lettuce and it's so bland. Did you know there are over fifty kinds of lettuce? It's really amazing, isn't it?"

Her son gazed at his salad plate, where Cici had artistically arranged various greens, zucchini and cucumber strips, and tomato wedges. *"Red* lettuce? This looks like a mutation."

Cici choked back a nervous laugh, aware of Bryan's frown across the table.

It was September 20, and they were having a "family" dinner, one of Cici's attempts to acclimate Bryan and Aaron to each other, to create some kind of common ground on which they could communicate. But so far no common ground had been established. Aaron still bristled at the man she wanted to marry, and went out of his way to resist anything Bryan might suggest he do.

"Eat your lettuce," Bryan commanded.

"Hey, a red mutation might turn me into a Martian or something," Aaron responded cheekily.

"What are you talking about?"

"Now, both of you," she began, placating. "Lettuce doesn't have to be an issue here, does it? I'm sorry I ever bought it. From now on, it's good old iceberg. Now, Aar, why don't you tell us what you're doing at school. Don't you have a big new project in art class?"

"Not really," her son mumbled, sliding down in his chair.

"I thought you were doing some sculpture."

"Yeah, I guess."

"What kind of sculpture?"

"Just some stuff."

Cici was annoyed that her usually verbal and articulate son should suddenly have clammed up. "Well, is it an animal of some kind? A dragon?"

She knew Aaron liked dragons. He doodled them constantly on all his school papers, and had begged her for a dragon belt buckle. She saw her son's eyes flicker with a spark of enthusiasm, but then his face became expressionless, shutting her out again.

"Aaron," Bryan snapped. "I've had enough of this. Your mother asked you a question."

Aaron jerked bolt upright in his chair. "Heil Hitler!" he cried. "Look, *Mr. Wyatt,* all we're talking about is what I'm doing in art class. It's not like it's the end of the world or something."

"Aaron!" Cici cried.

"I don't *have* to tell *you* anything I'm doing. I don't *have* to sit at the table and give out my activities like some stupid, dumb book report."

"Aaron Thomas Davis!" Cici's shock had swiftly progressed to fury. "I want you to stop talking like that and apologize to Bryan—right now!"

Aaron's eyes focused on hers accusingly, and she could see the bright glitter of tears in them. "I don't want to apologize to him. He always treats me like he's Hitler, Mom. He always acts like I'm some kind of a dork. I—"

"That's more than enough," she snapped. "We are all entitled to our thoughts, but we don't treat people rudely. I suggest you go to your room and start on your homework, and I'm going to come in before I go to bed and take a look at what you've done."

Aaron unfolded himself from the chair and walked stiffly out of the dining room, his unlaced, high-top Reeboks skidding on the polished wood floor. His head was held high; his back displayed the rigid straightness of one whose feelings have been deeply hurt.

Cici felt a twist of her heart when she heard the distant slam of Aaron's bedroom door. Damn! Why couldn't these two people, so important to her, get along with each other?

"Bryan," she began, turning to her fiancé. "Look, we really do have to talk about this. Maybe you're coming down on Aaron just a little too hard. His father is more laid-back, and, I guess, so am I. He hasn't been raised in such an authoritarian way."

Brian's clear blue eyes gazed into hers. "Kids shouldn't talk back, Cici. I won't put up with it at my table."

Oh, God, she thought. She knew Bryan had been brought up in a religious household—they'd attended some fundamentalist church, he'd told her. "But it isn't your table tonight," she finally said. "It's mine."

"It will be our table later, though."

She stared at him, not liking the severe tone in his voice, and liking it less that he had used it against her boy. "Bryan, Aaron hasn't been brought up to just sit there and not give his opinion. We've always talked about things. I've always given him reasons for things and listened to him."

"And I will give him reasons for things."

She shook her head. "I know you'll give him reasons, Bry. And that's good. But—does it have to come down like a pronouncement? Can't it just be, well, discussed in open conversation?"

Bryan stared at her for a minute, and then the rigidity she'd sensed in him seemed to drain away. He smiled at her, lines crinkling out from his eyes and bracketing the corners of his mouth. Her handsome lover, her adoring fiancé.

"Of course," he murmured. "Did you think it would be otherwise, Cici? I'm going to learn to get along with your son, I promise. In fact, maybe I'll get some tickets to a concert and take him. Would you like that?"

"A concert?" she said, surprised and pleased.

"We have free tickets floating around all the time at work," Bryan said vaguely. "I'll put the word out that I want some. Of course, I can't guarantee what they'll be. There's a jazz festival coming up. B. B. King."

Cici nodded politely, thinking that Bryan didn't understand Aaron very well if he thought he would like to attend a jazz concert. God! Combining these two was like mixing oil and water. What if it really and truly didn't work? What would she do then?

"What's the main course?" Bryan was asking now, as if their discussion were over.

"Oh, shrimp marinara," she said, her hopeful mood of the evening gone.

"Spicy?"

"Pretty spicy. Lots of oregano and garlic. Good thing we're both eating it."

"Anything you prepare will be wonderful," Bryan said, reaching out to take her hand and squeeze it tightly in both of his.

After a moment, Cici squeezed back. The pressure of their hands pushed the edge of her engagement diamond into her skin.

Kermit the Frog sang, in a burbling tenor, that it wasn't easy being green.

"God, I can't believe how well Aaron plays with the baby," exclaimed Cici's sister, Jocelyn. They were in Jocelyn's family room, where Fisher-Price toys and toddler-sized Lego blocks were scattered all over the carpet. At the other end of the room, Aaron was hunkered down on the floor, playing with eighteen-month-old Michael.

"He does, doesn't he?"

"Mark my words," remarked Jocelyn. "That kid is going to be a wonderful father someday, Cici."

"Aaron? A father?" Cici's laugh was dry. She added in a low voice, so that her son wouldn't hear, "Somehow I can't think that far ahead, Joss. I just want to get through these teenage years. I worry about him so much."

Jocelyn frowned. Two years younger than Cici, she was the epitome of the stay-home, bake-bread type of mother, already four months pregnant with another child. The T-shirt she wore proudly boasted *Baby Machine.* "Why, Cic? What's he been doing?"

Aaron had taken the baby into the kitchen for a drink of apple juice.

"Oh . . ." Cici's eyes abruptly glazed over with tears. "I don't know, Jocelyn. I think he might be vandalizing people's property. My neighbor mentioned it. And Bryan thinks he's involved with a group of kids that have thrown stuff at his house."

"No," Jocelyn said, one hand going protectively to her chest as if to ward off such misfortune from her own family.

"I don't want to believe it. But he's been so difficult lately, Joss—so moody. He hates Bryan, Joss! He just won't try to get along with him. I don't know what I'm going to do."

"Well, you've got to keep on trying. You can't let him wreck your chances with Bryan."

"I know. Oh, God, I know that. But it's so hard—he is *so* damn stubborn."

"Like you always were." Jocelyn smiled. "Remember when we had that knock-down-drag-out fight over the Barbie doll?"

"You drew with ballpoint on her forehead," Cici accused.

"That's because you dipped her hair in milk and it got all tangly."

"We were brats."

They grinned at each other. Jocelyn got up and began picking up the Lego blocks, putting them back in their box. "Cici, he'll come around, I know he will. You don't want to risk losing a man like Bryan. How many guys like that are going to come along for you? He's financially secure . . . he's accepting . . . he accepted your surgery. That counts for a lot."

"I know." But for the first time, Cici didn't say it with full conviction.

"Cici? Cic! There isn't anything wrong in your relationship with Bryan, is there?"

Cici hesitated, remembering Bryan's strange nightmare and the way he didn't really share things with her. She hadn't even known the name of his hometown until Ann dragged it out of him.

"No . . ." she told her sister.

"Well, you'd never know it to look at your face. Hey, girl, I want to be your matron of honor." Jocelyn was smiling as she rubbed her hands down her sides. "Preggers or not, I intend to be a mountain in ice-blue satin."

"You'll be beautiful," Cici said fondly.

"No, not me. You. *You're* going to be the most beautiful bride in town, Cic. God, a size eight yet, with lace, and little bugle beads, and one of those long, sweeping trains . . . you'll knock Bryan's suspenders off when he sees you."

"Right," said Cici, summoning her enthusiasm. But instead she pictured Aaron, dressed in a dove-gray tuxedo with blue boutonniere, scowling ferociously. And Bryan scowling back.

The next day, Cici walked into the lobby of Friday's to meet Bryan for lunch. The restaurant, located near Troy's "Golden Mile" of office buildings that included Kmart's national head-quarters and Bryan's firm, R.E.L. Manufacturing, was crowded with office workers waiting to be seated.

There was no sign of her fiancé.

Cici glanced at her watch. Damn—she was ten minutes early, unusual for her. She'd anticipated the lunch so much she'd jumped her schedule.

A host seated her on the lower level, along the bank of windows that looked out to a bistro garden and the parking lot.

Cici ordered a wine spritzer and unfolded the copy of the *Detroit News* she had brought with her. There had been another huge rally in South Africa, and more unrest in Azerbaijan. A Detroit housewife had set fire to a crack house. Then Cici's glance slid further down the page, where a headline at the

bottom read, ROYAL OAK WOMAN STILL MISSING. FOUL PLAY SUS-
PECTED.

Cici didn't read the article, but glanced at the accompany-
ing photograph. It showed a pretty blond woman in her mid-
twenties, with fluffy bangs and wide, sweet eyes. Even her smile
was eager.

Cici suppressed a shiver. Abby Tighe hadn't really lived that
far away. In Detroit all the suburbs ran together, and Royal Oak
was only a short drive on I-75 to the south, between twenty
minutes and half an hour away, depending on traffic.

The woman's warm smile seemed to reach out to her with
an intimacy Cici found unsettling. Where was she now? Lying
bloody and dead in some field or culvert? Could she be alive but
injured, an amnesia victim in a hospital? Or maybe a boyfriend
had beaten her, and she'd fled the city.

Cici read one paragraph of the article, which said that the
police had been searching for a body, then quickly turned the
page. It really wasn't fair that women were forced to live their
lives in constant fear of being victimized by men.

Glancing toward the front of the restaurant she was relieved
to see Bryan headed toward her table.

"Bryan! Bry!" She waved at him.

To reach her, he had to pass several tables crowded with
young female office workers, his tall blondness garnering appre-
ciative sidelong looks. Forgetting the article, Cici felt a small
glow. Other women coveted *her* man.

"Whew, what a day," Bryan said, sliding into the seat opposite Cici. He immediately reached out his hands to enfold one
of hers. His skin was smooth and warm. "You were here early,"
he accused.

"Only one or two minutes," she lied.

"What are you drinking?" he wanted to know.

"My usual spritzer."

"I'll just have coffee," Bryan decided. "I'm going to have to
make this a quick lunch, Cic. I've got a big meeting at one-thirty,
and I've got to get back to prepare for it. The new CEO is going
to be there, and he's a real shark."

"All right," she said, disappointed. She'd made time in her

own afternoon, juggling several appointments, so that they would have time to linger.

Bryan looked tense as he added, "They say two or three more managers are going to get the ax."

"But you're safe?"

"Honey, nobody is safe. But I'm doing better than most," Bryan explained, his jaw knotting as he frowned at the menu, which the waitress had already left.

Cici nodded. She felt sorry for Bryan for having to live under the gun at work as he did. How did a man cope with such pressures bombarding him every day? No wonder Bry seemed tense sometimes, even abrupt. She was lucky that the atmosphere was much more easygoing at her own agency.

They ordered, Bryan getting Cajun blackened fish, Cici a Cobb salad.

"I've got a little surprise for you," he told her, as the waitress brought their plates.

"Oh?"

"It's not much, but I thought you'd be interested." Bryan reached inside his suit jacket and pulled out a sheaf of travel folders, dangling it tantalizingly in front of her. One of them said MAUI. "I had my travel agent send me all the brochures."

"Hawaii!" Cici exclaimed in delight. "Oh, Bry—!"

"Would that please you for a honeymoon? We've got to make our reservations now, in the next few days anyhow."

"Oh, Bryan!" She heard her voice lift, and didn't fight the glad, greedy sensation of happiness that pushed its way up through her chest. For weeks she'd fantasized about their honeymoon, their special getaway, just the two of them with no problems of the world to interfere. A time for them to talk, to open up to each other and become truly intimate.

"I got brochures about all the islands," he told her, fanning the folders out in front of her. "Maui, Kauai, Hawaii, Lanai. And I think December is the beginning of the whale season off Maui. So pick out the hotel you'd like to stay in, honey."

"Have a good lunch?" inquired Becky, the receptionist at the Job Center, an attractive redhead of thirty-eight. She marked

Cici's return on an in-out list and handed her a sheaf of seven or eight pink message slips.

"Oh, the best," Cici practically sang. "We're going to Hawaii for our honeymoon, Becky! Two whole weeks!"

"Which island?"

"All of them, Bryan says. Especially Kauai. We're going to do some backpacking and take a helicopter tour, and visit at least two volcanos. And we'll do some snorkeling, and go on a fishing charter . . . sunbathing, mai tais on the beach . . ."

"Lucky, lucky," said Becky enviously.

Cici glanced down at the message slips, which were mostly routine except for one from her ex-husband, Tom, who wanted to stop by with her alimony check.

Renee Hoyt, one of the word processors, a leggy girl in her early twenties, came flying past clutching a folder that contained cover letters she had typed for one of the clients—by the speed of her footsteps clearly a rush job.

"It's Hawaii, Renee," Cici called to her.

The girl stopped, teetering on spindly high heels. A smile broke over her face. "Your honeymoon? Hawaii? Oh, fabulous! How long are you going to be there?"

"Two weeks! Two whole weeks! And we've already picked out our hotel! Whales! Bikinis! Fabulous sunsets! The hula!" Somehow it seemed even more exciting when she was away from Bryan. Cici couldn't help doing a little whirling dance, giddy with the pleasure of it. She was acting like a twenty-year-old but there weren't any clients in the hall right now who would see her, and Quint, the director of the center, was in his office with the door closed.

"Oh, by the way," Renee added, "there's a surprise in your office. Something very nice. I helped unwrap it."

Cici had a good idea what the "surprise" was, and continued down the hall to her office, a smile spreading across her face. She stopped expectantly in the doorway. Articles clipped from *Employment Weekly* were framed on the walls, along with a quote from Goethe about being ready for opportunity. But it was the lavish bouquet that drew her eye.

Another of Bryan's fabulous flower arrangements, pink roses and irises this time.

Cici hurried forward to find the card on its usual prong of clear plastic. *Love Always. Bry.*

She buried her nose in the flowery perfume, feeling a sudden, unexpected rush of fear. This was all like a fantasy, wasn't it, from the succession of bouquets and gifts to the Hawaii honeymoon? All of it wonderful but not quite real. Maybe Ann had a point. *Was* it really natural for a man to be that thoughtful, to shower a woman with so much?

A knock on her door interrupted her thoughts.

"Cici? I just passed you in the parking lot—followed you in. Thought I'd drop off the old checko."

It was Tom, her ex, jacketless and dressed in his work mode, wearing a white shirt with a pocket stuck full of engineering pens and pencils. Once handsome, Tom was getting a bit worn about the edges now—and knew it. This was a man who had been so traumatized by his fortieth birthday that he had an automobile accident, totaling his car. Who needed a twenty-two-year-old to make him feel truly alive.

She wasn't pleased to see him.

"You didn't have to bring it over. There is such a thing as the U.S. mail," she told him.

"When my office is less than a mile away?" He grinned, staring around her small, somewhat cluttered office with proprietary interest. "Nice flowers," he remarked.

"Yes . . ."

"Aaron says the guy sends flowers every other day. I mean, roses cost an arm and a leg these days. What is this man's florist budget, three hundred a month? A family could eat on that."

"I happen to love flowers," she told him stiffly.

"I guess, babes. Anyway, here's the checko." Tom waved the check around with a flourish before handing it to her. "Support a florist or two, and a couple of dozen rose growers."

"I don't appreciate your crass remarks. And I'm not your babes!"

"But you might not be his, either, babycakes."

"What do you mean by that?"

"I mean, hey, a thirty-four-year-old man is bound to have some secrets to hide. Maybe that's why he sends you all the flowers—so you won't start trying to find out."

She stared at her ex-husband, surprised and repelled by his statement. "Tom, I really can't believe you. Why would you say that? Do you have any facts to back up your innuendos?"

Tom shrugged. "Not a one, honey. Hey, the guy's probably as clean as Ivory soap. Looks kind of uptight to me, though. You know, the rigid, pucker-butt type. You might be sorry later when he makes you kneel down and lick his shoes clean."

"Tom!" Furious, she flew at him and punched his arm. The familiar tang of his aftershave filled her nostrils like a hurtful memory. "I can't believe you . . . I really can't! You're so disgusting, you turn my stomach."

Tom nodded, looking sheepish. "Hey. You turned out good, Cici . . . I mean, a lot better than I expected, if you know what I mean. Maybe I don't want any other guy to get you yet."

"Tom!"

"Well? Are you *that* locked in to marriage with this guy? Maybe you might want to come over to my condo sometime and we could maybe road-test things, see if our engines still work?"

Cici stared, shocked in a thrilling, gut-twisting way. Had she heard him correctly? Eighteen months ago he had told her that he "couldn't handle" her surgical scars, that she "disgusted him sexually." Now that some other man desired her, Tom wanted her again.

"I'm not going to have sex with you. Do you hear me?" She made her voice hard, glad when Tom flinched back. "You gave up a good thing and you're never getting it back. And one more thing. Don't ever hand-deliver my alimony check to this office again. Do you hear me? *Ever.*"

"Well, excuse the 'fuck out of me," Tom drawled.

Cici was shaking all over. "And don't use that language in my office! Get out of here, Tom—or I'll buzz for Quint."

"Oh, what a scare. Big, bad Quint, the head of the agency." But Tom sauntered out the doorway, giving her a little finger-waggling wave as he left, to show her he didn't care about the rejection.

After he was gone, Cici's knees felt watery with the release of tension. She sank into her desk chair with a heavy plop. She could hear Tom's progress down the hallway—his loud greetings to one of the clients he knew. She had tried to be forgiving, and sometimes achieved that objective, but at the moment she didn't feel very lofty at all. She purely and simply hated him. She could cheerfully dispose of his dead body in a swamp in the Everglades, dumping it out of the trunk of her car into a mucky sinkhole frequented by alligators.

The ringing of her desk phone interrupted her angry fantasy.

"Could you come down to my office?" said Quint Flannery, the head of the agency. "I want to ask you about the monthly report. And also that VandenBosche resume."

Settling down at her kitchen desk that night to implement Quint's suggestions for the resume, Cici reached out to switch on the small television set she kept on the counter. The six o'clock news was on, with a story about three arson fires set near Eight Mile Road in Detroit.

When the newscaster, Bill Bonds, began to talk about another demonstration at the Detroit Incinerator Plant, she picked up her red pencil, frowning at the resume. Three pages of turgid, technical prose that no human-resources manager would ever read. She began cutting out lines and words, marking the changes clearly so they could be read by the word processor.

The mention of a name over the air caused her to raise her head again.

"And now an update on the disappearance of a Royal Oak woman, Abby Tighe," said the veteran anchorman, who had been around most of Cici's adult life. "Royal Oak police have issued new information stating that bits and pieces of human skin and bone found at the scene indicate that the twenty-six-year-old woman may not have been alive when she left her home on approximately September twelfth."

Cici stiffened, her fingers tightening on the pencil.

"Police now say that as many as nine disappearances of

women may be linked to a perpetrator some are beginning to call 'The Basher.' "

The Basher. A singularly ugly name. Some *Free Press* columnist had coined it, and now all the media were using it.

Another shot of Abby Tighe appeared on the screen. She wore a pair of shorts and a halter top, her hair backlit by the sun. The photo showed glimpses of sand and someone's beach towel, a small picnic cooler. Cici shuddered. It might have been Abby's last picnic.

"Today Abby's mother, Mrs. Carla Tighe, held a press conference and pleaded for her daughter's abductor to bring her back," Bonds went on.

The picture switched to a head shot of a drained-looking woman of about fifty-five, with puffy eyes and skin blotched in a way that could only have come from days of crying. Cici felt her heart twist in painful sympathy.

Abby Tighe's mother had a raspy, smoker's voice. "I . . . I just want to say to him, whoever he is . . . Abby is a good girl, a sweet girl. She hasn't done any harm to anyone, and there are so many people who love her. Please. Please let her go. Let her come back to us. Let her . . ." Abruptly the woman collapsed in sobs, and an unidentified woman moved forward and put her arms around her.

Bonds was back on the screen. "Royal Oak police say the chances of Abby Tighe being found alive are growing increasingly more remote with each passing day. A shame. Such a shame," the anchorman added heavily. "They are asking all area women to lock their doors and use dead bolts, and to check their cars before getting inside. Now, in Farmington Hills, police are searching for two men who shot and killed a thirty-four-year-old Chaldean party-store owner and his wife . . ."

Cici flicked off the set, unable to listen to any more news of mayhem and death. She felt a wave of her usual news-story anger. There was no way to control it, was there, or to protect yourself? Crime existed all around you whether you faced it or not.

She didn't like feeling vulnerable. It diminished something in her and made her feel like a victim, too.

* * *

Her work week, filled with hundreds of telephone calls from recruiters and human-resource directors, and conferences with job seekers, slid on to Wednesday. At noon in the lunchroom, the women from the support staff pored over Cici's Hawaii folders, giving advice as to what Cici should wear on her December honeymoon.

"Bikinis, of course, and those one-piecers with the sarong skirts" was Becky's idea.

"And something incredibly sexy with a garter belt," added Renee, giggling. "You know, made of white lace. And get one for him, too, to match yours." She giggled again. "Only not with a garter belt."

Cici felt herself glow with the warmth of being among these people who cared about her. They had stood by her through her surgery and her divorce. Even reserved Quint had unbent enough to tell her where there was a good scuba shop on Maui.

Becky had brought in the *Detroit News*, and after the other counselors and staffers arrived, the talk turned to the missing Royal Oak woman.

"She's dead, all right," said Colin Spenser, a counselor, as he munched a turkey sandwich. "Bashed, just like the others. Didn't the *Free Press* call him the Basher? A great name. He beats them to death, drags them out of the house, and dumps them in the St. Clair River."

"Or buries them up north someplace," suggested Diane Perlmann, who ran entrepreneurial workshops. "The Upper Peninsula is full of good places to bury people, hundreds of miles of empty state forest. You could dig a grave there and the body would never be found."

Becky uttered a little sound of horror. "God! You people sound positively bloodthirsty. I don't think she's dead at all. I think she just had a fight with her boyfriend and ran off. It happens. People disappear all the time."

"A girl like that?" put in Quint authoritatively. "With all that blood left around the house? And didn't they say there were pieces of flesh, too? Bone and brain. No, there's foul play all right. I'm sure she's dead."

Cici, seated at the end of the table with her Greek salad, felt a shudder go through her. Since Abby's mother had appeared on the news, Cici had awakened several times with an oddly terrifying nightmare—a woman wrapped up in something smothering, her body being dragged.

"Please, could we change the subject?" she begged. "I don't like eating my lunch and talking about murder."

The topic of conversation changed, to a letter from a client the agency had placed at Mazda, and Cici forced herself to finish her salad. Her appetite had gone. She guessed she really identified with Abby Tighe. There was something about her photograph that reminded Cici of herself at a younger age, and there had been a sweetness, too, to Abby. Even in a grainy, amateur snapshot her *niceness* shone. It was such a tragedy that a girl like that should be dead.

Somehow Abby haunted Cici, like another path to her own life, a bad-luck path that only one slight misstep could send her onto, stumbling and screaming.

FIVE

The October 10 Job Fair was in full swing. A hubbub of voices filled the air as clients dressed in "interviewing suits" crowded into conference rooms where representatives from fifteen companies and six recruiters sat at long tables.

Cici eyed the sizable crowd with satisfaction. Despite the forty-eight-degree temperature outdoors, she had already been forced to turn on the building's air conditioning as body heat from more than two hundred people pushed the indoor temperature to well over eighty-five.

But even Quint, who was somewhere in the crush, admitted she had done a superior job of organizing.

"What a zoo," sighed Ann, taking a break from the table where she and another woman were representing her company, Executive Action, Inc. "And just think, tomorrow I get to go through all those stacks of resumes. Lucky me. Thank God I get to take some time off. I'm going to inflict myself on my mom—*if* my boss will okay the vacation."

Ann's mother, thrice married, lived in Connecticut.

Ann turned abruptly, spotting someone in the crowded entrance lobby. "Oh, there he is. I was wondering if he'd show up."

"Who?"

"Mike McVey. Come on! I asked him to come here. I wanted you to talk to him." Before Cici could protest, Ann had her by the arm and was dragging her through the crowd.

McVey turned out to be a man in his mid-thirties, with reddish hair and a wide body that was stocky without being fat. In contrast to the job seekers in their sober business wear, McVey wore a heathery tweed sports coat and a bright red tie.

"Mike McVey, Cici Davis," Ann said, glancing at her watch. "Oh, shit, I've got to get back to the zoo. You two make talk. Mike's a private investigator, Cici—he does insurance and arson claims."

With that, she disappeared into the crush, leaving Cici to stare helplessly at McVey. Why had Ann wanted her to meet him? Surely Ann could not be playing Cupid, could she? But, sighing, Cici realized that anything was possible with Ann.

"Are you here for the job fair?" she asked McVey tentatively.

"No, I just stopped in at Ann's request. She thought you might be able to use my services. I've done some work for her firm." He frowned. "You mean you didn't know I was coming?"

"No. And I—I'm not sure what you mean, use your services."

"Investigative."

"But I don't need an investigator. I don't know why you would—I mean, why Ann would—" And then Cici stopped. She did know. It had to do with Bryan. Oh, yes, Ann had casually mentioned this to her before, hinting about women who hired services to investigate their fiancés.

"I'm sorry," she murmured, stepping backward. "I didn't know anything about this. Ann had no right to do this. I'm sorry you were inconvenienced."

He was nice about it. "Well, anyway, keep my card for your collection."

Cici tucked the business card into her purse and quickly moved away, blending into the crowd.

She didn't want to argue with Ann here—not at the office with her boss nearby. So she invited her friend to follow her home in her car for some coffee, where at least they would have privacy.

"Tonight?" Ann demurred, glancing at her watch. "Cic, it's after eleven. I have to go home and call Larry."

"Why not? Anyway, we need to talk."

"We can't talk here? Or on the phone later?"

"Ann, I have chocolate chip cookies at home. I picked them up at Herschel's yesterday."

Ann grinned. "Well, in that case . . . You know I'm a chocoholic."

They made the drive north to Rochester, the roads nearly empty at this hour of the night. As Cici pulled her Mercury Cougar into her driveway, Ann in her Camaro behind her, she saw that next door the Pickards' house was lit up—every window. A shadow crossed one of the windows, looming against open venetian blinds—the wide, unmistakable form of John Pickard, Dustin's father.

"Wow, I hear rock music," Ann said cheerfully, getting out of her car. "And is that John Pickard I spot in the window? I didn't know he lived next door to you."

"Well, he does." Cici was in no mood for gossip about her neighbor. She wanted to have this out with Ann.

"You see him at all the singles dances," Ann explained. "He's a hunter."

"A hunter?" Cici said stupidly.

"You know—as in hunting down female prey. He goes out searching for the pretty ones, the new ones who haven't got their shit together. He dates a woman one time, and if she doesn't put out—pow, it's all over with. A really neat guy. They say he has a bad case of premature ejaculation. Typical of a Don Juan."

Cici stared at the house. She could see her neighbor, clad in jeans, walking into his kitchen, picking up the phone, and dialing. Hunched over the phone he seemed to be talking very intensely—bawling someone out, maybe.

Ann's glimpses into the singles world were sometimes very unsettling. But she didn't want to talk about John Pickard tonight.

"Come on in the house, Ann," she said. "I'll put the coffee on."

"Okay," Ann began as Cici was measuring the coffee. "Now, what's wrong? I see that look in your eye, Cici. You're pissed at me, aren't you?"

"Well, I guess I am a little. Dammit, Ann! I don't mind being nice to someone you invited to attend the Job Fair, but the way you just walked off and left me standing there talking to Mike McVey . . . I couldn't believe you did that. I certainly don't need any investigator."

"I wonder, Cici."

"Ann!" Cici stared at her friend. "You're saying that you think I ought to get him to investigate Bryan, aren't you? You think I ought to do a sleazy background check on Bryan!"

"Hey, hey . . . it's done all the time, Cici, it's the new thing now. Lots of women don't want to be taken financially, or they're afraid their partner didn't reveal his full sexual background. So they hire investigators. I'm telling you, some of the things they uncover make it all worthwhile."

"Ann, I *don't* appreciate your suggestion. For me to snoop around Bryan's background would be incredibly tacky. I couldn't. In the first place, it shows lack of trust. And what would Bryan say if he ever found out I'd done it? I don't even want to think about that. And I don't want to *do* it."

"He won't find out, Cic. Mike is very discreet, very thorough. He did some work for one of my neighbors, and she found out that her boyfriend was actually visiting massage parlors every Friday night when he told her he was in a men's golf league. And you know what they do in massage parlors. They actually jerk the man off with a hand job."

Cici dropped the coffee scoop back into the can, feeling a

sharp spurt of annoyance. "Oh, just great! You think Bryan is visiting massage parlors?"

Ann had the grace to look embarrassed. "No, of course not. But honey, you really don't know what he *is* doing, do you? I mean, here is this guy with this fabulous job and he travels all the time, and sometimes he's gone, what, three or four days at a time, and he—"

"I'm *not* going to listen to this," Cici snapped.

There was a long, quivering silence as both women stared at the coffeepot, now beginning to make bubbling sounds as the coffee perked.

"Okay," Ann finally said. "I guess I was way off base."

"Yes, you were."

"There's just something about him I don't trust."

"So the immediate answer is to hire an investigator and dig up all Bryan's secrets?" Cici began putting cookies on a plate. She spoke evenly. "Since my surgery. That's when you started getting this way, Annie. I'm *not* fragile. I'm *not* breakable. I weathered it pretty damn well and now I have to go on living— on my own."

They stared at each other, and finally Ann gave one of her wide, sweet smiles that made Cici remember why she loved her. "Okay, I stand corrected. I have been mother-henning you to death."

"More like Mother Doom," Cici said, laughing.

"It's like I can't stop myself. But Cic . . ."

"Hush," Cici said, putting a hand to her friend's mouth. "Let's sample these cookies, okay? They gave me a guarantee— any cookies purchased on Thursday have no calories."

In the kitchen the women's voices, at first sharp, had begun to rise and gentle with laughter. Aaron listened to Ann Trevanian's laugh. It was full and rich, and sounded like some-body you could really like.

Reaching out one arm from where he lay on his bed, Aaron rewound the Paula Abdul tape he'd been playing and flicked off the stereo. The minute the music stopped, silence seemed to rush into his room.

No, not silence, because the night had turned windy and he could hear a couple of tree branches hitting against the upstairs window. He was supposed to have gotten up on a ladder and trimmed them, but he hadn't done it because it had rained, and then he'd forgotten, and his mother had forgotten, too.

Scraaaape. Then a pause, and *scraaaape* again.

Aaron got down on the floor and reached halfway under his bed, where he had hidden the three cartons of large eggs he had bought at Kroger, along with a spray can of black paint. He fished them out and opened up one of the cartons to inspect the eggs. One was cracked a little, but it wouldn't make any difference. He shook the can of paint, listening for the rattle of the metal ball inside.

Carrying the stuff in a plastic Kroger bag, he walked through the back hall and cut across the living room, out of the line of sight of Cici and Ann.

Tonight was going to be great.

The others were waiting when Aaron got there, at their usual place, next door in front of Dustin's house. Dustin, Kevin, and Matt, his best friends. Especially Dustin.

"Hey, hey, man, we thought you weren't coming," called Dustin as Aaron trotted up. Dustin was fourteen, short, blond, and handsome, with pale eyebrows and very white skin. Tonight he looked tense and hyper.

"I had to get the eggs, man," Aaron lied. "I had to buy them at Kroger."

"Well, it took you long enough."

"I'm here, aren't I? Can we get, you know, Heather's car?"

"Old Leather-Heather's got a date, man. She's gonna go out and get *laid.*"

The other boys giggled, their laughter coming out in explosive chokes. After a second, Aaron joined in, too. Actually, he had a major sexual crush on Heather Pickard.

"What you got?" Kevin DeAngelo wanted to know. The youngest of the group, he was only thirteen but had already been expelled from school twice, once for swearing, once for drinking. His mom and dad were separated and getting a messy divorce.

"Oh, just eggs and some paint. Black. Real good for writing. We're gonna be graffiti artists," Aaron boasted.

"Yeah, graffiti artists," echoed Matt Weingartz, a thin boy with angry red zits on his face. He was the only one whose parents hadn't split up. "Yeah, man."

They gathered in a clump like football players, and then they scattered out along the sidewalk, sometimes running, sometimes huddling together, sometimes just walking, especially if a car passed them.

It felt good to be running free, lights and shadows all around them, the crisp, chilly fall air.

"Who shall we do?" Dustin asked. He was moving more slowly than usual tonight, his hand occasionally rubbing his hip.

"Oh, I know who, let's do old dickhead," Aaron suggested, putting on a swagger. "Dickhead needs some more eggs. Dickhead needs a whole omelette on his front windows. He thinks he's something, thinks he's hot stuff because he collects a lot of stupid old clocks."

"Tick tock," cried Dustin, running.

"Bong bong bong," yelled Aaron, catching up. "The clock man strikes again!"

They attacked Bryan's house like commandos, materializing out of the shadows of the big blue spruces in his yard, then darting across the grass in their high-topped Reeboks. Except for some wild giggles they managed to repress their laughter.

Aaron felt a rush of satisfaction as he threw eggs at the windows, white and yellow goo and pieces of eggshell dribbling downward.

He threw another one, which fell a little short and only hit the stone sill before dropping in the bushes. Eggs were incredibly hard to clean up after they dried, that's what everyone said, and Aaron happened to know that Bryan was out of town, so these were going to get good and dry. He could picture old Bryan outdoors making his mouth all tight as he tried to squeegee it away.

Why couldn't his mother see the way Bryan's mouth pressed itself into a thin line sometimes, his eyes getting all flat as if he were thinking of something else, something not nice at all?

"Come on! Move it!" hissed Dustin. A car was rounding the corner, about to turn into the cul-de-sac, so Aaron hurled one last egg, then joined the others as they ran across the grass and through the yards to the other street.

After doing Bryan's house, the rest of it wasn't as much fun. In fact it was kind of boring. But Aaron raced along with the others, running the point of a key along the trunk lid of a white Probe parked in the driveway of the Masters' house. They raced on so fast that by the time the people inside the house heard running footsteps, they were already five houses down.

"Man! Man!"

"Watch your ass, stupidass!"

"That guy, he's gonna shit . . ."

They were gone in seconds, Vietcong on patrol. Then they ran through the pumpkin patch, which they had already raided several times before. Tonight only a few big ones were left.

"I want a punkin! I want a punkin!"

They took four, one each, Aaron's so large that it felt as if he were carrying a watermelon, the woody stem of its top bumping his nose as he ran. He stopped and threw it down on the sidewalk, then picked it up and threw it again when it didn't smash well enough.

They heard a cry from behind. Turning, Aaron saw that Dustin had tripped with his pumpkin, flat out on his stomach like a little kid. His jacket and T-shirt had ridden up to reveal inches of bare white skin.

"Man! Man! It hurts!"

"What's wrong with you, man? Fall and hurt yourself like a little, wittle baby?" crooned Matt, dancing back, glad to see their leader showing some weakness.

"Shut up!"

"Baby, baby, baby-ass Dustin is crying, isn't he? Baby-ass Dustin!"

"Shut up, I said! I hurt my ankle, man. I did something to it." Dustin sat up, hunching over his leg and rubbing his ankle.

"Baby ass! Baby ass!"

"Shut *up,* you fuckhead! I'm not crying, you fuck! You're the one who cries. I heard you last week in the gym when you fell on the—"

The others danced and capered, caught up in the mood of the night and the anger that always seemed to run behind it, especially when they threw things or broke things. Aaron joined in a little, too. He had to. "Baby ass! Dustin's a crybaby! Dustin, Dustin!"

But then another car swung past them, headlights forming a white cone. The driver was staring at them. Matt and Kevin ran on ahead, leaving Dustin still on the pavement.

"Can you get up?" Aaron said, approaching his friend.

"Man, I think I just twisted it."

But instead of getting to his feet, Dustin just sat on the sidewalk, rubbing at his ankle. Aaron noticed a dark bruise along the pale skin that showed near his back. Dark crisscrosses of bruises, some covered with scabs.

"Hey, man?" Aaron asked. "You really okay? What's that mark on you?"

"Nothing, man."

"Jeez," Aaron whispered, taking a better look at it. "You've got scabs there, Dust. Black and blue."

"Nothing happened, dammit! I'm okay, man! Anyway, who cares, right?" Dustin's voice shook. "When I get old enough I'm gonna run away from home—and I'll go where *he'll* never find me."

"He?" Aaron stared at his friend, shocked. "You don't mean your dad hit you?"

"No," sneered Dustin. "He didn't hit me, he just sorta *disciplined* me with this big old wooden lath he's got. It's got edges that cut. And once I got it with a—" He stopped and gripped Aaron by the lapels of his jacket. "Hey, man, you won't tell, will you? You got to swear not to tell. He'd really kill me then. He says it's family, he can do what he wants to family."

Aaron swallowed, feeling sick. Once or twice he'd heard yelling from next door—someone crying and screaming and swearing. He'd thought it was Dustin beating up on Heather.

Dustin reached up a hand and Aaron hauled him to his feet. The other boy moved slowly, and he was groaning as he dug his fingers into Aaron's arm. "Shit, my butt feels like hamburger meat."

Aaron helped his friend walk along the sidewalk. Child abuse. Yeah, he'd seen it on TV. And now it was happening to his own best friend.

"You gotta call the police, Dustin," he began.

"Yeah, sure, right." Dustin's voice was bitter. "As soon as they leave he'd hit me again. Only worse. And I *ain't* goin' to one of those foster homes. No way am I doing that."

Aaron didn't know what to say. He'd never imagined something like this happening to someone he knew. And Bryan Wyatt—his thoughts inevitably traveled to Bryan Wyatt. Was he that kind of guy, too? Was that why Aaron couldn't seem to like him, because he got that feeling about Bryan? A picture in his head of Bryan hitting him—hitting him hard . . .

He walked Dustin to his front steps. John Pickard's Chrysler LeBaron was gone from the driveway, and Aaron saw his friend relax.

"Man, you can come over to my house anytime," he offered, not knowing what else to say.

"Sure," Dustin said, getting out his house key. "Hey, it's cool, man."

Aaron walked across the strip of grass that separated the two houses. The lights were on in his own house, warm yellow squares that lit up the windows and made it look like a cozy, Christmas-card home. Guiltily he realized that it *was* actually a fairly happy house, even with his dad gone now. His mom never yelled at him—well, not actually raising her voice. He had never been hit, not even when he was a little bitty kid.

Cici had just said good-bye to Ann when she saw Aaron come in, sneaking through the living room. Guilt seemed to surround him like a strong aura. Fear filled her. Midnight had passed an hour ago. And wasn't that a yellow egg stain on the front of his jacket?

She spoke sharply. "Aar? Where were you, honey? Why did you leave the house at one A.M.?"

"I just needed some air."

"Air? Then you should have opened a window. I suppose you were with Dustin and Matt and Kevin."

"Yeah," her son mumbled, digging his hands in his pockets. He looked miserable and troubled.

Cici drew in a deep breath, pointing to the telltale stain on the jacket front. "What's that on your jacket?"

"What's what?" Aaron looked down, bewildered, as if he'd forgotten he was wearing a jacket at all.

"That's an egg stain, son. Raw egg."

He was squirming, almost wriggling in his dance to get away from her, to get back downstairs to his bedroom and the ever-present stereo that he used as a wall to keep her out of his life.

"Aaron!" she cried.

"Hey," her son protested. "Hey, I can't remember all the stains and stuff I get on me. I have to eat in the school cafeteria, remember. The home of mystery meat and tomato slop and terrible tacos. Hey, maybe this stain came from an alien hamburger, huh? There's a lady in the cafeteria who looks like an alien—"

"Don't you dare make a joke out of this!" Cici snapped. "Aaron, Bryan told me that kids have been vandalizing his house ever since he first met me. Do you have anything to do with that? And I want a straight answer, not a lot of silly talk about alien hamburgers."

"Martian hamburgers," Aaron said sarcastically. "Hey, they're what good old Bryan eats for breakfast. How do I know it? Because I was walking past his house one day and I saw this little silver spaceship landing in his yard, and on the side of it was this sign, 'Alien Big Macs, We Deliver, Hot and Fresh.'"

She reeled back a little. Aaron's sarcasm was so adult. "You really hate Bryan, don't you?" she asked in a low voice.

"I don't hate him. I just don't like him. He's like Dustin's dad."

"What do you mean?"

"Nothing," Aaron muttered. "You think because I'm only

fourteen I don't know anything. You think fourteen-year-old kids aren't smart, they can't see things."

"Aaron, that's just not so—"

"Well, I'm not dumb. I'm not stupid." Moisture glittered in Aaron's eyes. "I just don't want Bryan Wyatt for a stepdad, that's all. I can't help it, that's how I feel. And you don't even listen. You don't care."

Each word felt like a punch in Cici's stomach. "Aaron, oh, Aar. I do care. I care so much. Bryan doesn't hate you, he wants you to like him. Not to love him, you don't have to do that, I'd never try to force that. But just to—"

"I don't want him," Aaron repeated, his eyes hard.

SIX

"No new leads on the mysterious attacker nicknamed 'The Basher,' " a voice intoned over the car radio as Cici pulled into the parking lot of Scallops, a seafood restaurant just north of downtown Rochester. It was five days later, and she and Ann were meeting here for dinner.

The WJR newscaster went on. "Police now believe as many as ten single women may have been victimized since 1980 by a mysterious intruder who enters their homes and savagely beats them to death. He is believed to have removed their bodies for burial elsewhere. Police in Wayne, Oakland, and Macomb counties are reopening the missing-persons cases of several dozen women, hoping to find more clues. In Detroit, Mayor Coleman Young has said that—"

Nervously, Cici switched off the radio. The Basher had been on all the news broadcasts, the media saturation on a level with that occurring in 1978 and '79 when the "Oakland County Child Killer" had been on the loose. The discovery of a woman's dismembered, nude body in a Macomb County trash landfill had spawned grisly front-page headlines, then turned out to be a drug execution. A feature in the Sunday *News/Free Press* had covered famous mass murderers in detail.

The other suspected victims, Diane Rose, Angie Sterner, Terry Hazen, and others, all women in their twenties and thirties, were pathetic enough, but it was blond, vulnerable, twenty-six-year-old Abby Tighe who still remained most vivid in Cici's mind.

Where was Abby now? Was she lying naked at the bottom of the Detroit River, weighted down with cement blocks or sandbags? Was she buried somewhere in a woods, or lying abandoned in some old culvert covered with dead leaves and dirt, her pretty white fingers curled upward?

Nearly every night Abby's face seemed to swim into her dreams, a pale and pleading ghost.

Cici switched off the Cougar's ignition and got out of the car. Although it wasn't even five-thirty, darkness had already fallen, a heavy black velvet shroud that seemed to smother everything. She shivered as she hurried inside the restaurant. My, she was getting fanciful, wasn't she, with her mental images of smothering and shrouds?

Ann was late.

Cici ordered her usual wine spritzer and sipped it slowly, ignoring the interested glances of a single man seated at a nearby table. The wine mixed with soda seemed too tart tonight, and finally she pushed the glass away. She was edgy, that was the trouble . . . and had been for several weeks.

She couldn't actually pinpoint the moment when her uneasiness had begun. Maybe it was the night she and Bryan had had the fight about Aaron calling Bry a dickhead. The night she'd stood in the shadows watching Bryan unload the oddly heavy rug that bulged so fatly in the center.

She frowned as she remembered he'd never really shown it to her, not officially anyway. However, she'd seen several new Oriental rugs, one in his study, another in his bedroom, so undoubtedly one of them was the one he'd been unloading that night.

She sat fussing with the wineglass, tracing patterns in the

beads of moisture with her fingertip. Her engagement diamond sparkled like the chips of ice in her glass.

What if there really had been something wrapped up in that rug . . . a human body?

Cici twisted impatiently, pushing away the idea almost immediately. What was the matter with her? Between Ann's questions and doubts, and the exploits of the Basher, she was letting her imagination run wild. Bryan was a fussy type, a neatnik, and he'd probably thought it was very efficient to carry some new purchase in the rug.

"Sorry I'm late, but the highway department decided to block a lane at the Rochester Bridge again," a voice said gaily beside her. "I think that bridge is going to be under repair until the year 2000."

It was Ann, looking anything but sorry. Her mane of dark hair was swept attractively back, and she wore an above-the-knee skirt and a red blouse that seemed to telegraph excitement.

The man who had stared at Cici now transferred his attention to Ann. Ignoring him, Ann slid into the booth and flagged down the waiter. "I need something to wet my whistle—a nice Bloody Mary, with double celery," she specified. "I like my vitamins with a kick."

Cici felt a rush of affection for her friend. "Ann, you are incorrigible."

"I know, but it's fun. Oh, did I tell you? Your neighbor tried to pick me up yesterday."

"Which neighbor? You don't mean John Pickard?"

"The very one. We work out at the same health club. You should see him in a tank top and shorts—he's actually not bad looking. Those physical types really can be. He really had a crude come-on, though. And I think he just dyed his hair."

Both women giggled.

"I mean, didn't he used to be almost gray?" Ann asked.

"Yes."

"Well, he's Mr. Clairol now."

They laughed again, and Cici told Ann how Pickard had approached her using the ruse of comparing notes on their children.

"Men," said Ann, shrugging. "They're so amazing."

"Let's flag down the waiter and order," Cici suggested. "I'm getting the sautéed bluefish. Did I tell you I ordered the wedding cake this week? It's going to be heart shaped, with three tiers, and flowers on top."

Ann raised an eyebrow. "No bride and groom dolls?"

"Bryan didn't really want them."

"Well, persuade him, then. When I get married I always have bride and groom dolls on my cake. I'm making a collection of them—they'll be worth plenty sometime." Ann spoke wryly.

It was when their meals arrived that Ann announced she had bought a gun.

"What?" Cici stared at her friend, shocked.

Ann mimicked shooting. "A nice thirty-eight, with a box of ammo, the whole bit. I even signed up for lessons on how to shoot it. Maybe I'll turn out to be a fantastic sharpshooter or something. The man said I had some aptitude for the whole thing."

Cici gave an uncomfortable laugh. "A *gun?* Jesus, Ann . . . you sound so—I don't know."

"Scared is what I sound. Haven't you been reading the papers? I have, and I don't particularly want to find some huge, muscular, screaming maniac in my house ready to club me down."

"But to have a gun in your house, Ann. Guns draw violence."

"Guns *prevent* violence, kiddo! Do you realize how close some of those victims lived to us? One of them, I think it was Terry Hazen, lived in Utica near Twenty-one Mile and Shelby. That's practically next door. And the Tighe woman was in Royal Oak near William Beaumont Hospital. I used to go to the doctor at Beaumont Hospital, Cici. I've probably driven right past her neighborhood."

"But to carry a gun with you . . . it's like the Wild West."

"I'm not going to carry it. I don't have a permit to carry. You have to have a special police permit for that. I'm going to keep it in my house, in my bedside table, just in case."

"What if you're not in your bedroom when the Basher comes?"

"*When* the Basher comes?" Now Ann was the one to shiver. "Hey, I don't know, maybe I'll seduce him and lure him up to my boudoir so I can get to my weapon. *I* don't know. I'd think of something."

"Well, I can't buy a gun, anyway," Cici decided. "I have Aaron in the house. I can't keep a gun with him around."

"If he doesn't know about it, you can. You can hide it in your closet."

Cici looked at her friend, who had never had children. "Get real, Ann. In the first place, kids snoop. They explore the whole house, they go through your drawers. Didn't you ever do that when you were a kid? I did. I knew everything my mother had in her dresser drawers. In the second place, well, Aaron is too moody to have a gun around."

The friends fell silent, both of them poking at their food with their forks, the festive mood of the evening—if there had been one at all—quite spoiled.

"Hey," Ann said after a moment. "Let's talk about guys. Did I tell you Larry's thinking about getting a Gold Wing Honda? Can't you just picture him, forty years old and tearing around town on a motorcycle? It must be midlife crisis."

When Cici came in from the garage the phone was ringing, and she hurried inside to pick up the receiver.

"Cecilia, is that you?" Her mother's voice sounded as if it were in the other room rather than in Forest Park, a suburb of Cincinnati.

"Who else would it be, Mom? How've you been? How's the reorganization at work? Did you get the floor you wanted?"

"Women's Surgical," Lila McKenna declared with some satisfaction. "A lot better than Emergency, believe me. So, what's going on with you and Bryan? Are you still getting married the day after Christmas?"

"Yes, we are." Cici deftly slithered out of her jacket while still holding the phone. Aaron had left a note on the refrigerator. *At Dustin's. Love, Aaron.* The note was embellished with a small drawing of a dragon.

"No second thoughts, honey?"

"None," Cici said after an infinitesimal hesitation.

"Are you sure, Cecilia? You don't sound a hundred percent sure to me."

"I *am* sure, Mom. And I wanted to ask you, are you still planning to come and stay with Aaron? I mean, they did give you the time off, didn't they?"

"Yes, everything's all set. I put in the schedule today. I hope Aaron will eat my cooking—I remember how fussy you were at that age."

Cici grimaced. Her mother's tales of her "fussy" eating had become augmented by time. "Aaron is a teenager, Mom, not four years old. Boys eat everything at his age—they're human food processors."

Conversation drifted to family matters, and finally Cici's mother, who subscribed to three daily papers, said, "And did you read the latest psychological profile of the Basher?"

"What psychological profile?"

"Cecilia, you *have* to read the papers every day. Otherwise you lose track. It's this psychologist, Dr. Fellows. They use him a lot in crime cases. He says that the Basher is probably in his thirties, very controlled, and he does the killings to relieve tension caused by stresses in his life."

"Mom, really. Police profiles are just guesswork."

"Those people study crime all the time, Cici. He may have had a severe upbringing, and was physically abused. In his childhood he wet the bed, and masturbated to excess. He was cruel to small animals—you know, dogs and cats—and he may have set fires. He hates women, hates his mother, and—"

Cici interrupted, shaking her head. Her mother adored true crime stories. "Don't they all hate their mothers? Isn't that the classic? I think it's baloney, just an excuse. Mothers take the rap for everything."

"Well, thank you for that, anyway. But I hope you're being careful. I worry about you living alone."

"Mom, I don't live alone. I have Aaron."

"Well, you *know* what I mean. He's just a child."

Cici sighed. "He's fourteen, Mom. And I do have Bryan. I'm not exactly alone."

"But Bryan's not over there at your house all the time. Do you have a weapon you keep in the house? I read in *USA Today* about these tear-gas canisters. All you do is aim it in the direction of your attacker and press the nozzle. I'm going to order one."

First Ann. Now her mother. Cici released her breath in a tight, nervous laugh. "Mom, I'm *not* going to buy tear gas. With my luck, I'd be holding the nozzle pointed right at me. I'd probably asphyxiate myself, not him."

"Still," Lila McKenna said.

"I can't spend my life worrying about some maniac, Mom," Cici said hollowly.

"Look, girl, you'd better start doing exactly that," her mother remarked with unexpected firmness. "I'm a nurse, Cici. I worked Emergency for ten years. I've seen a lot. I've seen women come in beaten half to death, and it's enough to turn your stomach. I've seen pretty faces turned into hamburger. Broken noses flattened and pushed to one side of the face. I've seen women with all their front teeth missing, and burns from cigarettes all over their—"

"Mom," Cici managed to choke, stopping the tirade.

"Well, it *is* reality," Lila said. "Cecilia, sometimes I worry about you. You have a tendency to deny reality, to push things aside and try to pretend they aren't really there."

"I'm not that way!" Cici exclaimed, stung.

"Aren't you? What about your marriage to Tom? It was in trouble long before he deserted you because of your mastectomy, Cici, you know it was. And then there's Bryan, your fiancé. I'm not saying anything against him, but I listen to the tone in your voice, Cecilia Marie, and it does not sound like that of an ecstatically happy bride floating on cloud nine."

Was that true? Cici hung on to the phone, feeling perspiration dampen her hands. "Anything else?" she inquired sharply. "While we're going over my entire life for flaws, I mean."

"Now, Cecilia—"

"Mother," Cici said. "I love talking to you and I'm glad you called, but I'm leading the life I want to lead and I *am* happy. I'm very, *very* happy. And now," she lied, "I think I hear Aaron coming home, so I've got to go. I'll call you next Sunday."

"All right, but—"

" 'Bye, Mom," Cici interrupted, hanging up. She replaced the phone in its cradle and stood staring down at it. She hadn't liked the shaky tone in her own voice just when she'd insisted she was happy. Her mother had undoubtedly heard it too, and would keep it in reserve for future lectures.

Oh, God, *was* she happy? Or was she just going through the motions, pretending she felt what brides were supposed to feel? She just wished that Bryan would open up to her more. For instance, that nightmare he'd had several weeks ago. Had he really forgotten what it was about, as he'd told her? How could he have a terrible nightmare about someone he called "Pa" and not remember what the dream had been about?

Of course I'm happy, she assured herself. *This is just prewedding jitters, that's all. Everyone has those.*

SEVEN

On Friday, Cici had agreed to return some of the membership materials to the Friday Nighters club. She and Bryan had decided that he would attend, too. It would be their last visit to the singles club—a sentimental commemoration. Cici's idea, really. She wanted to dance cheek to cheek with Bryan again and recapture the same rush of feeling, the same euphoria as on the night they had first met.

However, Bryan called her that day at work, telling her he had several meetings and would be late. Rather than pick her up, he would meet her at the banquet hall.

She was disappointed. "On our last night there, Bry? I've been looking forward to this."

"I'll be there," he promised. "But it'll be after ten. Just don't go dancing with any other guys, at least not any slow dances. You're mine now, remember."

There was a short line at the sign-in table, as members paid their entrance fees and showed their membership cards. A few had brought guests. As Cici filled out her name tag, she felt a twinge of her old vulnerability, as if she were still the same timid and panicky Cici who had first come here to the Friday Nighters expecting rejection.

Several women greeted her, and Cici showed off her engagement diamond. There were envious cries. Displaying the elegant, two-carat emerald-cut stone, she flushed with pride. These other women would give anything to be in her shoes. Not only was Bryan handsome, but he held an excellent job, was straight, and had his act together. How many catches like him were available in the singles world? From talking to Ann, she knew that single men were often riddled with commitment problems or substance addictions.

Lynn Petit, a heavy woman who was the membership chairman, came up to her. "Cici, since Bryan isn't here yet, have you got a few minutes to help out? We've got a couple of membership foul-ups to straighten out. About twenty-five people aren't getting their newsletters."

"Sure," Cici said. Lynn told her what to do, and she took the membership roster and a stack of sign-in sheets to an empty table at the back of the meeting room.

While several officers prepared for the meeting, she began comparing the lists of signatures, some of which dated back to the previous February, several months before she had met Bryan. She spotted her own signature several times, and Ann's, and that of John Pickard, her neighbor.

Then a name jumped out at her, seeming almost to leap up off the page.

Abby Tighe.

She stared down at the pretty, ballpoint signature of the Basher's victim. The *A* was a big, round loop, the *i* dotted with a round circle. It was the handwriting of someone sweet and unassertive—almost a high school girl's writing.

Seeing the signature brought Abby uncomfortably to life. She'd been in these very rooms, on—Cici glanced at the date— August 5. Over two months ago. She'd worn something pretty, no doubt, maybe a new dress or a short skirt and blouse. Those fluffy blond bangs had probably been moussed and curled with a curling iron.

Had Abby met someone here?

Had she met the Basher here? It *was* possible.

Now, stop being overdramatic, Cici told herself, slowing her breathing and reaching for the next sheet. There didn't have to be any significance in the fact that she had found Abby's name. It *was* a popular local club, its total membership numbering over fifteen hundred.

Still, her conversation with her mother came flooding back, Lila's vivid description of beaten women. She could picture Abby, cowering away from battering, punishing blows. Blood gushing from her mouth where there were broken teeth . . .

"You look positively white," Ann said beside her.

Cici jumped.

"You've been staring at that piece of paper for the past four minutes," Ann teased, sitting down beside her.

"Oh . . . have I?"

"Yes, you have."

Wordlessly Cici pushed the sheet with Abby's signature toward Ann.

"Holy crow," Ann said, whistling.

"It's Abby Tighe. It's her. She was *here,* Ann. She came to the Friday Nighters."

"But that was way back in August," Ann pointed out. "She hadn't disappeared yet."

"*Yet.* What if she met someone here? What if he was the one? I mean *the one.* He could have picked her up here, Ann. He could have made the connection with her here."

"Oh, Jesus, Cici." Their eyes locked, sharing the same ugly thought.

Cici rose, more from a need to do something, to move around, than from any urge to be a detective. "I've got a couple of old issues of the *Detroit News* in my car—I think there's a picture of her. I'm going to go out to the parking lot and get it. I'm just wondering if someone might have seen her here, seen who she was talking to."

Cici glanced at her watch. It was 9:50, and Bryan had said he would try to arrive sometime around ten. The speaker was still at the mike, a dynamic young man talking about personal crime prevention, a topic that Cici considered eerily appropriate. At the back of the room, she whispered a question to Lynn Petit, who thought she might have seen Abby.

"You say she was here most of the evening?"

"Yes . . . I noticed her because she seemed so new."

"Did you see anyone talk to her?"

Lynn shrugged. "Lots of guys talked to her. She was pretty. She danced every dance. You know how it is when they're young and pretty and all the guys hit on them." There was envy in the heavy woman's tone.

Cici sighed, thinking that this information was far too general to be useful. Should the police be told about the signature? Undoubtedly so. They would be better equipped to ask questions of club members. She gave up and turned her attention to the speaker, who was now telling the women in the audience how to defend themselves against a potential rapist.

"Remember, ladies, you might have to get a little closer to your rapist than you might want. But the trick is to GRASP HIS TESTICLES, PULL, AND SQUEEZE!"

There was a collective gasp in the audience. Then nervous laughter.

"Look at all the men," remarked Ann. "Look at their faces. They're turning white."

"PULL! AND SQUEEZE!" All the men in the audience winced, while the women laughed loudly and nervously.

Cici hugged herself, watching the reactions of the people around her. She wondered if Abby Tighe had had time to make such a maneuver or had even thought of it. Or been capable of it at all. It was easy to sit in a crowded room and figure out how you were going to be a heroine. But when the attacker was actually *there*, what would you really do?

Later, during the enthusiastic applause, Ann nudged Cici. "Hey, come on in the other room. We can talk a little before Bryan gets here."

Cici followed her friend to the room the club used for dancing, where the disc jockey, T.J. the D.J., was setting up his equipment. They sat down at a table spread with flyers about upcoming club activities.

"I found a woman who remembered Abby," Ann began. Her eyes glittered, and her mouth was in an unusually straight line. "Jayne Kepplinger. She sells real estate here in town. She says Abby was dancing quite a few dances with a light-haired man. Well built and blond. Handsome."

Cici felt a strange chill. "There's tons of blond men who come here, Ann. He could be any of them. Even John Pickard from next door. He's blond."

Ann's eyes bored into hers. "You're not going to like it, but I know another person who matches that description, and I happen to know that right after you met him he did come to the Friday Nighters a couple of times by himself. And he stayed for the dancing, too. He danced every dance."

God, Ann meant Bryan.

Cici stared at her friend, too startled to speak.

"I didn't tell you before. I didn't want to upset you," Ann added.

Cici swallowed. "Ann, I'd just *met* him. We weren't serious yet. We weren't exclusive yet."

Ann shifted, looking exceedingly uncomfortable. "Cic, no one can talk to you about this man, can they? He's secretive about his background and he's given more than one person bad vibes. Not just me, but Aaron too, and even Tom—you told me what Tom said about him."

"Ann!" Cici felt a burst of real anger, more so because that very fact had worried her, too.

"Doesn't it mean anything to you that more than one person doesn't like him?" Then Ann sighed. "Hey, all right. I'm pushing this too far. I'm sorry I—"

"Sorry about what?"

Both women turned. Bryan was approaching their table, smiling one of his wide, beautiful, sexy smiles that grabbed at Cici's heart. He was wearing a pale-gray suit that emphasized his broad, athletic shoulders and narrow waist. His shirt had narrow blue stripes, and his silk foulard tie was also blue. He looked clean-cut and fabulous . . . a dream fiancé.

"Are you talking about me?" he asked in a jocular manner. "Come on, now, I want to know what you two are saying about me."

The music had begun, a slow Kenny Rogers ballad. Cici and Ann glanced at each other.

"Just what a desirable hunk you are," Cici said quickly, matching his light tone. "And I hope you remember how to dance, because I love Kenny Rogers slow dances."

"And I love *you*," Bryan said deliberately.

The music was sweetly sentimental, almost sad, mingling with the tang of cigarette smoke and perfume that floated in the air. Cici danced close to her fiancé, enjoying the smooth texture of his cheek against her own. The aftershave he wore, which she had given him, enhanced the more subtle aroma of his own skin.

The past months had given her a familiarity with his body that was extremely sexually stimulating tonight, she had to admit.

"Well, what does Ann think of me?" Bryan wanted to know when they had been dancing a few minutes.

"She thinks we're getting married too soon," Cici admitted.

"I gathered that. But what was she saying about me in particular?"

God, she couldn't repeat what Ann really had said. "She just thinks we're not ready."

"Cic, I'll tell you what, your friend Ann has a very bad case of sour grapes. I don't notice her with an engagement ring on her finger. We are talking about jealousy here."

"I don't know," Cici said, troubled.

"Trust me, Cici. I think she's a man hater. Women like that don't want to admit any man could have some good in him."

"Ann likes men!" Cici heard herself protest. "She does. She—"

"She hates men, Cici," he interrupted, ending the discussion.

John Pickard was one of the single men standing in the stag line, stylishly turned out in a blue blazer and gray pleated pants, the cut of the blazer emphasizing the wide, weightlifter's span of his shoulders.

In the dim light of the dance floor, the newly dyed blond hair looked golden. John stared at Cici and Bryan as they walked off the dance floor, his expression curiously brooding.

It gave Cici a chill, although she wasn't quite sure why. It was almost as if he was staring at Bryan rather than at her. Was he jealous that she was with Bryan? *A hunter*, Ann had called him.

Cici was tired, Pickard's stare was unnerving, and the cigarette smoke in the room was suddenly making her eyes burn. "We don't belong here at these dances anymore, Bryan," she remarked. "An engaged couple doesn't really fit in. It's not like it was when we first met and you used to come here alone."

"I never came here alone."

She stared at him. "You did, Bry. Ann saw you."

Bryan's eyes looked cold. "Ann lied, Cici. You just can't see it, can you? She is jealous of you and trying to tear me down."

Cici stood silently, not wanting to argue with Bryan anymore. Ann said he'd come to the dances alone, he said he didn't. Which of them was she to believe? It was easy enough to check the sign-in lists for his signature, but did she really want to do that? Anyway, Bryan had barely met her then and had a right to do as he pleased.

"I . . . I think I could use a glass of wine," she said finally. "Maybe a spritzer."

Bryan nodded and excused himself, heading across the room crowded with mingling singles to the table where bar tickets were being sold. Pickard also went to get in line, and Cici averted her eyes from both men.

"Okay," Ann murmured, materializing at Cici's elbow. "I guess we're going to have to have this out, aren't we? I mean, I can see by your face you're ready to kill me."

"Yes, I am," Cici said stiffly. "But I don't want to talk about it now, not with Bryan right here."

Bryan was returning from the bar, making his way through knots of people, guarding the two plastic glasses of wine he carried. Several women smiled at him hopefully.

Ann and Cici watched him approach.

"Smile, Cici," Ann said. "God, he *is* good-looking, isn't he? He definitely is a head turner. I guess I can't blame you for being smitten—half the world would think Bryan Wyatt is wonderful. Well, I guess I'll go find Larry. He's got that nice little spare tire . . . just enough to be cuddly, if you know what I mean."

Ann blended into the crowd, and Cici waited as her fiancé approached, bearing her drink, his face open and handsome.

They left the dance at midnight, driving home in separate cars. As they turned into the subdivision, a sudden wind tore at the dead leaves that still hung on the trees, lashing them back and forth in an eerie, sweeping rustle. One dead leaf had become trapped in Cici's windshield-wiper blade and fluttered desperately, like a live creature trying to get free.

Cici turned on the wiper blades to free it. It went sailing off into the night, pulled by the strong wind.

She parked in her driveway, Bryan's van immediately behind hers, then got out of her car and went to sit in the Aerostar with him.

"It was a great dance, wasn't it?" Bryan murmured, sliding his arm around her. "Good music. And it felt so good to hold you close."

"Do you want to come in the house?" Cici asked.

"Not tonight, honey. I've got an early morning—a big report to finish. I'll have to go to the office."

"Oh . . ." She fought her spasm of disappointment. Somehow the dance hadn't re-created any of the feelings she'd hoped for. In fact, it had made her feel even more distant from Bryan than before. And the fact that he'd once danced with Abby Tighe . . . why hadn't he ever mentioned it to her? Or didn't he even remember?

"Now, come on, Cici, you know it's an important time at work for me—I can't afford to lose sleep. We're seeing each other tomorrow night," he was saying. "We have tickets to Meadowbrook, remember?"

"Oh, yes . . . a good-night kiss, then," she said, feeling like a pouty child.

Bryan enfolded her in his arms for a long kiss, his tongue probing within her mouth and toying with her lips in a manner that sent shivers straight to her crotch. But somehow the sexual feelings were getting short-circuited. Instead, her thoughts kept spinning, back to what Ann had said at the dance.

"I've really got to go, hon," Bryan said, pulling away. He reached to his left to unlock the automatic door button, the sound a loud, metallic *ping*.

Cici slid out of the car. "Bry . . . are you going to miss me tonight?" something made her ask.

He looked surprised. "Of course. I always miss you."

"Are you looking forward to December?" To their wedding, she meant.

He looked at her, his eyes made opaque by her yard lights shining in through the windshield of the van. "You know I am. I love you, darling. I'll always love you, and I'll take care of you. You'll never have to worry."

Exactly the words she wanted to hear. Damn Ann for her doubts. She did not need Ann's nagging questions. *Or your own?* a little voice added in her head.

Cici gave Bryan another kiss and went hurrying up to her front door.

As soon as she stepped inside the house, the pounding rhythms of her son's rock music grabbed her by the gut.

The house smelled strongly of popcorn, and Aaron's school jacket lay in a crumpled circle in the center of the hall floor. Her own life seemed to reach out and enfold her in its solidity.

"Aaron," she called to her son over the too-loud music. "Aar? I see a jacket that needs picking up."

She walked around it, resisting the urge to do it for him, and went into the kitchen. Aaron's typical popcorn mess greeted her.

"Aaron!" she called, annoyed.

She began automatically to clean up. But then her thoughts scattered, and she thought of Ann again. She and Ann had always discussed every up and down in their relationships with men. They'd told each other everything—they'd laughed and they'd cried. Surely this tiff with her friend would blow over soon, once she made Ann understand there were areas of her life Ann had to leave alone.

But when she dialed Ann's phone number, she got the tape.

"Hi, this is Ann. I can't come to the phone right now, but your call is extremely important to me, so at the sound of the—"

Cici hung up before the beep. She rubbed tiredly at her eyes. Ann must have gone out for a late drink with Larry—or had she simply turned on her tape while they made love? Cici happened to know this was a practice of Ann's. Tomorrow they would laugh and tease each other about it.

She rubbed her temples where a sudden headache seemed to be trying to knock its way out through her skin. A bad feeling was squeezing her . . . a premonition of some bad thing about to happen, something terribly wrong.

Will you stop? she told herself, annoyed. The disagreement with Ann had somehow colored her perception of everything, she realized. Even being with Bryan felt different, less secure. She supposed Ann's opinions were only bringing her own prewedding doubts to the surface. Well, those doubts were going to have to stop.

She decided to go down the hall and check on her son, try once more to get him to talk to her. *Please,* she found herself praying, *don't let the bad thing be about Aaron. I couldn't take it if it was. I can take anything but that.*

It was one-thirty A.M. when Ann Trevanian pulled her car into the driveway of her condominium. As she flicked the opener for the single-unit garage, a set of car headlights cruised slowly down the street, casting crooked, moving shadows on the row of condos before turning the corner.

She wondered which of her neighbors it was. Most of the people who lived here were older couples or retired, but there were several nurses who worked afternoons.

She waited impatiently for the door to move up on its tracks. Tomorrow she was leaving to visit her mother—she'd cleared it with her boss, and she was looking forward to the trip. Her mother, still beautiful at age sixty-two, had promised to take her shopping at Trump Tower in Manhattan, and they planned to see a few Broadway shows, which Larry had slightly mocked.

Thinking of it, Ann made a little face. Larry was her own age, but had a habit of thinking old. Or else, she told herself thoughtfully, she was the one out of whack.

She pulled the car in, flipped the door remote again, and went inside.

Her condo was carefully decorated in mauve and cream, and she'd spent hours searching out the paintings and prints she liked best. An artist called Nell Revel Smith was her favorite.

Ann went immediately to her answering machine and played back the tape, which contained two hang-ups. Shit. Why couldn't people leave *some* kind of a voice print, even if it was only a "hi," or even heavy breathing?

She reset the tape and went to the hall mirror, examining herself with severe scrutiny. Dancing made her sweat so much. Her makeup looked streaky, and her eyeliner had run a little, too. She noticed that she had also spilled something on the front of the teal-blue blouse she wore. She rubbed the splotch, feeling annoyed. And further annoyed at the fight she'd had with Cici.

For fight it had been.

Dammit! Why couldn't Cici see what she was doing? Ann didn't want to watch what was going to happen—a hasty marriage, a painful second divorce. Anyone who had been single a while had observed the crazy rebound marriages that lasted only two or three or, at best, fourteen months.

People grabbing, searching to fill a void in themselves.

Ann sighed and began undressing, tossing her short black skirt on a chair and peeling off her sheer black panty hose. She took off the blouse last and then, clad only in bra and bikini panties, started through the kitchen to the small laundry area. Her weekly maid had taken two months off for major surgery and Ann hadn't replaced her. As a result, her housekeeping was beginning to fall apart, and about five loads of laundry waited to be done.

In the cramped but adequate laundry room, a condo-sized washer-dryer in goldenrod yellow awaited her convenience. She spot-treated the blouse, then added it to a load of colored clothes that included two weeks' worth of panties.

She added a dollop of blue liquid soap, and punched the button to start the machine humming.

Bryan Wyatt was definitely *strange,* she was thinking. The way he had looked at her as he came across the room. Eyes like cold blue marbles. Why hadn't Cici noticed that absolutely killer expression? She was blind to him, that was why. Besotted! He overlooked her mastectomy scar and poured romance into her life, and Cici lapped it up like a starved cat.

Water was now pouring loudly into the washer. Ann padded back into the kitchen, deciding to get some frozen yogurt out of the freezer and eat it slowly out of the carton.while she waited.

She was standing at the refrigerator when she felt a presence behind her.

Not a sound, not exactly. Just a sensation that the air was being filled up, that someone was breathing very near her.

She turned.

A man wearing a pair of panty hose stretched over his face was standing in her kitchen by the dinette table. Seen through the brown nylon mesh, his features were mashed and flat. He was tall, well built, and wore something she saw only as a blur of beige. Coveralls? Some kind of suit.

"Ann," said the intruder hoarsely. "Ann, come to me."

She staggered backward, a scream freezing halfway up her throat.

He knew her name. Had he found it on some of her papers? How had he got in? Had he been here all along, waiting for her?

And then, with a horrible chill that reached all the way down her throat to her stomach and genitals, she saw what he was holding in his hands.

"Say your death prayer, Ann," he ordered in a voice that seemed high, artificially pitched and yet deathly familiar. She knew this man. She'd heard his voice before.

"No! No, oh God . . ."

He read her lips. "Take not the name of the Lord in vain." *The Basher. He was the Basher!*

The gun, she thought wildly. Thank God she had the gun . . . but it was upstairs in her bedside table, just the worst place for it, she realized. She had to somehow get away from him, get upstairs so she could use it.

"Ann," he kept saying. "Ann . . . Ann . . ."

"Please." At last she found something that passed for a voice. "God wouldn't want you to do this. God says not to. God says—"

A mistake.

Even behind the mesh of the panty hose, she could see the angry flash of the eyes. He hated her to use God against him; he thought God was on *his* side. Oh, god, oh, Jesus, this was so incredible, he was going to kill her right here and now, like he had all those other women.

He was going to beat her to death.

Suddenly the intruder swung the massive wooden club that was thicker and flatter than a baseball bat. It whistled through the air and smashed into the center of Ann's glass dinette table, sending papers, place mats, coffee cups, and shards of glass cascading down through the triangle of wrought-iron legs that had supported the table.

CRASH! CRASH! CRASH!

The huge, deadly paddle pulverized the remains of the table like a slow-motion scene in a cop movie.

"Please, please, please!" Ann sobbed. She felt terribly naked, defenseless in her lacy bra and blue bikini panties. With his body, he blocked her flight. She began backing away from him in the only direction she could go, toward the laundry room, which had no outside exit.

CRASH! The club hit the doorjamb just beside her, splintering it like matchsticks. Ann cowered away, terror flooding her. This was insane . . . insane . . . Why, oh why had she bought a condo without enough decent exits? The design of her damn condo was going to kill her.

"Bitch!" he shouted. *"Cunt!"*

She half-fell against the washer. It was still tumbling her blouse, sheets, and panties, vibrating with cheerful domesticity.

Desperately Ann's hands groped behind her, closing on an aerosol can of stain spray.

She hurled it at him with all her strength.

It hit his chest and bounced to the floor, its lid clattering off.

Ann wept with fright. Such a puny, ridiculous weapon when she had a gun upstairs she couldn't get to. She'd have to fight him somehow—fight back. She was tall, 5'10". But she was already weak with a sickening terror that had drained the energy from her.

Her attacker swung the paddle again.

SMASH!

It landed in a hideous smash of wood slivers and paint chips, the sound simultaneous with Ann's high-pitched scream.

SMASH! CRASH! She felt vomit choke up in her throat. Hot moisture gushed down her inner thigh—she'd wet herself. She no longer cared.

Like a cornered animal, she backed further into the laundry, going the full length of her possible retreat. He followed her, swinging the club like a wrecking ball. SMASH! CRASH! Every stroke was maniacal. The doorjamb again. The top of the washer. Then the plastic controls, which broke off like chips and went scattering. She shrieked as a high blow demolished the overhead light. Pieces of milky glass fell all around them like crazy rain.

"Don't," she whimpered. *"Don't, don't, don't . . ."*

He seemed not to hear her pleas.

Each blow landed closer to her, pulverizing, shattering, exploding fragments of wall and ceramic in her face. Ann staggered, twisting away from the club. She thought fleetingly of her mother, in Danbury. Of Cici. Yes—

And then the club raised again.

Ann bent her head, protecting her scalp with her forearms and hands.

She barely saw the paddle descending. It arrived in a whoosh like a shadow in the corner of her eye. It hit so hard that the explosion it caused was far beyond pain. It was a catastrophe of *nothingness* from which she could only fall backward, becoming a rag doll, and into the universe.

More blows, not so sharply felt. Things flew in the air. Her own blood, pieces of her.

Lying on the floor, all the feeling in her body gone, and her breath exhaling from her, Ann could still see briefly through one bloody eye. What she saw was him holding the club between his legs, rubbing it back and forth, back and forth.

You bastard, she thought, her thoughts sifting like mist.

EIGHT

That night Cici slept poorly. For some reason her dreams were of Ann. Ann walking up a hill, pausing to stare back at her with sad eyes.

She awoke, shivering, got out of bed, and pulled on her shortie robe, switching on her bedside lamp. Although the air was cool, she had been perspiring and her skin felt clammy. The branch from the birch tree had been banging on her window again, and that was probably what had wakened her. Why would Ann's trip to Connecticut have spooked her, given her unpleasant dreams?

She went downstairs in bare feet. The house was in its nighttime mode. There were unexpected cracks and pops in the drywall, and the refrigerator motor chose that moment to begin its mechanized humming. A little *click* made her jump, and she realized it came from the kitchen clock.

Four A.M.

She switched on the kitchen light and made herself some instant cocoa. She sat sipping it, remembering last night, the pointed sound of the automatic door locks as Bryan unlocked the door for her to get out of the van. She'd hoped to feel closer to him last night; instead she'd felt farther away than ever.

And had he really danced with Abby Tighe, as Ann insisted?

She felt another wave of anger at Ann for her refusal to accept Bryan. She wanted to enjoy her prewedding weeks, not worry about Ann's "vibes" and "hunches."

Finally she went back to bed and managed to fall uneasily asleep.

The following morning was Saturday. Cici decided to do some long-overdue housecleaning. Working all week in an office, she enjoyed the physical activity of vacuuming and scrubbing, and even decided that she would wash some of the kitchen windows.

Her mother called at eleven-thirty. Cici completed arrangements for her to stay with Aaron, thinking that in the daylight her concerns of last night seemed superficial, the product of tiredness and prewedding tension. Bryan too was tired, stressed from pressures at work. None of it carried much significance— all engaged couples, if they'd been married previously, went through their periods of doubt and soul searching.

Even Ann ought to know that, with her two marriages and all her relationships.

As she was hanging up, Aaron slouched into the kitchen, his eyes still puffy from sleep. He wore skinny jeans and an Aerosmith T-shirt, and looked young and smooth-skinned— very vulnerable this morning.

Cici felt a rush of love for him. "Hey, good morning, sleepyhead."

He mumbled a greeting, managing a crooked grin. "Who was that on the phone?"

"It was Grandma," Cici began, thinking that this couldn't be a better opening for her to explain her plans. "She's coming here for Christmas, and she'll stay over for the next two weeks while Bryan and I are in Hawaii."

Aaron scowled, hunching his shoulders over and staring at the floor. "You mean to babysit me?"

"I wouldn't put it that way exactly."

"I'm *not* a baby, Mom. Can't I stay by myself? Or I can stay at Dustin's house—his dad said it was okay. I'd go to school every day with him, and there wouldn't be any problem. I'll do all my homework, I promise."

"I don't want you staying there," Cici said sharply.

"Aw, Mom . . ."

"That's the final word. Now after you have breakfast I would appreciate it if you would go and get the stepladder out of the garage, and the hedge clippers, and go up and trim that knocking branch."

"No!" her son suddenly shouted.

Cici stared at him, startled.

Red splotches stood out in angry relief on Aaron's cheeks. "I *don't* want you to marry Bryan, Mom. Can't you listen to me just for once? He's a weirdo and mean, and a jerk."

"Aaron!"

"If you really marry the guy, then I'm going to go and live with Dad."

Cici recoiled. "Aar. Please," she managed. "Let's talk about this later, when we're both calmer."

"I'm not going to *be* calmer!" he shouted, whirling and running off to his bedroom. Cici heard the door slam. After a few seconds there was the familiar blast of the stereo that he used as a protective wall.

She stood shaken, thinking about Aaron's threat to live with his father. Tom could barely stand to visit Aaron for a couple of hours. He certainly wasn't going to open his home to his son—not with a new, sexy girlfriend in the picture. She was ashamed of herself for taking comfort from that. God, she didn't know what she'd do without Aaron.

When she had finished the kitchen, she dialed Ann's number but got the answering machine again. Obviously her friend had already left for the airport. Cici knew Ann would pick up the messages later, using her remote.

She waited impatiently for the beep. "Ann. Annie. I just want to say . . . I'm sorry we had words . . . that we didn't agree. I wish you could be happier for me. If you're with your mom right now, I hope you're having fun. Call me when you get back and we'll go out for drinks or something. I . . . I need to talk to you, Annie. I mean, I *really* do."

Saturday night was the play at Meadowbrook—*The Boys Next Door,* about retarded men living in a group home, not as depressing as it sounded. Later Cici and Bryan just talked about the play, Bryan's job, and the latest gossip from the Job Center where Cici worked. But, Cici consoled herself, didn't most married couples have similar, very ordinary conversations? Maybe she was expecting too much, that he share everything.

Hadn't she known from the beginning that Bryan was the way he was?

On Sunday ngiht, Cici had bought tickets for herself, Bryan, and Aaron to attend a "monster truck" event at the Silverdome that Aaron had been begging for weeks to see.

Aaron was still in his rebellious mood.

"With *him?*" he questioned. "Do we really have to go with *him?*"

Cici's heart sank. "Yes, Aar, we do. I've had the tickets for a week and I can't return them—besides, you need to get to know Bryan better."

"I already know him well enough," her son insisted.

Aaron was glumly silent as they drove to the Silverdome, and his mood didn't improve as they found their seats. The show began in a thunderous roar of "Big Foot" motors, the air filling with blue smoke from their exhausts. The four-wheeler trucks were grotesque looking, some of their tires twelve feet tall, pushing the cabs ridiculously high in the air. They were painted in gaudy Day-Glo colors, with names like "Screaming Machine" or "Godzilla."

"Aar? Do you want popcorn?" Cici asked after an hour of watching the huge machines try to race each other over rows of flattened cars.

"I guess."

"Here, take ten dollars. Bring some for all of us," she said, pressing a bill into his hand. "And Cokes. Diet Coke for me."

Aaron left, blending into the crowd of youngsters that ceaselessly went back and forth to the refreshment stand. He was gone twenty-five minutes. He returned with a cardboard tray loaded with soft drinks and containers of popcorn. His face showed the first expression of enthusiasm since they had arrived at the Silverdome.

"I saw Dustin out at the concession stand. He wants me to sit with them."

"Aaron. Not tonight. This is a family outing—I don't want you going off with Dustin."

"Mom, he's my best friend."

"But we're here together," Cici began.

Aaron lifted his chin. "Please? I want to sit with Dustin and Heather and Matt. They've got better seats, they're a lot closer, and I'd rather be with kids my own age."

"Sit down," Cici started, but her son had already set down the food tray on his empty seat, taking out one drink container and one popcorn box for himself.

"I'm going," he announced. "I'll get a ride home with them."

"Aaron!" she called, but he was already descending the stairs toward the aisle door, out of her reach as he had been for five months.

"He's being insolent," Bryan remarked. "You should have called him back and made him sit with us."

Cici shook her head, her eyes filling with unexpected tears. "I just don't know, Bry. It feels like I'm losing him. I don't know what to do."

"You don't assert yourself with him, Cici. You don't make him do things. You're spoiling him."

Was she? Had she spoiled her son? Was that what the problem was? Cici didn't think so. Until five months ago—until Bryan—Aaron had been fine.

The traffic jam outside the stadium was massive, with policemen standing at intersections blowing whistles and waving cars on, their expressions angry looking.

The five of them were crammed into Heather's car, with the radio turned up loud, the speakers vibrating to a rap song by

Tone-Loc. Dustin seemed edgy tonight, and there was another bruise on his cheek.

"You okay, man?" Aaron asked under his breath.

"Sure, man," Dustin said loudly.

Tonight Heather wore her hair crimped into masses of hard, tight curls. A very pretty sixteen-year-old with pale skin, she wore a black leather jacket with fringe across the front, and a matching pair of very tight leather pants.

Seated beside her in the front seat, Aaron could not keep his eyes off those pants. Man . . . the leather curved around her thighs like black paint.

Jesus, Aaron thought. *Oh, hot.* He was still a virgin, but Dustin had had sex four times already, or so he claimed. The boys had thoroughly pored over the big collection of *Penthouse*s owned by Dustin's father, with a selection of even dirtier magazines that showed women being whipped and tied to the bed.

Aaron was more than a little intimidated. Did girls expect you to know everything? Did they move or did you have to do the moving? Did it hurt them? What if the girl didn't want to do it?

But Heather wanted to do it. Even Aaron knew that, and the realization made him acutely nervous. He was only fourteen; she was sixteen. Dustin said Heather had done it a lot, with a lot of guys. Dustin said she fucked any guy who had a car.

Which left him spectacularly out, since he had no car and no prospect of owning one for two more years. In fact, Heather was their transportation, when she was in a good mood as she was tonight.

"Wild thang," she crooned sexily, in tune with the rap song. "I wanna do the wild . . . thang. . . ."

"Well, we can't do it here, man," Aaron said, flushing bright red.

"I can." Heather giggled. She diddy-bopped in the driver's seat, gyrating with such energy that two guys in a Toyota truck next to them blasted on their horn.

They finally got out of the worst of the traffic, heading north on Opdyke. "I wanna go wilding again," Dustin began, leaning forward from the backseat. "Do a few mailboxes, man.

Hey, remember that one last week? The guy came running out, screaming? I thought he was going to fucking kill us."

"Yeah, man . . ."

"Yeah . . ."

"He would've, too, if he'd caught us," Matt said. "My dad, he told my mom, he told her once if he ever caught guys doing stuff like that, he'd shoot 'em in the ass with shotgun pellets."

"Woo! Woo!"

"Pow, man, pow—right in the butt!"

"Right in the old ass cheeks."

"Right in the fat glutes, man!"

They were raucous tonight, full of adrenaline after the loud four-by-fours. Heading north toward Rochester, they started drinking beer from the twelve-pack Dustin had stashed in the backseat. Dustin had "borrowed" it from his dad.

Aaron took long swallows from the can. The beer was warm and made him feel faintly sick. Beer actually tasted kind of crappy, but they would have to kill him to get him to say so.

"Hey, man, I needed a hit with this," he boasted loudly, passing another can to Heather. "All that exhaust smoke made me *dry.*"

"Warm beer," the girl giggled, accepting the can. "That's sexy, right? Warm beer is sexy."

"You should know," Dustin cackled.

At University they headed east, toward the twinkling lights of Oakland University. There were big dormitories with hundreds of windows lit up. Rumors were if you drove past the dorms you might get a show, so they made the tour.

They didn't see any girls. All they saw was a couple of guys standing around in one room drinking beer. They also had an excellent glimpse of some vending machines.

"Hey, there's some, there's a couple of bare boobs!" Dustin shouted, then squawked with laughter as the other boys craned and gawked. "Just kiddin', guys. Hey, no action here tonight. I want *action,* man! *Action!*"

"We could drive by my dad's," Aaron suggested.

"Your dad's? What the fuck for?" There was a chorus of disapproval.

"Because he has a girlfriend who looks like a *Playboy* Bunny, that's why."

"*Playboy* Bunny? Man . . ."

"Has she got, you know, a couple of big ones?"

"Big, man . . . like huge?"

"Bigger than Heather's?"

They all giggled and waved their beer cans around, and Kevin, from the backseat, flipped a spray of foam on Heather's hair.

"Quit that!" she cried angrily, rubbing it off. "Quit that, dammit! Or you can just walk."

"Sorry, sorry, sorry," Kevin crooned. "I want my wheels, I want my beer, I want a *Playboy* Bunny."

They drove by King's Cove, the condominium complex where Aaron's dad lived, off Tienken Road. But when Aaron urged her to turn into the development, Heather balked. "*I* don't want to look at any bunnies."

"Just turn," he begged. "I just want to drive past once. I want to look in the windows."

So they cruised into the complex. A mood of gloom sank over Aaron as they approached the corner unit where his father lived. Even from here they could see the light in the big window, and no drapes pulled.

What if his dad's girlfriend, Tara, really *was* there?

He'd joked about her looking like a Bunny, but she really was too much like one for his comfort. Her breasts were full and pointy. And she was only twenty-two years old. That was eight years older than Aaron himself. Not even old enough to be his mother, not that he'd ever want her for his mother, with her skin-tight jeans and all the eye makeup she always slathered on. Why'd his dad want a person like that anyway, when he could have had Cici?

Because she had two good boobs, Aaron knew with an angry feeling. His dad had thrown his mother away like a broken department-store dummy.

Ugh. Sometimes he thought about Tara too much, and other times she made him sick. And if she was visiting his dad tonight they'd both be sitting right by the window, probably necking or even feeling each other up, getting hot.

Heather slowed the car. As she did so, someone walked in front of the window in Aaron's dad's condo. It was a woman wearing nothing but an electric-blue, shortie satin bathrobe that had been so carelessly tied in front that most of her breasts were visible.

All of the boys except for Aaron began to whistle and make remarks. "Man," Kevin kept saying. "Man . . . man! Give me some! Woof! Woof! I want some of that!"

Aaron slid down in the seat until his spine was practically on the seat cushion. This was the woman that his father fucked. He felt waves of anger and hurt and lust, all of them pounding him simultaneously.

"What's wrong, Aarie baby?" taunted Kevin.

"Leave him alone," Dustin suddenly said.

"Whatsamatta? Poor Aarie baby can't stand the sight of his dad's pussy? Poor Aarie wants to go and live there so he can look at fancy pussy all the time."

The boys were excited, jumping around in the backseat, and Aaron heard the popping of another beer-can tab.

"Hey, he can't go live there . . . his dad's afraid Aaron might get to the pussy!"

"Hey, he might take all there is!"

"Hey—!"

Someone shook up a beer can and whooshed it out, spraying it on Aaron's jacket and over most of the car.

"Will you guys just shut *up*," Heather snapped, backing up the fourteen-year-old Bobcat with a squeal of transmission and tires. "You guys are just so rude, you make me sick. And don't spray *any* more of that beer on my car seat, or you assholes can just get out and walk from here. And I mean it."

"Rude, oh, rude . . . rude . . ." They teased her, imitating her tone of voice, while Aaron sank further into the seat, gazing glumly out the car window.

Were the guys right? *Did* his dad want him? Aaron had a horrible feeling that he knew the answer.

* * *

Aaron was in a foul mood when he got home, a mood that did not improve when he saw his mother's note on the hall table.

Wake me up when you come in, Aaron. Don't forget. I love you. Mom.

He went upstairs and knocked cursorily on Cici's bedroom door, making sure that he heard her sleepy murmur before going back downstairs to his own room. He didn't want her to wake up enough to smell the beer on his breath.

Shit . . . no one trusted him, did they? And now he was going to have his grandmother babysitting him for two weeks after Christmas just like he was still in grade school. Well, he wasn't a baby anymore. Anyone who drank beer was no baby. And Heather had promised him he could drive her car sometime. And Aaron knew "driving her car" meant a hell of a lot more than just that.

Incredible.

He scuffed into his bedroom, flipped on the light, and threw himself on the unmade bed, which was scattered with dirty clothes, several empty Pepsi cans, and an issue of *Four Wheeler* he'd bought at Perry Drugs. He stretched out, accidentally kicking one of the cans onto the floor. Then his hand—almost by itself—reached out for the telephone.

He punched in his dad's telephone number, waiting as it rang three, four, then five times.

"Yeah?" His dad's voice sounded breathless, as if he had been running.

"It's me. Aaron. Your son Aaron," he heard himself say, and then hated himself for being a dork. Did he have to act like his dad might not remember his name?

His father was still panting. "Aaron! Jesus Christ, do you know what time it is? It's—shit, it's two A.M.!"

"Yeah, do you know where your kids are tonight?"

"Aaron, what the hell are you doing calling me at this hour? Is there some emergency?" In the background, Aaron heard the protest of a woman's voice.

"How's Tara?" he asked, sneering.

"Tara? She's—Aaron, what the hell *is* this? It's the middle of the night, we're in bed, we're asleep."

Yeah, right. Aaron held on to the phone, some of his bravado deserting him. Why had he called, anyway? To get on his dad's case about his stupid girlfriend? Divorced men were studs, everyone knew that. Dustin's dad had three or four girlfriends in one week sometimes. He used women like they were Kleenex.

His dad went on, "Aaron, does your mother know you're on the phone? Did she put you up to this?"

"No, she didn't, no way. Dad . . ." Aaron's voice cracked a little. "Dad, I want to come and live with you."

There was dead silence on the other end of the line. In the background Aaron could hear Tara asking, "What is it? What does he want? Tom?"

"Aaron," his dad finally said in a heavy, scratchy tone. "Aaron."

"Yeah?"

But Aaron already knew what was coming.

"Aar, you know it's not possible. Don't put me on the spot like this. You know what my life-style is. I'm a partner in an engineering firm, I've got to bring business into the firm, I've got to bring money in. I've got to go out at night and wine and dine those people, and what would I do if I had you to take care of?"

Aaron responded sullenly, "I'm not some baby that needs someone to take care of them."

"No, you're not a baby, but you're only fourteen, and you like to eat, don't you? I don't cook, Aaron. I eat out all the time. All I've got in my refrigerator is cheese."

"I like cheese. I could help you shop, Dad. I wouldn't mind eating out." Aaron's eyes watered. He knew he was pleading, and he hated himself for his weakness, his neediness.

"Your mother has custody, son, and that's for a reason. She's got a less demanding job and she has time to be there for you when you need her. I don't. That's the bottom line. I'm just too busy with my job to have you full time."

Aaron lay across the bed gripping the telephone, clenching it in his fingers.

"Aaron? Aaron? Are you still there? Dammit, Aaron!"

"Yeah."

"Put your mother on the line, will you? I want to talk to her. She put you up to this, didn't she? She wanted to make me feel like a jerk and she sure succeeded. Oh, brother, did she." As his father talked, Aaron began holding the phone farther and farther away from his ear, until finally the voice emerged as a small, tinny bray.

"Aaron? Aaron? Aaron?"

"Fuck you, Dad," Aaron muttered, bringing the receiver up again.

"What? What?"

"Hey . . . *fuck you.* And one more thing, Dad," he said, enunciating very clearly. "You ever stop to think about AIDS, man? It kills, Dad. And you know how you get it? From girl-friends, Dad—from SCREWING! From damn, shitass, stupid, ugly PLAYBOY BUNNY GIRLFRIENDS!"

He slammed down the phone in his father's ear.

Then he picked up his pillow and began slamming it down on the mattress, pounding it with his fist, pounding and pound-ing.

NINE

The following Monday night Cici was in the kitchen working on a stack of resumes when Aaron came skidding past her. He was dressed in his jacket and a pair of jeans torn in parallel strips at the knees, the laces trailing from his high-topped Reeboks.

Cici glanced at her watch. It was eight-thirty.

"Aaron? Aar? Where are you going, honey?"

"Out."

"I know you're going out, I saw your jacket. But I meant, where?"

"Oh, out. That's all. I'm going out with the guys."

She eyed him carefully. Was he hiding something underneath his jacket? He seemed furtive somehow, and was fidgeting in his haste to leave. "Aaron, what have you got in your jacket?"

"Nothing."

She got up, putting down the resume. "I want to see, Aaron. If those are eggs—if you're planning to go out and throw eggs—"

"I'm not going to throw anything." Aaron evaded her

grasp, purloined two brownies from a plateful on the stove, stuffed one in his mouth, and was gone. The back door slammed behind him as he made his escape.

Cici returned to her work, but her eyes did not focus on the listing of the client's previous jobs at General Motors. An uneasy feeling spiraled up from her stomach. *Did* Aaron have something hidden under his jacket, like raw eggs or spray paint?

She was getting so tired of this! Aaron was becoming so secretive and angry. Maybe she should have Tom talk to him. If his father spent more time with him . . .

Decisively she reached for the phone and dialed her ex-husband's private office number.

"Yes, Cici?" Tom sounded impatient. "I've got to leave in five minutes to take a customer out to dinner, so we'll have to make this fast."

"It's Aaron," she said. "I wish you would talk to him, Tom. I don't know, I think he needs a man to relate to."

Tom snorted. "I just talked to him last night, babe. Two A.M. He called me in the middle of the night. And he insulted me, got obscene with me, that's what happened. He doesn't need talking, he needs a damn belt applied to his backside."

"He called you? What are you talking about?"

"You mean you didn't put him up to it?"

"No."

"Well, let me give you the bottom line. He wants to come over here and live with me. Are you sure you didn't ask him to call me? Are you sure you aren't getting a little tired of having him around?"

Shock punched her in the stomach. Not that she hadn't expected this. Aaron had even told her he wanted to live with his dad. But somehow hearing it from Tom . . . she felt a wave of wild grief.

"No, I'm not tired of having him around," she said, her voice shaking. "Oh, Tom."

"Well, I told him no. My life-style, Cici. I can't cook for a teenager. And clean up, and have pizza every night, and be there when he comes home from basketball practice or whatever."

"Aaron doesn't play basketball, Tom," she said acidly.

"Well, whatever. You know what I'm talking about. I've got to be blunt with you, Cici. I can't handle having him here. I'm not one of these guys who's all hot for fathering—know what I mean? It's a weakness I have. I mean, I know I'm not great that way. But did he have to confront me on it? At two A.M. with Tara right there? Shit, we were right in the middle of—well, you can guess."

Cici pressed her lips together, imagining it all too well. Tom's cruelty really knew no bounds. How dare he tell her that he and Tara had been in the middle of sexual intercourse when Aaron called? She could just imagine what he had said to his son. No wonder Aaron was so angry.

"You're such a shit, Tom."

"Hey," he said aggrievedly. "What? Cici—?"

"Such a *royal* shit. I'm glad Aaron called and interrupted you in the middle of the night—you deserved that. Someday, Tom, you're going to feel very, very distant from your son, and don't come running to me when that happens. Don't ever feel sorry for yourself, because you brought it all on yourself."

It was not Devil's Night yet, but it would be in only a week. The air already tasted icy, like November. The night shadows were as inky as the black paint in the aerosol cans the boys carried. Many of the homeowners had turned on gaslights or porch lamps, but the effect was to make the rest of the night seem deeper, blacker, more dangerous.

Dustin was driving tonight. Heather had grudgingly loaned her car, and now he kept to the exact speed limit on the main roads, terrified of getting picked up for driving without a license.

They drove around for nearly two hours, covering not only their own subdivision but several others, including Grosse Pines, off Walton. Mailboxes, paint, sod, soap, the works.

Aaron clenched his hands, feeling the pinch of his fingernails against his palms. He was still angry—almost sick with it, an anger that filled every vein in his body, every capillary. His dad didn't want him; his dad wanted some stupid bimbo instead, some no-brain with big boobs. His dad didn't even care if he had to live the rest of his life with Bryan Wyatt.

It wasn't fair. He was only fourteen. They never listened to him; they didn't care. But Aaron knew, without knowing how, that Bryan Wyatt was *bad*. Not just a little, but major bad. The kind of guy who snipped off the ears of puppies with garden shears . . . yeah, that kind.

They finally pulled up in front of Dustin's and all piled out of the car. As they did so, Dustin's dad came out on the porch holding a beer can. The porch light gave him an eerie look, like an older, uglier Bryan. By the glowering expression on his face, it was obvious this was not John Pickard's first or even fifth beer.

"Oh, shit," Dustin muttered under his breath. "My dad's in the bag."

"Dustin, you little craphead, what are you doing with your sister's car?" John Pickard wanted to know. "You park it here and toss me the keys—now."

To Aaron's shock, Dustin didn't even protest. He just pulled the keys out of the ignition and obediently walked over to the porch where he tossed his father the keys. Pickard caught them with a swipe of enormous bear paws.

"You little turd," he said, eyes glittering. "You're gonna end up in jail, aren't you? And I'm not gonna bail you out."

"Yes, sir," Dustin mumbled, looking at the ground.

Aaron stared at his friend, struck by the total change in his appearance and behavior.

Only one thing could make Dustin *humble* like that. The fear of being hit. Dustin's dad really did hit him, maybe worse, whenever he wanted. Aaron had known this before, but now the reality hit him like a slap in the gut. Right next door to him all this time, Dustin had been crying and getting abused, and saying *yes, sir,* because he was afraid.

Pickard finally went back in the house with a slam of the door, and Dustin gave an explosive sound that might have been a laugh or a sob. Then he went in the garage and returned lugging a metal can. The liquid inside sloshed ominously.

"Hey, what's that, man?" Aaron wanted to know. "*Gas?* Jeez . . ."

"It's for us."

"Hey," Aaron said uneasily.

"What do you mean, 'hey'? We aren't going to do anything real bad, we're only going to torch his garage."

There was a whistle of excitement among the boys. *"Torch his garage? Whose garage?"*

Out on Walton, a siren screamed its way to Crittenton Hospital.

"Bryan Wyatt's," Dustin said. "Old dickhead, remember? We've been chicken in doing him, and now we're gonna get serious."

Aaron laughed nervously, and after a second Kevin and Matt joined in. Aaron felt an uncomfortable mix of emotions—fear, anger, and relief that it was Dustin who'd thought of it, not him. Not that they'd really do it. They probably really wouldn't.

Dustin added, "Hey, who's got a match?"

Aaron reached in his pocket and pulled out a book of matches from Greektown, left over from last summer when he and his mom had eaten at Pegasus and ridden the People Mover. Dustin reached out, trying to snatch it from him.

"No, man," Aaron said, pulling away. "You have the gas. I'll carry the matches."

"I gotta pee," wailed Kevin. "I gotta!"

"Piss in the grass," ordered Dustin.

"But I can't see to—"

"You don't have to see it to pee with it," Dustin commanded. "Now do it, 'cause we don't want you messing this up for us."

There was the streaming splatter of a bladder being emptied and the pungent smell of urine.

"Pew," griped Dustin. "You got stinky piss. I can smell it in the air, man."

"Shut up," Kevin said, zipping. "I can't help it."

Aaron felt in his pockets again for the matches, feeling a spasm of nervousness. This was just a minor deal, right? They weren't planning to do anything major like set the house on fire.

They ran like commandos in the dark to the cul-de-sac

where Bryan Wyatt lived. Bryan had switched his yard lights on, but between the lights were dark patches of night.

Aaron stared at the house with hatred. It was frugally lit, and the glass-brick basement windows seemed to glow from behind. Visible at the curb was a row of garbage and leaf bags and other things left for the trash pickup. He glimpsed the outline of a big cardboard box from Montgomery Ward, folded flat. It was the kind of big appliance box Aaron had loved to play in as a child, making it into a GI Joe fort.

Once his dad had played in the fort with him. They ate peanut-butter and honey sandwiches, scrunched up inside the cardboard.

The pang that squeezed Aaron's heart was so powerful he had to stifle a sob.

"He's home," Dustin said, poking Aaron. "Maybe down in the basement."

"Wait a minute," Aaron said quickly. "I want to look. I want to make sure he *is* down there. Before we . . . you know."

He ran forward, his Reeboks crunching down the hard, frosty spears of grass. When he reached the first window, he bent down to see, but the bricks were wavy, the thick glass fracturing the light, and he could make out nothing but some shapes.

"Shit," he muttered and ran to the next window. There were the same dark shapes, maybe a person bent over a table. But then he saw the shape move and realized with a thump of his heart that it *was* Bryan Wyatt, working on some project down in his basement. Maybe drawing one of those weird, fussy pen-and-ink pictures of clocks with faces on them.

"Hey . . . hey . . ." Dustin was motioning to him to come. Kevin and Matt giggled; they were ready for any adventure.

Aaron hesitated.

"Come *on,*" Dustin urged.

They left the gas can under a bush and broke into the detached garage through a side door. They pushed inside, crowding together for security. Aaron lit a match, waving it around for a brief look.

Bryan's Aerostar van was parked in the left-hand space, but

the other side held no car. Shelves had been built into the walls, and on them were dozens of neatly stacked cardboard storage boxes, marked with neatly typed labels that said things like *Ship Kits* and *Bottle Books*. There were also the usual tools, lawn mower, and snowblower, along with another machine that Aaron thought might be a generator.

"Guy's a damn neatnik," Dustin whispered, tipping one of the storage boxes off its shelf. It tumbled onto the floor, spilling out old books. Dustin found a large flashlight on a shelf and began shining it around the garage in loopy arcs.

"He's a jerk," Aaron muttered.

Dustin kicked over another box, and with a cry the boys were on the boxes, dumping some over, tossing others outside onto the lawn. It was like New Year's Eve. Papers swirled madly, baseball cards scattered, books fell out, and old ships in bottles fell sideways.

"I want this one! I want this one!" Kevin crowed, picking up one of the ships.

Aaron shoved it out of his hand. "You can't, asshole— they'd catch us." Suddenly he was anxious to get this done with, to be home again, safe.

Dustin found an old magazine and ripped out a couple of pages, scrambling them into a ball. Then he took a stick he'd picked up and stuffed it into the paper, creating a kind of handle.

"What's that? What's that?" Matt squeaked.

"Nothing. You'll see. It's our firebomb."

Dustin got the gas can and drizzled the liquid all over the floor, careful to leave a path for himself to get back out. He left the side door wide open, and went to stand outside on the grass.

"Gimme a fucking match," he hissed to Aaron.

"No. I want to light it."

"*I* want to."

"I wanna, too," cried Kevin in imitation.

Aaron hesitated, then lit a match. It flared hotly, creating a tiny circle of heat. For a second, cold sanity rushed in. He shouldn't be doing this—it was arson, a crime.

"Gimme that," Dustin said, reaching out and grabbing

Aaron's hand to pull the match toward the crumpled paper ball. Aaron reached out to take the stick, and both Dustin and Aaron gripped the paper ball, struggling over it.

The paper blazed up.

All four boys uttered an indrawn gasp. The yellow flame was tongued with red and blue, giving Aaron a brief, painful memory of campfires and marshmallows, his mom and dad together, loving each other.

But the heat quickly grew too intense, and Aaron knew they had to drop the burning ball of paper—or throw it.

"Come on!" Dustin snapped. "Come on, come on, come on!" Dustin gave him a shove, and then somehow the burning paper ball fell and landed beside one of the runnels of gasoline. Aaron waited with crashing pulse for the fire to erupt.

Nothing happened.

"Shit," Dustin hissed. "You turkey. Fighting me for it. You should've let me throw."

Then the gasoline went up, with a frightening, sucking whoosh that ran along all the puddles and blazed up red.

They had planned to run away but Aaron couldn't pull himself away from the sight of what they had wrought.

"Wow," breathed Dustin, gripping Aaron's arm.

"Hey, man, hey, man," Kevin was saying, pulling anxiously at Aaron's left sleeve. "That house over there, they switched on a light, man. What if they're callin' the police?"

"Wait, wait," Aaron begged, unwilling to leave.

The flames leaped higher, a lot higher than Aaron had envisioned. There was a lot of smoke. Hot orange flames licked, and little things popped and exploded. Any minute the van would go up, too, its paint cracking and blistering before the gas in its tank blew it up.

"Man!" Kevin was in a panic, almost crying. "Man, we gotta run. Come on, come on, come on!"

Within seconds, Kevin's running form had faded into the shadows, with Matt at his heels, and now Dustin was pulling at him, too. "You're crazy, Aar . . . come on, come on, we gotta split. This is heavy stuff, man . . . *we set a fucking fire.*"

Fleeing, they nearly fell over some of the boxes they'd thrown. They reached the trees, panting, excited, frantic. Aaron gazed back. The garage now billowed smoke, but the house looked just as it always had, unharmed, perfectly normal. The lights in the basement still glowed behind the glass bricks. Bryan Wyatt must still be down in his hobby room.

Did Bryan even know that his garage was on fire?

The question was like a fingernail scratch across Aaron's mind. Maybe he didn't. That basement room was airtight. Shut up down there, could he smell the smoke? What if he couldn't? The garage was separate, but what if the sparks, the flames, leaped across to the house? Stuff like that happened. Aaron had seen it on cable.

Burning up a garage was just vandalism, the kind of crazy stuff kids always did on Devil's Night, that kids in Detroit did all the time, but burning up a house . . .

That was arson.

Worse than arson—it could be murder, because what if Bryan couldn't get out of his basement in time? What if he got burned up, became a flaming human torch like on TV?

Oh, shit.

A cold panic began to run through him, and for a brief second he hated Dustin for grabbing his hand and lighting the paper ball.

The light in the house next door casually flicked off again. The neighbors hadn't seen the fire yet, Aaron realized, and the turning on of the light had only been a coincidence. Maybe no one had even called the fire department yet. Oh, shit, shit, and more shit.

This wasn't funny, man, it wasn't happening like Aaron had envisioned because he wasn't a killer. *Jesus.* They never should have done it. If someone didn't hurry—

"Hey, where you going, man?" Dustin whispered.

But Aaron was already running toward his own house, taking the shortcut through lawns and backyards.

Aaron hung up from making the phone call to the fire department. His throat felt sore, his chest hollow. He'd sounded like a damn baby on the phone, his voice quavering, going suddenly high and squeaky as he blurted out the news about the fire.

"Your name?" the female dispatcher had snapped. Her voice sounded nasal and official like a policewoman's or a prison guard's.

"I . . . I can't tell that."

"Address?"

Aaron panicked. His voice did the squeak again. "*My* address?"

"The location of the fire."

"Oh, that's . . . I don't have the house number." Aaron managed to give cross streets and an approximation, then hung up before the dispatcher could ask if he was the one who had set the fire. Shit, she knew he was. Who was he kidding? Did the police tape-record calls to the fire department? He'd heard they did. He felt sick and on the verge of throwing up. In fact, he went in the bathroom and managed a few dry heaves. He was shaking all over.

Cici was now in the TV room watching some flick on Cinemax. He could hear the sound of car wheels squealing and exciting "chase" music. For once he felt like going in there and watching with her.

Yeah, they'd sit on the couch and maybe he'd get out the popper and make popcorn. Everything could be normal, and there wouldn't be the bad thing in the air, the possibility that he could have killed or hurt Bryan Wyatt.

He started toward the TV room, but he got only as far as the door. His feet felt restless, dancy. He could not make them stop moving.

"Aaron? Aar?" Cici called. "I'm glad you're back. I'm watching *Blue Steel.* This is a really good movie. Jamie Lee Curtis is fantastic, you should see her, Aar . . . it's just like a male cop movie. Do you want to come and watch?"

"I—I've seen it," he muttered. He loped to his bedroom and cranked up the stereo, putting in a new tape by Tone-Loc. Carefully he turned it up loud, but not so loud that Cici would get annoyed and ask him to turn it down.

Then he bolted out of the house. He had to get back to the fire. He had to see.

The smell of smoke hung over the block, thick and exciting. The sky near Bryan's cul-de-sac was pink with flames and police flashers. The fire trucks were already there, two of them, and several police cars were parked in front. A crowd of ten or fifteen neighbors and neighbor kids had gathered.

Yeah, and there was Bryan Wyatt, out on the lawn, wild-eyed as he ran back and forth, yelling to the firemen, something about power lines.

Seeing Bryan, Aaron felt his stomach suck hollowly inward, relief overwhelming him. At least he wasn't a murderer. Dustin's dad was also there, gazing around with swift, angry looks, as if he suspected who might have set the fire. Aaron edged into the shadows, unwilling to be seen by either of these men.

His foot hit something, and he noticed that the boxes they had thrown earlier still lay all over the grass. Some had been crushed under the wheels of the fire trucks, their contents spilled out.

Even as Aaron watched, Bryan went up to John Pickard, gesticulating angrily. Bryan looked—well, wild. One tail of his shirt hung sloppily out of his pants, and there was black soot all over the shirt, all over Bryan's hands, and on his face, too, where he'd been rubbing it.

Aaron stared, fascinated by this change in someone he thought he knew. Gone was the uptight man with the stone-cold eyes. Bryan's angry movements were big, loose, clumsy, like . . . yeah, just like guys at school. Yeah, that was it. He moved like a kid, Aaron thought, not a grown man. Which was definitely creepy.

"Hey, man," someone said beside him. Aaron recognized Mike McKenzie, a guy he knew from school who lived several houses down.

"How'd it start?" Aaron asked, pretending he didn't know. He coughed a little. The smoke was thick and he had a slight smoke allergy.

"I don't know. I was watching TV when I heard the sirens."

"Me too," Aaron muttered guiltily.

"Man, this fire was *great.* It had explosions and everything. They say somebody might have set it."

"Mmmmmm," Aaron said.

The fire was out now, just some smoke left, and the firemen were rewinding their hoses, tramping around importantly. Water was puddled everywhere, soaking the lawn. More kids from school appeared, along with some older neighbors, and everyone milled around, talking about the fire. It was almost a carnival atmosphere. People were even laughing.

Aaron edged closer to the burned garage shell. He knew he shouldn't; what if one of those cops started asking him questions? But it was as if he was drawn by some compulsion.

Soon he was standing close to the garage and could look inside the broken windows. Bryan's Aerostar van looked blackened and unfamiliar. It was totaled; no one would ever be driving it again. The sight gave Aaron a chill.

He'd done it. Well, he and Dustin. They'd killed a car.

A policeman was starting to ask questions, talking to Mike and a couple of other guys. They shook their heads, excited to be a part of things, yet nervous too. *What if they questioned him?* They probably would. Old dickhead already suspected Aaron of vandalizing his house.

Shaking, Aaron began to back away. As he did so, his foot caught something and he looked down to see one of the boxes they'd thrown on the grass. The cardboard was water-soaked, the flaps of the box taped tightly shut with old, yellowed tape. The typed label said *Clyattville.*

The box seemed to bulge with secrets.

Impulsively, Aaron reached down and picked it up. Hey, who knew what might be in it? Maybe there was something weird that he could use to prove to his mom what a dork Bryan Wyatt really was.

TEN

Returning home, Aaron let himself in the side door. Cici was still watching TV and hadn't even noticed his leaving. Obviously she hadn't heard the sirens, or thought they were just part of the movie she was watching.

Good, he thought.

He carried the *Clyattville* box to his bedroom and closed the door, adjusting the sound level on the stereo again to prevent the noise drawing Cici to his room. He didn't want her knocking on his door right now. The more he handled the box, the surer he was that there was something fishy and creepy inside, something that would definitely prove that Bryan Wyatt was a real weirdo.

He lowered the damp box to the floor, rubbed off the wet dead leaves that were clinging to its bottom, and pulled away the tape.

He pried open the damp lid. A smell came out at him, a sour, powdery odor of mildew. Aaron's heart speeded up. This was getting better and better. How long had it been since this box was opened? Twenty years? It sure looked like it. Spiders had gotten inside and it was full of their webs, all thick, gray, dusty, and dead.

But he was disappointed when he looked at the contents. He didn't know what he had expected, but it was something more exciting than just a bunch of old letters and electric bills, a couple of black books, and some religious cards and pictures.

He picked up one of the letters, which was yellow and old and carried with it that moldy smell.

> "This is to notify you that regulations of the Roscommon County Health Department require that all children five years of age who are entering the school system be vaccinated for the following diseases: diphtheria, pertussis, polio . . ."

It was signed by an Almon Drucell, M.D.

Puzzled, Aaron put the letter down and picked up another one.

> "Dear Mr. and Mrs. Wykotsky: It has come to my attention that you have kept your son out of school for more than six weeks . . ."

All of the letters seemed to be like that.

> "If you refuse to have your child vaccinated according to regulation . . ."
> ". . . medical attention for your son . . ."
> ". . . if you refuse, then a Court Order signed by Judge William D. Cook . . ."

There was a big stack of religious junk—photographs of a real human man dressed up as Jesus nailed to the cross, his face twisted with agony. Red blood was splashed on Jesus' hands and feet, from which a big, realistic iron nail could be seen protruding.

Aaron examined the photos closely, his mouth going dry. Violent Jesus pictures! He had never seen stuff so real looking. On the back of one of the photos was writing in some foreign language, maybe Italian. Weird! He never thought old Bryan would be the kind to keep stuff like this.

He explored the rest of the box, finding an old diary, the kind that had a leather flap that locked with a key. White mildew had mottled its binding. The lock lent the diary an air of excitement and mystery, like a clue from a Hardy Boys book. Aaron had been addicted to the Hardy Boys when he was in the fourth grade.

Aaron slit the flap with a steak knife he kept in his room to peel apples. The pages flipped open to the center, the binding nearly coming apart in his hands.

He stared down. The printing looked as if it had been written by a witch. The letters were jagged, some so tiny and cramped that he had to squint to see what they were, others huge. There were rips in the paper, as if the writer had jabbed too hard with the pencil.

He began to read the page.

> ". . . Pa made the Boy get out the wood burnin set and he put the letters in, He whuped him until he did it, then He whuped him with the hamer too . . ."

Hamer? Aaron thought. What was a hamer? And what did whuped mean? Was that a word for whipped?

He turned to another page.

> "No way to burie the dog bacuz it is feberary and the ground is froze. Had to whup the Boy again today for Cryin. He has a bad seed in him, he does not listen to God . . ."

"Aaron? Aar?" It was his mother's voice in the hallway. Aaron jumped guiltily. Quickly he threw a blanket over the box, hiding it from view. He went to open his bedroom door a crack. "Yeah?"

"Aar?" She was staring at him, puzzled. "What's that smell, Aaron? It smells like an old ashtray. Or smoke."

Smoke. He squirmed, realizing he had to say something, and fast. "I, yeah"—he improvised—"Dustin and Matt and me, we lit up a few. We inhaled them. We smoked a whole pack."

The lie had the desired effect. "Smoking! Oh, Aaron! Please don't start smoking, Aaron. Not at age fourteen. Do you realize what incredible damage that will do to your body? You'll be short of breath all the time. You'll shorten your life by twenty or thirty years. You'll always regret—"

"I didn't smoke that many," he said quickly. "Just four or five. And I didn't smoke them down to butts."

"Oh . . ." Cici looked hurt, anxious, and worried. Aaron felt a pang and wondered what she'd think if she really knew. She was very pretty, with her curly blond hair, her big, blue eyes. All the guys said she was too young looking to be a mother.

Cici spoke in a soft voice. "Aaron, one afternoon doesn't make you a smoker. You don't have to take it up if you don't want to. I just want you to know, I really love you. No matter what."

"Mom . . ." he began miserably.

"I know it's tough being in your shoes right now. Things haven't always gone just like you want them to. It's been rough, my getting cancer and having the surgery, and then your dad leaving us."

"Mom . . ." He squirmed. Her expression of her feelings was too open, creating hollow holes in him, vulnerable places that he couldn't expose.

"I just want you to know, you can always come to me, Aaron. I promise I'll listen. You can talk about *anything*, no matter what it is."

"Except Bryan," he flared.

She stared at him. Aaron squirmed again uneasily. And he almost did tell her about the box. But how would he explain where he'd gotten it? Could he show her without actually telling about the fire?

Shit, he thought. He had to think about it a little.

"Remember, Aar."

"Yeah. Right."

As soon as Cici left, Aaron picked up the box again and tried to shove it under his bed, but it would not fit underneath the low metal frame that supported the box springs. So he set it on his dresser, draping a dirty shirt over it.

In the corner of his room, Aaron's nocturnal gerbil, Cookie, moved noisily about its cage, chewing up pieces of newspaper for its nest. The meaning of the word *hamer* came to Aaron just as he was about to drift off to sleep. He sat up, throwing off the blanket.

It wasn't *hamer*, it was *hammer*.

Aaron's heart started to pound.

He sat up in his Jockey briefs, his usual bedtime wear, and gazed around the darkened bedroom. Nighttime, aided by the outdoor floodlight near the garage, had wrought changes in his comfortable and familiar clutter. The big plush gorilla that sat on his dresser top had become a dark, furry bulk lit by two pinpoint glass eyes. The open closet door revealed a yawning dark hole. Even the *Clyattville* box looked starkly black, ominous. The shirt he'd tossed over it had fallen to the floor.

Nervously, Aaron reached out and switched on his bedside light. In the exact second that the warm, comforting yellow light took away the darkness, a horrible thought hit him.

What if Bryan Wyatt was the Basher?

Aaron gripped his own forearms, clenching himself tightly with the sheer surprise of the thought. His eyes traveled to the box he had taken from Bryan's lawn. He'd been right, there *was* weird stuff in that box. Bryan himself was weird.

Then Aaron flopped back on his pillow, squeezing his eyes shut. Hey, what was wrong with him? Setting that fire had made him crazy. The bloody religious pictures were scary, but so what? And a diary written twenty years ago probably didn't mean anything. Being weird didn't make Bryan Wyatt the Basher.

Aaron cuddled himself into a ball, still smelling the smoke on himself. It must be in his hair.

Anyway, he thought, Bryan Wyatt couldn't be the Basher. He just could not picture it. The man was too neat, too proper, too good-looking, and had too good a job. And he collected clocks. Stamps, too, because Bryan had once shown him his collection. He owned about five thousand stamps.

No, Aaron thought sleepily. A real Basher would be ugly, like a movie bad guy. Or at least big and strong. And he certainly would not collect dorky things like stamps, clocks and old music boxes. Maybe instead he would be someone like . . .

Like . . .

But Aaron drifted asleep before his mind could complete the image.

Cici woke the next morning feeling uneasy. She could not put her finger on exactly what might be the cause, but there was definitely a knot clenched in the center of her stomach.

She lay in bed stretching her legs under the sheets, wriggling her fingers and toes in her usual wake-up ritual.

Her thoughts went to her son. Aaron had lied to her last night, she felt sure. Why did she get this feeling that her son was growing farther and farther away from her? That something bad was happening or had happened?

Suddenly she longed desperately to talk to Ann, to relieve her tension by spilling out her concerns to someone who would care. But Ann had never returned her call. Maybe she and her mother, Jeanette, were having so much fun Ann hadn't had time to check her messages.

She reached out her hand for the bedside phone, and swiftly punched in Ann's number. After four rings, her friend's tape picked up again, repeating the same message.

"Your call is important to me, so at the sound of the beep . . ."

Cici cleared her throat. "It's me again, getting persistent, so I hope wherever you are you'll call me because I don't like to have things hanging between us." She paused, then went on, "Aaron smoked some cigarettes, Ann, can you believe it? I was sick when I heard. I know it's normal, I know kids experiment, but I'm just thinking not *my* son. I'm worried about him . . ."

She had intended to go on, using the machine as an electronic letter box, as was their frequent habit, but something stopped her. Somehow it didn't seem as if there was really a person at the other end of the tape.

Yes, that was exactly it. It felt as if she was talking to—nothing. As if Ann might never call back.

She moved violently under the covers, pushing away the thought. "Ann!" she cried into the phone. "Ann! Please call me back, will you? I'm going to my aerobics class at Vic Tanny and I'll be back around eleven. Please . . . *call me.*"

The lobby of Vic Tanny's was hung with posters for a Halloween costume party. Seeing them, Cici paused. How many weeks now until her marriage to Bryan? She did some hurried calculations. Less than *ten weeks.*

The room where they held the aerobics class was lined with mirrors that reflected forty jumping, kicking, leaping bodies, all clad in high-fashion spandex. Cici flung herself into the can-can kicks and jumps, feeling the healthy pump of her blood.

God . . . she really needed to let some of her tension loose. She hadn't felt relaxed in days, she realized. An engagement was stressful. And having a rebellious teenaged son added immeasurably to that pressure. She'd be so glad when Aaron finally settled down. She hoped the horror stories told by friends with teenagers weren't all true.

"Cici . . . Cic!" She heard a familiar voice as she left the dance area, heading for the locker room. She turned to see her sister, Jocelyn, looking chubby in another oversized T-shirt decorated with cats. She had her hair pulled back in a matching headband and carried a blue workout bag.

"Hey, I was wondering if I'd run into you here," Jocelyn said. "I just joined last week . . . I want to use the pool. They say swimming is great for pregnant people. How is Bryan bearing up under the fire?" Jocelyn added.

"Fire?" Cici froze. "What fire?"

"You mean you didn't *know?* I happened to drive past there

this morning—I had to pick up some silk flowers I ordered from a woman in your subdivision. A gorgeous arrangement, Cic, I'll give you her phone number, and so cheap. He had a big fire in his garage, Cici. It was pretty badly totaled."

Cici walked to her locker and stood opening the combination lock, her back turned to her sister to hide her shock. It must have happened the night before and in the excitement he'd been too busy to tell her.

Jocelyn plumped down her bag at the adjoining locker and began pulling off her T-shirt. "He didn't call you, huh?"

Cici nodded, busying herself with changing out of her aerobics clothes. She didn't want Jocelyn to see that she was upset, and changed the subject to little Michael, about whom her sister could talk happily for hours.

"You tell that Bryan he'd better keep you more up to date," Jocelyn finished as Cici prepared to go to the showers.

"Yes, dear," Cici said lightly.

"I mean, if Ed ever hides *anything,* I get suspicious. I might act like Happy Suzy Homemaker, but I know how many men fool around. Ed told me it's about eighty percent of the men where he works."

But later, as she was driving home, Cici knew that she didn't take it quite so lightly as she'd implied to her sister. She was a little hurt—more than a little—that a fire could have happened and her fiancé did not call to tell her about it. Was it because he thought Aaron might be involved?

Oh, God, she thought, clenching her hands on the steering wheel so strongly that the car wobbled toward the center line.

She turned down Bryan's street, driving slowly past his house. The garage looked a sad, smoke-blackened mess, with broken windows and garage door at half-mast as if the automatic door opener had malfunctioned during the blaze. Inside she glimpsed the wreckage of Bryan's van.

She pulled into the driveway behind the Hertz car Bryan had apparently already rented. He had time to rent a car, she thought, but not to call her. The grass was muddy, the sod welted with tire marks and boot prints, and debris was scattered about, pieces of paper and cardboard.

She went up to the door and rang the doorbell. Within a few minutes Bryan appeared, his face drawn with tiredness. He had not shaved since the previous day, and there were bags of exhaustion under his eyes. Cici eyed him in surprise. She had never seen him looking this distressed.

"Cici," he said.

"Bryan! Bry . . ." She went into his arms. "I had no idea you had a fire! Why didn't you call me? I would have come right over. I would have helped you clean up—it looks a mess."

"It was a mess. Is a mess." His arms went around her but not with any real firmness; it felt as if he was just going through the motions. She smelled smoke on him.

"You've been up all night, haven't you?" she accused, pulling back.

"Yes, I worked all night. I had the generator going; I had a power outage for about six hours. Detroit Edison just left. I didn't want to be without power. A house shouldn't be without power. I have things—my security system depends on electricity."

Bryan rubbed one hand across his face as if a fierce headache pang had suddenly squeezed his temples.

"Well, I think you need to go to bed and get some sleep," she said gently. "Whatever the damage is, it can wait now. Have you had breakfast? Would you like me to make you some?"

"Breakfast?" He stared at her as if she'd started speaking Russian. "I'm not hungry."

"All right, but Bry, this happened last night . . . I was home. Why didn't you call and tell me? I had to find out from Jocelyn at the health club. She was driving past this morning and saw the mess."

Bryan's eyes evaded hers. "They found a gas can, Cici. They've been questioning kids in the neighborhood. I didn't give them Aaron's name. I thought about it but I didn't."

"Aaron? You think Aaron might have—" Cici stopped, appalled and horrified. She remembered the smell in Aaron's room last night—the smell of smoke.

Bryan studied the floor. "I don't want trouble," he said. "I don't want him over here anymore. I don't know what to do. You know what happens when you punish kids for vandalizing—they come back and get revenge and it's a hundred times worse. I can't take that."

Cici felt a wave of nausea. She couldn't believe Aaron would have done such a thing. Pranks, yes, soaping of windows and throwing a few eggs, yes—she could believe he might have done those things. But that was all. Her son wasn't a criminal.

"Torching a garage," Bryan went on angrily. "Kids these days. They stop at nothing, do they? They don't care."

Cici's voice shook as she promised to go home and talk to Aaron. "I'll get to the bottom of this."

"Don't."

"I'm going to, Bryan!"

"No," he snapped. He gave a little movement of his arm that actually seemed to push her away. "I don't want vandalism here, Cici, I can't tolerate it. My . . . my collections, my things. All the things I have in my house. What if my house is next, Cici? What if they set fire to my house?"

Cici left, walking heavily out to her car. She didn't blame Bryan for being worried about a house fire. Still, something was very wrong, she sensed. Perhaps had been wrong for weeks . . . and it was not just Aaron, it was her relationship with Bryan, too.

He didn't act like a fiancé.

He didn't need her, not really. Most men would have phoned when something as major as a fire had damaged their property. But Bryan acted as if he wanted her to stay away, and he had even tried to push her physically away from him.

Why did Bryan love her, anyway? Did he even like her?

She had never questioned Bryan's love before, and a mood of depression settled on her as she drove slowly home, trying to marshal her confused thoughts. It was a golden October morning, one of the last before winter, yellow and red leaves flaming against a sapphire sky. People were raking their lawns, piling the dead leaves into enormous garden-sized plastic leaf bags.

As she drove into her driveway, she heard the loud, thunderous roar of a leaf blower. John Pickard was blowing the dead leaves off his lawn in a hurricane of brown. Already he had ten leaf bags lined up at his curb. The huge black bags, loaded heavily with crushed and ground-up leaves, seemed ominous and bulky, big enough to hold a human.

Cici scowled, averting her eyes from the row of bags. Where were her thoughts lately? Fixated on death. What was wrong with her, anyway? She was getting married in only weeks; she was supposed to be happy, ecstatic, hopeful. Instead she was letting doubts torment her.

The roar of the leaf blower followed her as she went inside the house, to discover that Aaron had already gotten up, eaten most of a box of doughnuts, and left. Today there was no note on the refrigerator, but Cici had little doubt where her son had gone—over to Dustin's again.

This was too important to wait. They had to talk now. She had to assure herself that her son was innocent of setting the fire in Bryan's garage.

She picked up the phone and dialed the Pickards' house, getting Dustin's older brother, David, who attended Oakland University. "Man, they drove over to Lakeside" was the laconic reply.

Lakeside Mall, he meant—a large shopping mall in Sterling Heights, about twenty-five minutes' drive away. Cici hung up, debating whether she should drive over to the mall to search for Aaron herself. She supposed if she walked the central mall corridors she had a fifty-fifty chance of finding him. If all else failed, she could cruise the parking lot looking for Heather's scrofulous old Mercury Bobcat. She was sure she would recognize its distinctive rust patterns.

Finally she managed to calm herself, sinking into a kitchen chair and rubbing her eyes tiredly. She could chase around town all day and never catch up with her son. Had Aaron really set that fire?

If he had . . .

Oh, God . . . was all of this really her fault?

The wave of anger that overtook her was so sudden and strong it strangled her breath. It was the breast cancer that had really begun all this! Without the mastectomy, Tom would never have left, and there would never have been a divorce. Meeting Bryan—everything else followed from that. *The damn cancer!*

She sat shivering under the surge of hatred, waiting for it to recede enough so she could think clearly again. It wasn't fair—none of it was. And now Aaron would pay a price, too, for an illness that had happened to her.

Cici, don't be an ass, Ann would have said. *You didn't ask for cancer. You were warm and loving, weren't you?*

Being warm and loving wasn't enough!

It is enough. You tried your damnedest. No one could have made that asshole Tom stay in the marriage. As for Aaron, well, he is a separate person from you. Don't take the blame for everything in the whole goddamn world!

Cici relaxed a little, feeling a slight smile touch her lips. Ann. God, yes, she needed to talk to a real friend, someone who'd talk straight, who didn't take any bullshit, who saw the world through plain glasses.

She dialed Ann's number but got the hollow-sounding tape again. But she didn't leave another long message, just left her name again and asked Ann to call.

For Cici, housecleaning was a way of dealing with worry and aggression. She got out the heavy vacuum cleaner, pushing it through the house with firm strokes, glad of the exercise to take her mind off Aaron and Bryan. She even did the stairs, getting out the attachments, worrying the long, slim aluminum wand into corners that hadn't seen a vacuum in six months.

After the vacuuming she did three loads of laundry, hand-washed five or six sweaters, and ironed several blouses. By two-thirty she was carrying a stack of clean jeans and T-shirts up to Aaron's room.

Putting the clothes on his dresser, she was stopped by the sight of an old, waterlogged cardboard box. It looked as if it had been carried out of someone's flooded basement. In fact, it actually stank of mildew.

Cici stopped, puzzled, alarm twingeing through her again. Had Aaron deliberately left the box here for her to see? It almost seemed so.

She reached out to touch a piece of torn tape, seeing the neatly typed label affixed to the side of the box. It said *Clyattville.*

Clyattville. Wasn't that the town where Bryan grew up? She remembered Ann quizzing him the night they had all gone to Chaplin's. She sucked in her breath. If Bryan had grown up in Clyattville, then this box must be his.

She reached out a forefinger to touch limp, pliable, almost sticky pasteboard. Why would the box be so wet?

Then the answer came to her. Cici swayed backward, shaking.

Fire hoses could water-soak a box. Aaron had stolen this box from Bryan's garage.

She thought only briefly about not opening the carton, then threw her scruples aside. Her son came first and every instinct told her that if she didn't look, she'd regret it.

She sorted through the contents of the box with a growing feeling of alarm and unreality. There were letters from civic authorities to a couple called Wykotsky, taking them to task for not having their son vaccinated, for not getting medical attention for him. There were copies of several court orders that they permit their son, Boy, to be treated by a physician.

Cici stared at the papers, remembering her own safe childhood growing up in the village of Rochester. How could any parents deliberately withhold medical help from a child?

And the name, *Boy*. Was that a nickname, or could it be the child's legal name? What did a boy ludicrously named Boy have to do with Bryan? Could it possibly be Bryan himself?

And then there was the diary, written by someone named Junie. "Boy's" mother? The uneven, psychotic printing gave Cici a case of the chills. She flipped through the pages, reading random phrases and paragraphs. *"He Whuped the Boy . . . The Boy's wickid . . . wickid . . . God's hamer . . ."*

Whoever Junie was, she was a rotten speller, Cici told herself, trying to find some humor in this. Her eyes moved to the next page.

> "Whuped him agin with anythin he culd
> get . . . Cryin for the dog . . . We would permit
> no Atopsie . . ."

That last phrase stopped her, and she turned back to the beginning of the page, reading a disjointed account, something about an older relative, maybe a grandmother, who had apparently died alone in her home.

> "God don't want no disturb of her Bones.
> Ungodly! Unpease! We would pertect her, and
> they took her, they do not see, they are the
> Wones who are wickid."

Cici replaced the diary in the box, thinking that there was actually an aura of evil around that mildewed little book. Cici, reared a Methodist, had always found religious fanaticism frightening. The Inquisition, religious cults . . . How far away, really, was this diary from the Reverend James Jones and the poisoned Kool-Aid?

But most chilling of all was the realization that if this was Bryan's box, stolen by Aaron from his house, then all the contents of the box had to relate to Bryan in some way.

Grabbing the diary again, Cici searched the pages more carefully this time, looking for any references to the boy by name—either Bud or Bryan.

She found nothing. He was always "Boy," "the boy," or even "he," as if he had no name at all. Once, it was "Bud Boy."

"Mom?" came Aaron's voice behind her.

Cici jumped violently.

"Mom? What are you doing in my stuff?"

Cici whirled, her heart slamming up into her throat. Her son stood in the doorway of his bedroom, holding a greasy paper sack from Mrs. Field's Cookies, which had an outlet at the mall.

His eyes met hers defiantly.

ELEVEN

Aaron," Cici began in a low, strained voice. "Aaron, I have to talk to you."

He stared at her, appearing both defiant and frightened. Even now she felt a wave of love for him so strong that it swayed her, making her knees weak. She saw him tighten his grip on the bag of cookies as he prepared to edge into the hall.

"Don't you dare back away from me," she cried. "We have to talk, Aaron. I'm not leaving until we have this out!"

Unwillingly her son slouched into the room. He flopped down on his bed, balancing the Mrs. Fields bag on his stomach. His fingers fiddled with it nervously.

Oh, something was wrong, all right, and it was major. Cici felt her throat tighten with dread.

"Aaron, where did that box come from?"

"What box?"

She pointed furiously. "You *know* what box. It's right there on the dresser in plain sight. Waterlogged."

"Oh," he said in the maddening way of teenagers. "I didn't know you meant that box."

"What other box would I mean? Aaron, where did you get it?"

He was silent.

"Aaron!" she snapped. "You knew I'd have to come in your room to put the laundry away. You left the box right in plain sight. You are not a stupid boy. You knew I'd see it! You must have wanted me to see it!"

"Okay, okay, okay, okay." He sat up, scowling. "You want to know where I got that box? Well, I'll tell you. I got it over at El Jerko's garage."

"El Jerko? Aaron, if you're referring to Bryan—"

"*El Jerko,*" her son repeated with sarcastic emphasis. "Mom, he's weirded out. Look in that box. Look at all that crazy stuff. Bloody Jesus pictures. Your fiancé Bryan is a freak, Mom. He's whacked out. Whacked *out.*"

Cici gazed at her son. The adult lines of his features were beginning to show through the adolescent babyishness. Peach-fuzz hairs already grew on Aaron's upper lip and chin and soon would be a shavable beard. His soft, ruddy mouth was tightened now into a stubborn line.

"I don't know what to say first." She forced the quiver from her voice. "Aaron, you admit you got this from Bryan's garage. So that must mean that you had something to do with the fact that his garage was set on fire last night."

"I heard the sirens and went down there. I found the box lying on the grass."

"Aaron! I want the truth!"

"That is the truth." Suddenly Aaron unfolded himself from the bed and stood up. He was two inches taller than she. "Mom, you just don't *get* it, do you? You just don't see the significance."

"What 'significance'? What are you talking about?"

"I'm talking about your boyfriend, Mom. He's got a screw loose! But you don't want to see it, do you?" Aaron's voice rose. "Mom, you're desperate. That's what's wrong with you. You're too damn desperate!"

"Aaron!" she cried angrily, stung to the heart.

"Well?" Her son reached over and swiped up the bag of cookies, twirling the neck of the sack between his fingers. When he turned to her again there were tears in his eyes. "I'm not going to live with him, Mom. You can try to make me, but I won't. I'll go and live with Dad, and if he won't let me live there, I'll . . . I'll . . . I'll *do something else!*"

Her son ran down the hallway and she heard his footsteps clatter across the kitchen floor, then the angry slam of the back door.

Cici slumped down onto her son's bed, which smelled faintly of smoke.

Desperate.

Was she? Had she been?

She picked up a corner of Aaron's pillowcase and began creasing it between her fingers, seeing it all through a diamond prism of tears. Desperate wasn't for thirty-seven-year-old women who still looked good. Desperate was for women in their fifties and sixties, fearful that they'd never find another partner.

But . . . the breast surgery.

That changed everything, didn't it? That placed her in a different category, because she *had* worried about that very thing, hadn't she?

Being alone.

Being unwanted. Considered repulsive. Never again having sex with a man, never again being intimate with anyone.

Cici lay back on Aaron's pillow and slitted her eyes shut. The tears spilled through, weaving a path down her cheeks. What if—just what if—Aaron could possibly be right? And Ann's instincts, too.

What if her fiancé was a different man from the one she'd thought he was? A stranger who didn't really like her as much as he said he did, who had whole, vast chunks of his life he had not told her about. A man with eccentric or even psychotic parents. Like Ann, she'd taken psychology too, at the University of Michigan. She knew how deeply a person's background and genes could shape him or her.

And there was the rug, too—the odd "trick" of the moonlight she'd seen that night as she walked to Bryan's house.

And the fact that Bryan had danced with Abby Tighe.

And Ann's "hunch" about him. Ann was a clever person who read people very well.

Cici raised her head and brought her left hand up. The engagement diamond that Bryan had given her glittered on her ring finger, catching and refracting the light.

Oh, Bry, she thought in agony. *I loved you. I do love you still.* And then her mind added, *But . . . I have to know.*

"Cici Davis. Oh, yes, Ann's friend. We met at the Job Center." Over the phone Mike McVey's voice sounded pleasantly ordinary, certainly not that of a professional investigator.

"I hope I didn't interrupt your day," she managed to say. For a wild moment she thought about making an excuse and hanging up. She should have talked to Bryan first!

But what would she have said to him? How could she possibly ask him about the contents of a box that had been stolen by her son? Or about a rug she'd seen weeks ago?

"No, my day needed interrupting. I was in the middle of some very dull paperwork."

"I'm sorry. I can call back—"

"No, no. You got me at a very good time. I love having my work interrupted by a pretty lady."

"I need to talk to you about something," she blurted.

"Oh?"

"It's—it's about an investigation. Of—of my fiancé." The words fell heavily from her mouth.

"I see," McVey said slowly. "Well, my office is in Southfield, which is a pretty long drive from here. But I'm working at home today, and I live about a mile from the Big Boy restaurant in Rochester. Do you want to meet me there? In, say, twenty minutes?"

Cici gathered up her purse and left immediately, sitting in her car in the garage while the electric door rattled upward on its tracks. Backing her car out, she automatically glanced next door to the Pickards' house.

A shadow on the large picture window caught her eye. Distorted, yet unmistakable, it appeared to be that of a big man hitting a boy across the buttocks and upper thighs. The boy struggled and writhed, and the man hit him again, using a long object of some kind.

The sudden anger that Cici felt was so intense that it rocked her backward against the car seat. That was no spanking. It was child abuse.

Without thinking Cici shoved open her car door and jumped out. She ran across the lawn and hurried to the Pickards' front door. Angrily she leaned on the doorbell, ringing it repeatedly.

Inside the house she could hear Dustin yelling "Shit! Shit!" and sobbing.

"Yeah?" The sobs abruptly stopped. John Pickard appeared in the doorway, glowering. His hands were empty. He wore a pair of khaki slacks and a white shirt loosened untidily at the collar. There were sweat stains under his armpits and the man reeked of angry perspiration.

"I heard the . . . crying," she managed to say, fighting the urge to turn and run.

"I was giving the kid some discipline," Pickard growled.

She stared at him, feeling way out of her element. "Physical discipline? With a ruler or stick?"

"Hey, this is a tough kid, and you'd better think about it for *your* boy, too, Mrs. Davis. It's the only thing these kids listen to nowadays. Authority."

"I don't believe in physical punishment, Mr. Pickard," she said as strongly as she dared. "I consider it abusive."

His eyes challenged her. "Yeah?"

But she had reached the limit of her courage, and she turned and hurried down the steps, half running to her car, expecting at any moment to hear Pickard's footsteps behind her. Reaching her car she jumped in and snapped the door locks.

But looking back toward the Pickard house she saw that no one had followed her. She put her Cougar in reverse and backed out of the driveway. She was shaking all over, her hands trembling. It was one thing to read about child abuse in the newspaper, quite another to realize it was going on right next door, happening to her own son's friend.

The hitting and beating of children made her feel furious, enraged.

Oh, God, what was she going to do about it? Did he beat Heather, too? Should she call the police? Or would that only make it worse for Dustin? She realized that she'd acted impulsively, but now she was going to have to slow up a bit, make sure she did the right thing.

Troubled, she drove toward town, and ten minutes later was pulling into the parking lot of the Big Boy on Rochester Road. She was shown to a booth in the garden room, where a green canopy of plants hung from hooks overhead. A family group in the booth next to hers was just leaving. The father was holding a six-month-old baby, adjusting its denim jumper. The tenderness, such a contrast to what she had just witnessed, made Cici start shaking again.

She ordered coffee and, sipping it, struggled to get her perspective again.

"Well, you certainly do look like there's something on your mind," Mike McVey said, sliding into the booth opposite her. He wore jeans and a blue cotton sweater, and looked fresh and smiling, his reddish hair glossy clean. He ordered black coffee from the teenaged waitress who had just reappeared.

"I was just pulling out of my driveway when I saw my neighbor abusing his fourteen-year-old son," Cici said. "I . . . I lost it a little, I guess. I went up to the door and told him I'd heard the crying. I confronted him."

McVey whistled. "You have guts."

"It's not a matter of guts. I hate child abuse! It's sickening and terrible!" She cleared her throat to get rid of a tremor. "Sometimes I think the human race, *some* of the human race, is pretty frightening."

"Well, you're right. But you may find this is a real can of worms, Cici. The boy may deny everything—an abusive parent can threaten kids with a lot worse if they tell. And some ethnic or religious groups view corporal punishment as a normal way of life. To them, it's not abusive, it's simply accepted procedure. Unpleasant but necessary."

"I refuse to believe it's necessary." Cici stared into her

coffee, where cloudy swirls created a vortex pattern. "Anyway..."
She drew a deep breath. "I've been thinking I might want to use
your services."

McVey's eyes moved briefly to her engagement ring, then
met hers. "All right," he said, nodding. "Maybe I should outline
for you exactly what I can offer, and what I charge. Just so we
have it all up front. I will give you a reduced hourly rate, since
you're a friend of Ann's."

"This all sounds so . . . so official," she began in a low voice.
"So, I don't know . . ." She laughed nervously. "I can't believe
I'm really sitting here talking to you about investigating my
fiancé."

"Is it better to marry him and then find out things that, if
you'd known about them, would have changed your mind about
marrying him? Things that might be very unpleasant?"

Cici pressed her lips together. "I'm sure you're right," she
said uneasily.

"Cici, I was a police officer for fifteen years, and I've been
a P.I. for four. There are a lot of secrets a man can have. For
instance, marriages he never reveals. I had one client who discovered her fiancé had been married ten times, with only six
divorces. That made him a bigamist."

"Oh—"

"There are lawsuits a man might be hiding, or bankruptcy
proceedings, or homosexual contacts, jail terms, you name it.
It's amazingly easy to lead a secret life—a lot of men do it.
Mistresses on the side, regular visits to massage parlors, the use
of 'escort services.' Selling drugs, being a peeping Tom, sex
rings, sexual abuse of young boys—"

"Enough, enough," she said. "Please don't scare me anymore. Just tell me what your services are going to cost, and then
I'll tell you as much as I can about Bryan."

Half an hour later she'd outlined it all for him, a story that,
even as she told it, seemed pathetically ordinary. Single woman
swept off her feet by handsome, single man, now having doubts.

McVey had produced a small notebook and made detailed
notes. When she told him about the fire, and the box, the

religious materials and the diary, McVey nodded, jotting down phrases.

"I'd like to see that box, if I may. Do you still have it?"

"Yes. Aaron took it from the scene of the fire."

"Well, it might provide some clues as to where to proceed from here." McVey went on, "So let me go over all this again. You met the man at the Friday Nighters singles club. He works in Troy and travels quite a bit. He's an antiquer, a collector, and says he was born in Clyattville, up near Houghton Lake."

"That's right."

"You never met any of his family?"

"No. He said both his parents are deceased. He never had any brothers or sisters—he said," she found herself adding.

"He's lived in his present house how long?"

"I think about four years."

"And before that?"

She shook her head, realizing how little Bryan had really told her, and how little she had asked. "Well . . . I think Royal Oak, and Warren, he mentioned those. And of course Ann Arbor, where he went to school."

"Any previous marriages? Relationships?"

Cici was beginning to feel more and more uncomfortable under the scrutiny of this professional. He must be wondering why she had accepted the ring of a man she knew as poorly as this.

"He never spoke much about previous girlfriends. He had a brief marriage when he was in his early twenties, but he never talks much about it. He—he isn't the kind to share much," she explained with difficulty. "The strong, silent type. Oh, please . . . you don't really think there is anything, do you? I mean, anything *really* bad."

"Cici, I never make conclusions this early in the game. When you do an investigation you cover all the bases, in all the cities the subject has lived in. You do a police check, a credit check, you check the courts to see if there are any legal cases, you talk to neighbors and fellow employees—"

"Oh, no!" she exclaimed. "Oh, please—he'll get suspicious."

"There will be no problem. When I talk to the employees I'll be an executive recruiter, and he'll think nothing of it. Men in jobs like his get approached by recruiters all the time. This *is* going to take me a few weeks, though. Some of this stuff takes a while. We'll talk later about whether you want him followed."

"Followed?" she cried.

"It's often necessary if there are blank days or suspicious behavior. But we can just keep it as an option for now."

"I . . . I see."

"When is your wedding date, Cici?"

She flushed. The confrontation with Pickard had upset her. Now this conversation seemed so very unreal and repugnant. Did she even have the right to do this to another person? "December twenty-sixth."

Mike McVey raised a sandy eyebrow. "That soon? I'd advise you to postpone it if you can. If you feel the need for an investigation, then I'd say you have no business getting married that fast."

Numbly Cici nodded.

"I'm going to ask that you keep up your normal behavior with this man. Don't do anything unusual, don't start suddenly pulling away from him or asking a lot of questions. I'll do all that. I guarantee you, if there is anything suspicious, I'll get a handle on it."

She bit her lip. "Please . . . don't let him know you're doing this."

"I'm very discreet. You can trust me."

Two tense days passed. Cici fought the urge to phone McVey and ask what he'd found, or better yet, call off the whole search. Hiring him made her feel incredibly dishonest and sneaky, a sensation she disliked.

Worse, her stomach was in knots just thinking about what he might uncover.

What if he *did* find something suspicious? What would she do then? Would she confront Bryan with what she had learned, ask him for explanations? Say nothing and just break their engagement? If she did that, what excuse could she give?

Several times she made an attempt to talk to Dustin, but the boy studiously avoided her. He seemed ashamed she had seen him, and almost scuttled away from her. She hadn't mentioned the incident to Aaron, not wanting to upset him further.

Cici wanted desperately to talk to Ann. Ann's perspective was what she needed. Cici keenly felt the lack of that best friendship, on which she'd depended. Why hadn't Ann responded to her several messages? It seemed odd to her, and she tried to remember Jeanette's last name. Bogart, was that it? No, that had been the previous marriage. Frustrated at her memory lapse, Cici searched through her address book, but apparently she had not recorded the newest name and number.

Damn! she thought.

On Tuesday she phoned Larry, Ann's boyfriend, to see if he had heard from Ann. According to his secretary, Larry was in San Francisco on business. When he called in, the secretary would relay Cici's question.

Bryan was in Cincinnati this week, a fact that made pretending much easier. At least she did not have to pretend to be at ease when she wasn't.

"I'm up to my ears in work," he told her when he called on Thursday night. His voice sounded calm and normal again, and it was hard to imagine his temporary upset on the night of the garage fire.

He went on to tell her some of the things that had transpired at his business meetings, while Cici closed her eyes, pretending to listen. She spent a lot of time, she realized, listening to Bryan tell her about business.

"Are you okay?" he asked during a pause for breath.

"What?"

"I said are you okay? You seem quiet tonight, Cici."

"Oh, I—I'm fine. A hard day at work, and a sinus headache . . . you know."

"Well, take something for it then. What do you want me to bring you?" he added. "I've already looked at a few things for you but I need to make up my mind."

Uneasily Cici shifted the receiver to her other hand. He was shopping for gifts for her while she was paying money to have him spied on. "Please, Bry," she said in a low voice. "Don't bring me anything. I wish you wouldn't."

"But I always bring you something."

She remembered McVey's admonition. "All right, then."

"You'd better go and take some headache pills," Bryan told her. "You definitely sound under the weather."

Later that night Larry called. He hadn't heard from Ann either.

A large bouquet arrived the following day, several dozen peach-colored roses that seemed to burst out of a sparkling Waterford crystal vase, the arrangement stunning enough to be an illustration in *Town and Country*.

"I see he sent roses again," Aaron remarked, this time refraining from using Bryan's name or any other insult, or even sarcastically emphasizing the pronoun *he*.

"Yes. I love roses, Aar, and Bryan knows that."

Aaron did not comment further. She and her son had reached some delicate and temporary balance. *Was* he innocent of setting the garage fire? Cici hoped and prayed so.

A one-day trip to Chicago with Quint to visit the main office of their agency took her mind off the waiting. In Chicago, Cici would train a new job developer for that office.

They spent the flight to Chicago going over several reports and discussing a new software program Cici wanted the company to purchase that would assist clients with cover letters.

At O'Hare Airport on the way back that same night, she and Quint stopped at the concession stand to buy magazines. Cici impulsively purchased a postcard of the Chicago night skyline to send to Ann.

> *In Chicago on trip with Quint. Work great, love life questionable. I called McVey. Hope you're having a great time in Connecticut. Don't you ever return your calls? Please, PLEASE call me. Always friends? Cici. P.S. Please call!*

She bought a stamp from the salesgirl and found a mailbox on the way to the gate. As she dropped the card in, it gave a little papery rattle against the metal of the chute, then went down into the maw of the postal box. It would be waiting for Ann when she returned from her visit.

"How're the wedding plans shaping up? That Hawaiian honeymoon?" Quint wanted to know after they had settled themselves in their tourist-class seats.

She hesitated only a second.

"Oh, excellently," she said. "We're taking a helicopter tour of Kauai, and a couple of snorkeling trips. Lots of sunning on the beach and some golf on Maui. Also a fishing charter. Bryan wants to go fishing."

"Don't forget to take something if you get on any boats. The waves over there are humongous between the islands, very, very choppy. It's seasick time otherwise."

"Right," Cici said, forcing a smile.

The day after Cici returned from Chicago, Aaron and his father had planned to attend a World Wrestling Federation match at the Palace, featuring Andre the Giant, Brutus "The Barber" Beefcake, and Million Dollar Man, names that meant little to Cici but caused Aaron to talk excitedly.

"Brutus the Barber carries these huge scissors, and when he beats his opponent he gets 'em out and clips off his hair—right there in the ring! I wonder if he's gonna cut off the hair of Million Dollar Man. Man, I can't wait."

But returning home from work on the night of the match, Cici found her son sprawled in front of the TV, a tight, hurt look on his face.

"I thought you were going to the wrestling match," she said in surprise.

"You thought wrong, Mom."

"You mean your dad cancelled?"

"Yup. He had a 'big push at work,' his favorite phrase. I got dumped."

"Oh, Aaron!" She moved toward her son, intending to give him a sympathetic hug, but Aaron pulled away.

"No!" he cried. "I don't want hugs. Just leave me alone."

"Aar? We'll drive over to your dad's and pick up the tickets and I'll take you myself." She wanted to go watch wrestling about like she wanted to gain forty pounds, but she couldn't stand that look of devastation on her son's face.

"No."

"But you were looking forward to it. I really wouldn't mind—"

"Come *on,*" her teenager said dully. "You know you hate wrestling. Besides, I don't want to go now, anyway."

"But I'd be happy to take you—"

"Forget it," Aaron said, unfolding himself from the couch. "Dad's a jerk, too, Mom. How come you ever married a guy like that, anyway? He doesn't know how to keep his word, does he?"

"Oh, Aaron, Aaron." Children saw life with such cruel, black-and-white clarity. "There are just things that your father doesn't handle very well. He doesn't know how, Aaron. It's not that he doesn't care—"

"Yeah, right," Aaron said bitterly.

After her son drifted off to his room, Cici began straightening up the couch cushions her son had tossed onto the carpet, thinking that she was being far kinder than Tom deserved. For once, she should be honest with herself. Tom had always been that way.

She remembered once when Aaron was small. She had gotten three tickets for *Annie* at the Fisher Theater, a big treat then. On the night of the play, Tom arrived home from work telling them he was "too tired" to attend. Aaron cried—he'd wanted to sit next to Daddy. But Tom didn't relent and even snapped at the little boy when he begged.

Cici took Aaron to the play herself. They had excellent seats and *Annie* was wonderful, even with that empty seat next to hers. Later, Tom didn't even ask them how the play was.

Was indifference a kind of child abuse too?

The following day, Cici received another call from Larry. "I've been tied up in nonstop dealer meetings, and it's hectic as hell," he told her. "I'm taking a quick break."

"Has Ann called you?"

"No," he said, "and I'm getting worried."

Cici felt a frisson of alarm. "Her answering machine remote *does* work, doesn't it? I mean, maybe it's malfunctioned."

"As far as I know it works. I'm wondering if she's mad at me. You know, using her answering machine to screen out my calls."

There was a silence as Cici digested this. Now the alarm was growing into a blossom of fear. On the other end of the wire she could hear Larry's breathing, along with a tinny, long-distance hum.

"Larry, did she leave you her mother's number?"

"No—and if she had, I would have already called it. I know we aren't—I mean, I don't have any claim on her, but she usually calls me every couple of days."

Cici tried to reassure Larry, citing Ann's independence, her fear of commitment, but the words sounded hollow, and when she hung up she was more worried than before. She sat at her desk staring at a stack of printouts from the job bank.

Wayne Sturdevandt, a fifty-three-year-old client who'd been early-retired from GM, was lurking in the hallway outside Cici's office, hoping for an impromptu counseling session.

"Cici, do you have a few minutes to go over a cover letter?"

"Yes, Wayne," Cici called cordially. "I'll be with you in just one second."

She scowled at the phone, and finally picked it up again, punching in Ann's office number. She asked to speak to Royal Thorsson, Ann's boss.

"Ann?" he said, with a note of puzzlement in his voice. "Why, no, she didn't leave a number where she could be reached. In fact, she was supposed to take some files with her, to review, but they're still on her desk."

"I see," said Cici, again experiencing that hollow feeling. "When's she supposed to return to work?"

"She was supposed to be back today, actually."

"And she never showed up, and didn't call?"

"No . . . is something wrong?" Thorsson sounded concerned.

"I don't know," Cici said, and hung up.

She decided to stop at Ann's house on the way home. Maybe she could find Ann's address book and call her mother.

Even though it was only five-thirty, it was dark as Cici joined the hordes of commuters on the drive north on Crooks Road into the suburban bedroom communities of Troy and Rochester Hills. Traffic was stop and go, every traffic light requiring a long wait. By the year 2000 it was predicted that Oakland County would be gridlocked, and the process seemed to be well under way.

Nothing's wrong, she told herself as she fiddled with her car radio, switching nervously from one station to another. *I'm being silly; this whole thing is very silly. And I'm going to be late getting home.*

It was thirty minutes later by the time she reached Ann's condominium complex, a new luxury development built off Hamlin Road.

Ann's was a corner unit, with a brick wall enclosing a tiny front patio, and a wooded view out back. Cici pulled into the driveway, feeling a knot clench in her stomach. There were lights on in the house. Not just one window but several—and the lights burned brightly.

She parked on the driveway apron in front of Ann's one-car garage. Car headlights passing on the street behind her suddenly lit up the garage door, which had a row of decorative windows in it.

Cici gasped.

There was a car parked in the garage. Ann's car.

She pushed back the sudden anxiety. The presence of Ann's car in her garage wasn't necessarily that sinister. After all, maybe Ann had been picked up by an airport limo service and left her Ford Taurus at home.

She got out and walked up to the small patio, pulling open the wrought-iron gate and stepping inside. The tiny enclosure had been attractively landscaped with small evergreens and plants in tubs. A curved bay window revealed Ann's living room.

Cici peered through the glass, thinking that the room looked like a pleasant stage set waiting for the actors. Ann's new furniture was piled with tapestry pillows, and her collection of paintings and prints glowed from the walls. Cici had been with her when she purchased some of the art.

But somehow the sight of the quiet room wasn't as reassuring as it should have been. Cici walked out of the patio and around to the back of the building.

At the back of the unit, there was a sliding glass door that looked into Ann's formal dining area. Here another light burned, as if someone was home. Cici walked up to the glass and gazed in. Again, the scene looked normal at first glance. It was an attractive dining room wallpapered in a yellow Laura Ashley print. An arrangement of silk flowers decorated the table, and there was a small stack of unopened mail and circulars.

Then Cici saw Ann's purse sitting on a chair.

It was her friend's gray leather Stone Mountain purse, which she always carried, claiming its color went with practically everything. Ann never left home without that purse.

And there was broken glass everywhere.

Oh, Jesus, Cici muttered, fear spearing her heart.
Oh, Ann.

TWELVE

Cici decided to use a rock to break a section of glass in the sliding door, but when she tried the latch it slid easily open. Had Ann left it unlocked? Or had someone broken in?

The wind had come up, concealing the sound of her entry, and the dark shadows cast by trees at the back of the condo hid her from view. Being a burglar was ridiculously easy, she thought. She probably should have called the police but she didn't want them coming in first, until she'd seen . . . whatever there was to see. Ann deserved at least that privacy.

She opened the door.

The minute Cici stepped into the condo, she felt the presence of something evil. Badness seemed to crackle in the air like a tiny, electrical force field.

"Ann?" she called, her voice cracking. "Ann, please, if you're in here . . . *Ann?*"

She walked through the dinette area toward the kitchen itself, seeing that the refrigerator door was standing ajar. She opened it and saw food containers half putrefied, a container of yogurt on its side. The door had obviously been open for days.

Dread freezing her, she continued on, toward the door that led to the small laundry area. That was when she saw the massive hole smashed in the drywall. Insulation and wires gaped from it.

"Ann," Cici whispered.

The room had been wrecked, as if by a giant with a club. The light fixture hung in splinters. More holes had been violently smashed in the drywall, and the washer was wrecked, the plastic control panel hanging loose. Its crushed knobs were scattered on the floor. A stain-spray can lay awry, and soap powder was scattered everywhere.

But that wasn't what caused Cici to draw in her breath in a strangled scream of horror.

It was the blood.

On the washer, on the wall, and puddled on the floor.

Dark brown and coagulated, like paint that had been drying too long.

"Ann! Ann!" Screaming, Cici ran through the condo, searching for her friend, but even as she hurried frantically from room to room, she knew that Ann wouldn't be there.

And she wasn't. All of the rooms were empty. Ann's bedroom was horrifyingly vacant, her bed unmade, items of lingerie strewn across a chair and flung on the floor. This room didn't smell like death, but rather of hair mousse and Ann's distinctive, spicy perfume. Cici stood in the middle of the room shaking violently.

The Basher!

What other explanation could there be? Ann's house looked exactly like Abby Tighe's, and like the other women's homes shown on the endless news broadcasts. Somehow the Basher had attacked Ann.

Cici knew she had to call the police, but first she went into Ann's bathroom and was violently sick, spewing up her lunch into the commode. She knelt in front of the toilet and hung on to it while the bathroom spun dizzily. Ann had hung some panty hose over the shower rod to dry, and they dangled like little coffee-colored, shrunken legs, looking ridiculous.

Then she saw the towel draped across the towel holder, with

a dried bloodstain on it. He must have come up here to this bathroom to wash away the blood afterwards.

He.

Oh, God, where was Ann? *Was she dead?*

Still crying, Cici fled back into Ann's bedroom to use the phone. The answering machine was positioned beside Ann's bed, and Cici saw that its red message light was blinking. Some of those messages were undoubtedly her own and Larry's. The police would listen to them now.

Averting her eyes, she reached for the phone and dialed the police.

Uniformed police officers and plainclothesmen trooped through the condo. Technicians arrived with cameras and other equipment and set to work. A detective, Ben Oleson, didn't bother to conceal his annoyance that Cici had left fingerprints, especially in Ann's bedroom, where the attacker had been. He was especially irritated that she'd vomited in the toilet, possibly destroying evidence.

She sat in the back of a police cruiser and answered his questions. Then she was driven to the police department and questioned again, even more exhaustively.

Where did Ann work? What were her daily habits? Who were Ann's boyfriends? Was there a steady one? Had she been receiving any obscene phone calls, or unwanted male attention? Was Ann promiscuous?

"Now just wait a minute!" Cici cried. Oleson was about forty years old, with dark eyes, graying hair, and the look of a sleek, competent ferret. "I resent that. What does Ann's sex life have to do with this? She's single, but that's not exactly a crime. She dates, but she isn't promiscuous at all . . ."

Cici's voice trailed off. Ann *was* a flirt. Men did come on to her often. Even Cici's neighbor, John Pickard, had made a play for her.

John Pickard. Cici's thoughts seemed to grind to a halt.

"Mrs. Davis," Oleson began patiently, "Ann Trevanian's sex life has everything to do with this. We have to investigate all of her contacts. It's routine and no reflection on her character.

Now you say she belonged to a singles club. What singles club?"

"The . . . the Friday Nighters."

"Was she a regular?"

"Yes, she—she was their vice president at one time. On the Board of Directors."

As Oleson continued to question her, asking for details, Cici felt a deep chill. *John Pickard attended the Friday Nighters, as well as Bryan.* Where Abby, as well as Ann, had gone to dance.

She gathered her purse close to her body and sat hugging it, shivering despite the warm furnace air coming in through a vent under the detective's desk.

Oleson noticed her shiver. "Anything wrong, Mrs. Davis? Did you think of something?"

She spoke reluctantly. "There is someone . . . my next-door neighbor. He attended the Friday Nighters. He was interested in Ann; in fact she said he came on to her. He's quite a—a stud." She moistened her lips, afraid, but knowing she had to say it. "He is also abusive to his son. I—I saw him hitting the boy with some kind of ruler or stick."

"I see. This man's name?"

"John Pickard." Cici gave the address and Oleson wrote it down. She watched his pen move with a feeling of disbelief. My God, now the police were going to question John Pickard, and what if he was innocent? Of being the Basher, anyway.

Cici remembered the Pickards' big backyard, with the new plant beds John had dug in the summer, the installation of various bushes and shrubs around his new deck. Another shiver crawled over her. A flower bed—the perfect place to bury someone.

Then she shook her head, forcing the idea away.

Get real, she told herself. Pickard didn't exactly live alone. He was the father of teenagers. How could he bury a body in the yard without one of them noticing? And there had been at least nine women, with Ann making ten.

Ten chances to get caught.

She realized that Oleson was staring at her. "Mrs. Davis? Are you all right? I realize this is very difficult for you. Please, just bear with me. Any other contacts you know of at the singles group?"

Cici reluctantly gave him Larry Watts's name and phone number, which she was sure he would get anyway from Ann's papers and from the fact that Larry's voice was on Ann's answering machine.

"Ann was very well liked," she added. "She had dozens of friends, male as well as female. I can provide you with a list. But there is something else," she went on with a stab of guilt. "I did see Abby Tighe's name on our club sign-in sheets."

"Abby Tighe?" He looked at her sharply.

"Yes."

Oleson frowned, looking angry again. "If you saw her name on the list, *why* didn't you call us about it, Mrs. Davis? We can't work without help from the public. When the public sees something and just ignores it, then we have nothing to work with."

"I was going to," she responded, flushing. What must he think of her? Of course she had known it was important. The reason she hadn't told the police was because Ann had said she talked to a woman who saw Bryan with Abby. She'd been trying to protect Bryan.

Bryan. Who hadn't liked Ann. Who'd been angry at Ann because of her constant questions and cross-examining, who'd overheard Ann warning her against him.

Cici's empty stomach squeezed hard, and she felt another rush of nausea. She knew she should mention Bryan's name to Detective Oleson as well.

But Bryan wasn't just anyone; he was the man she was going to marry. What if the police actually brought Bryan in and put him under arrest?

It was unthinkable!

She realized that Oleson was still questioning her, but she hadn't heard any of what he'd said. In fact, the room was beginning to do a slow, wobbly spin.

She crossed her legs again, breathing deeply. "Sorry," she managed. "I . . . this is so upsetting to me. Ann was my best friend. Could I go home now?"

He frowned, the ferret eyes alert. "Mrs. Davis, are you *sure* you're telling us everything you know?"

"Yes! Yes, I am." She twisted her hands together. "If you want more names, of men I mean, maybe you should go through Ann's things. She had a big Rolodex, and she saved almost everything. She was kind of a pack rat."

Dully Cici noticed that she had used the past tense, *was.*

"We're going to do all of that. It's routine procedure." Oleson rose, glancing at his watch. "Well, Mrs. Davis, I'll have someone drop you off to pick up your car, and you can go home. I'll be in touch, though. And I want you to do some thinking about any other men in Ann's life, anyone who might be in any way at all suspicious. Call us if you think of any more names."

"All right." Cici rose, too. Her mouth tasted terrible. She hadn't had time to rinse it out. "Mr. Oleson . . ." She stopped near the door. "What do you think happened to Ann? Do you think . . . she's still alive?"

He gazed at her grimly. "No. There's too much blood around, and the force of those blows—the ones that wrecked the washer and put holes in the walls—was just too massive. Those were killing blows, Mrs. Davis. I'm sorry."

She thought so, too, but to hear a police officer say it was like a blow to her stomach.

"Frankly, we think that the attacker kills the victim, then showers in the woman's bathroom, maybe changes his clothes, then carries the victim out to his car. The victim may be alive at that point, but we don't think so. Some of the tissue we found was—" The detective stopped, apparently realizing his words were turning Cici a sickly shade of white. "Sorry," he added.

"It's all right."

Oleson's phone shrilled. The detective picked it up, and Cici fled into the corridor, where a young police officer was waiting. Another spasm of nausea clutched at her stomach. She excused herself and hurried to the ladies' room.

After being dropped off at her car, Cici drove the short distance from Ann's to her own home. She felt weak, shaky, and drained, her mouth sour with vomit. The night seemed very black and clear, every light so sharply delineated it hurt her eyes.

At Ann's, she had seen a van from Channel 7 parked in front of the condo. A female newscaster was giving a news update, wind flapping at the hem of her smart cloth coat. Seeing her, Cici had felt a spasm of sharp, irrational anger. Now Ann was going to be a part of the whole Basher story, the endless, grisly speculation.

At home, she found another florist's package waiting on her front doorstep. The sight seemed bizarre, a relic from some other world, some normal world to which she no longer belonged.

She unlocked the door and carried the flowers in. They were from Bryan, of course—who else? She didn't even want to open them. However, when she set the package on the hall table, it was unsteady and started to tip over, so she ripped off the green paper.

Inside were more roses, dark red, a perfection of fat, velvety buds and just-opened blooms, their scent garden-sweet.

Cici stared at them, shuddering. Red . . . blood-red . . . She snatched up the bouquet and carried it to the kitchen, where she hurled the bouquet, vase and all, into the trash. A thorn scratched her arm as she threw, the pain needlelike.

Her own violent act against the helpless roses shocked her. My God, was she losing her mind? Tears pricked her eyes and began to flow, gathering momentum as she leaned against the wall, her entire body shuddering.

Ann gone . . . and what about Bryan? Wasn't he a suspect too? Wasn't that really why she hadn't mentioned his name to Oleson? Because he had been at the Friday Nighters club at the same time as both Ann and Abby Tighe. Because she had seen him carrying something bulky and heavy, wrapped in a rug . . .

She suddenly felt terribly, terribly afraid.

She could hear Aaron's stereo playing, more Paula Abdul, and stopped to knock on her son's door. Briefly she told him about Ann, trying unsuccessfully to make it sound less horrible than it was.

Aaron's shock was profound. "You don't mean . . . the Basher?" he said, going white. "The *Basher* did it?"

"I don't know," was all she could tell him.

"Oh," Aaron said, his lips trembling, emotion he immediately tried to hide by sliding another tape into his player. Aaron had loved Ann's breezy jokes, her "cool" interest in the same kind of music he liked.

"Aaron, we don't necessarily know that the Basher did it."

"He did it."

"Aar, the police aren't sure—"

"It isn't fair!" her son burst out, turning his back to her. "Ann didn't do anything!"

Cici felt her throat close, knowing her son was railing against the essential injustice of life. "Aar, all we ever really have is each other," she finally said. "Ann knew you cared about her. She—" But she could go on no more with hollow words of comfort.

She knew that her son wanted to be alone, so she went upstairs and changed her clothes, reaching for the first garments she found, some jeans and a much-washed blue chambray shirt. As she was buttoning the shirt, the phone rang.

For a horrid instant Cici stared at the telephone. She let it ring again, then again. She didn't want to pick it up. If it was Bryan, what would she say to him? Too much had happened. She could stand no more.

But the ringing continued. She forced herself to reach for the receiver.

"Hello?"

Of course it was Bryan. "Hi, honey. Seven rings? Where were you?"

"In . . . in the bathroom," she replied faintly.

"I can tell by your voice your day's been like mine, long, tough, and aggravating."

For an instant she couldn't speak, exhaustion flooding her like an anesthetic.

"Cici? Cic?"

God, she had to say something or he would suspect. "I'm sorry," she said, choking back guilt. "I was just putting on some jeans," she said vaguely. "How was your day? How did the meetings go?"

He responded to her question, not seeming to notice anything wrong. "It's been the usual, a long, long meeting, and then a couple of disagreements I had to iron out between supervisors."

He went on to explain in detail the ramifications of the latest politics at work, while Cici listened numbly, thinking that she really knew very little that was significant about this man. Most of their conversation had been about superficial things— work, computers, antiques, movies. And she'd settled for that.

"Did you get the roses I sent?" he finally asked her.

"Oh—oh, yes, I did. They're beautiful," she responded, remembering with another spasm of guilt that the roses were now at the bottom of a garbage bag.

"I sent red ones this time," he told her. "It's the language of flowers, you know." He was talking to her about the language of flowers when Ann might be dead somewhere. "Red, deep red, shows intensity of feeling, Cici. It's the strongest statement, the strongest color of flowers you can send."

For the first time she wondered where he had got such information. What other man she knew actually bothered to look up the language of flowers? It was so calculated, somehow. She wanted so much for Bryan to be what he seemed. What would she do if he wasn't?

"Cici?" he prompted.

"The—the roses," she said quickly. "They were so pretty. Bryan. Bry—" She started to tell him about Ann, then stopped, the words stuck in her throat.

"I'll be home in a couple days, honey, I'm not sure just when. I'll bring you a nice gift, and we can go out for dinner— how about the Summit?" The Summit, in downtown Detroit atop the Renaissance Center, was a revolving restaurant with a stupendous, sparkling view of the lights of the Detroit River and Windsor, Canada. Just what Bryan would choose, she realized dully.

She didn't think she'd ever be hungry again.

But she choked back her repugnance and told Bryan she

was looking forward to the dinner. McVey had told her to act natural, and she supposed it was natural for her to go out with her fiancé. Hadn't she accepted dozens of other such dinners? Been proud and thrilled that she had a man like Bryan beside her?

She hung up, and sat for a long time staring into nothingness. She wanted Bryan to be blameless . . . to be exactly what he seemed. Now everything was spoiled as she was caught in her own web of suspicions, unable to think clearly anymore.

A scrap of paper beside the bed caught her eye, and she realized it was the one on which she had jotted down Mike McVey's phone number.

Relief sagged through her, mingled with the burgeoning of hope. McVey! She'd felt so guilty when she hired him, but maybe he had already cleared Bryan. Then there'd be nothing to worry about, would there?

She needed to know that everything was all right, that Bryan was an ordinary, strong-but-silent type who was simply reticent about his past.

She reached for the phone again, and punched out McVey's number.

She arranged to meet the private investigator at the Big Boy that same night.

"Are you sure you don't want to drive down to my office? We'd have more privacy there."

"No." She didn't want to wait that long.

It was nearly ten o'clock when she arrived. McVey was in the nearly empty garden room again, the sports page of the *Detroit News* spread out in front of him. Resting on the seat beside him was a leather folder. Glancing around, Cici saw that they would have some privacy. The only other diners in this section were two hand-holding teenagers.

"Hi." She slid into the booth.

"You look a bit frazzled," McVey said after a moment of studying her.

"I'm living under a lot of stress," she said. She drew breath to tell McVey what had happened to Ann, but caution stopped her in time. He'd find out about Ann soon enough—it would be on the news.

But if she drew a connection between Ann and Bryan, then McVey would know her suspicions and he might even notify the police himself. No, it was too early to do that! She could destroy Bryan with just a few words. She didn't want to say those words until she was very, very sure.

She went on, "I feel guilty that I hired an investigator, and I—I guess I just need to know what you've found out, if anything. I want to get back to my normal life."

He nodded. "You know that the investigation isn't complete, don't you? I told you that over the phone. I still have things I'm tracking down—the death certificates of Bryan's father and mother, for instance."

"I understand that, but I want to know what you do have."

"All right." McVey took out the folder, consulting a yellow legal pad on which he had scribbled notes. "First of all, I followed up on the Clyattville lead. He was born Bryan Ed Wykotsky, in 1957, to June Kallika Wykotsky and Ed Wykotsky. Apparently his father owned a small furniture shop. They made porch and patio furniture, crude pine stuff mostly."

"I see," Cici said, moistening suddenly dry lips. So the "Junie" who had written the diary *was* Bryan's mother. Was the "Boy" in the diary Bryan? "But—I mean, he must have changed his name then?"

"Yes. He had it legally changed to Bryan Wyatt when he was twenty-one, in 1978, in Washtenaw County. He was a very bright boy, Cici, and won a full scholarship to the University of Michigan. That's where he had the papers drawn up, in Ann Arbor. But there's a lot more. As you know, the parents were heavy-duty religious fanatics who refused to have their son vaccinated, and they were cited several times for contempt of court."

Religious fanatics. Yes, she remembered the papers in the box. Those garishly realistic photographs of a bloody, crucified Christ.

Cici took a sip of coffee. The cup shook a little, sloshing dark liquid up to the rim. "He didn't tell me any of this. Not about the name change or the contempt of court. He never mentioned a word of it."

"Hardly anyone reaches adulthood without some secret, Cici. People have vulnerable areas, or events in their lives they consider less than flattering." McVey consulted his notes. "Okay. It was definitely a strange family. There were at least three occasions I found when the parents bucked the court system by refusing to get medical attention for their son.

"Twice the child had croup, another time it was pneumonia, and the Wykotskys refused to allow a doctor to treat him. What happened was, finally June's sister, a woman called . . . yes . . . Betty Schwartz, would get a court order so the kid could get a shot of penicillin."

The whole thing sounded like a Social Services case history, one of the chronic kind. Cici caught her breath, filled with a stifling pity for Bryan. No wonder he never wanted to tell her— could she really fault him for that? But how much else hadn't he told her?

She remarked, "I can't understand how parents could just let a child die—even if they thought they were following God's law. I've never understood that kind of blind belief."

"Well, the mother spent some time in Ypsilanti State Hospital. Another thing, Ed Wykotsky's mother died in 1965—that was Bryan's grandmother, Evelyn. Apparently she drank herself into a stupor, fell down, and broke her hip. The county wanted to do an autopsy and the family fought it tooth and nail. Said they didn't believe in autopsies, cutting apart the body, that sort of thing. Wykotsky was jailed for thirty days for obstructing the county medical examiner. He illegally tried to remove the body."

Cici felt a chilly shiver lift the nerve ends of her skin. "You don't mean . . . *body snatching?*"

"If you want to use those terms, yes. Well, attempted, anyway. I can show you copies of the court papers. I'll provide copies of everything for you."

"I—I'll take your word for it." Cici struggled to assimilate this information. "Oh, boy."

"Yes, you can see why Bryan might have wanted to change

his name and dissociate himself from all of that. And then in 1971, when Bryan was fourteen, the family just upped and moved to Detroit. The father sold the shop; they moved away and were gone. All the case records and court records stop."

"Oh," she said heavily. Confused thoughts swirled through her head. On the one hand, Bryan had risen out of that ugly environment, which was all to his credit. On the other hand . . .

A picture flashed into her mind: Bryan lugging that heavy, bulging rug into his house. And he'd never really shown her the rug, had he, or told her what he'd had wrapped up in it.

Could it possibly have been a dead woman?

McVey was taking out a stack of legal-size papers from the folder. "Here," he said, handing them to her. "These are Xerox copies of everything I've obtained so far. I'd strongly advise you to put them in a safe place."

She gazed at the legal papers. They formed a stack nearly three inches thick. What would Bryan say if he saw them? He'd know she'd hired an investigator, that she didn't trust him. It would kill their relationship.

But how could there even *be* a relationship now that she no longer trusted him?

She handed the stack of court records back to McVey. "I can't take them home with me. I don't want any evidence around—anything to show that I've started an investigation."

McVey sighed. "It's the best thing, Cici. Now, I have more information coming in. I've made a number of contacts in other areas, but it should take two or three more weeks for them all to come through. Don't make any major decisions until then."

Two or three weeks! How could she possibly stand the tension until then?

A thought struck her. "You mentioned an aunt. Is she still in Clyattville?"

McVey consulted his notes again. "Do you mean Betty Ann Schwartz? She runs a dress shop in town, I believe."

Cici felt a little thrill of sick excitement. An aunt, still alive, who actually remembered Bryan as a boy. And living only three hours' drive away. Maybe she could ease her mind a little, take away the awful feeling that Bryan was hiding vile secrets from her.

"I think I might drive up to Clyattville," she began.

"What? No!" he snapped. "Don't. That's my job. I'd really advise against it."

"I want to go myself," she insisted. "I need to talk to her, get a picture of—"

"Cici, you *don't* know the situation. What if he hears you've gone up there? What will he do? I would not advise it at all."

"I'm not going to say I won't."

McVey scowled at her, and she could see the policeman he once had been. "Look, this isn't TV, this isn't *McGyver* or *Murder, She Wrote*. This is the real world, and shit happens, if you'll pardon my language. The best thing you can do is stay out of it, and let a professional handle these things for you. Now, I want you to promise—"

"I'm not going to promise anything. That's why I'm paying you for the information—so I can use it."

"Cici . . . just be careful, then. Don't let him know you went up there."

"I'm not a fool," she said.

By the time she arrived home it was almost midnight, and Cici was deeply exhausted. Her muscles ached as if she had been clenching them for hours. In fact, it felt as if months, instead of only hours, had passed since she had discovered Ann's wrecked home.

She thought about what McVey had told her. But the aunt had to be a decent person if she had defied the Wykotskys to get the court orders. Were there things she would tell another woman that she would not tell a male investigator? Cici knew that she had a trustworthy face and a goodly supply of "people abilities"—people liked her. People talked to her. She felt sure she could convince another woman to confide in her.

Anyway, why had she hired an investigator except to get information she could use as *she* saw fit?

In the TV room Aaron was sprawled on the floor with

several textbooks strewn in front of him, watching a movie on the VCR. It was *Harold and Maud.*

"This is excellent, man," her son exclaimed, his laugh suddenly cracking apart. His face looked tense, his hair rumpled, and there were tear streaks on his face. He began explaining some of the plot to her. She vaguely remembered that *Harold and Maud* was a cult movie among teenagers.

"I don't suppose you watched the news?" she said. "Was Ann on?"

On the TV, a girl raced out of Harold's mansion, screaming. Aaron seemed mesmerized by the sight.

"Aaron?" she questioned sharply.

He looked up. "No, I didn't watch the news. I hate the news, Mom. It's so false!"

Ann, she knew, was the reason he hadn't watched it. She looked at him. "Aaron, I'm taking a day off work tomorrow. I'm going to drive up north to Clyattville, up near Houghton Lake. I'll probably be back sometime after dinner, I'm not sure."

Her son nodded, absorbed in the movie.

"Aar? Are you listening?"

"Yeah, right. I'll nuke something in the microwave. You don't have to worry."

"And finish your homework," she added automatically. "Right now, Aaron—before it gets any later. And lights out at twelve-thirty."

She went upstairs to her bedroom, and wearily began getting ready for bed. Putting her watch on her bedside table, she noticed a little ceramic basket filled with hand-painted ceramic tulips. Ann had given it to her for her birthday two years ago, the year they drove down to Greektown, ate *saganaki* and drank *ouzo,* and Ann did a belly dance in the parking structure. They had laughed themselves silly.

She'd always assumed her friendship with Ann would last her lifetime.

She threw off her bra and panties and went naked into the bathroom to soak in the tub. Somewhere in the process of soaping her face, she began to cry.

* * *

Cici woke at six-thirty, her stomach still clenched in a hard knot. The previous night's dreams had been chaotic, filled with a Bryan who changed shapes and became dark and menacing, his face twisted with agony like the garish pictures of the Christ that were in the *Clyattville* box. And then his face changed and became John Pickard's, leering and grinning.

She wrenched herself out of the nightmare, and switched on her bedside lamp. Was she making a mistake in deciding to drive north today? Would Bryan find out what she had done?

But, she reminded herself, Bryan probably hadn't been back to Clyattville in years. After all, if you changed your name to get rid of your background, then you certainly didn't make lots of trips back.

She showered, dressed in slacks and a cotton sweater, and breakfasted. Aaron left for school looking scrubbed and endearingly sleepy, his hair still shower-damp.

"Did you finish your homework, Aar?"

"Yeah . . ."

"*All* of it?"

"Well, all but five pages and I can read those before the bell, man," her son said. "It's cool." He trotted out of the house to catch the bus, which stopped a block away on the corner. Cici watched him from the window as he took long, lanky steps exactly like his father's.

She gave Quint a phone call at home to tell him she would not be in today.

As she was backing her Cougar out of the driveway, a sharp rapping on her left fender startled her. She jammed her foot on the brake, squealing the car to a stop.

Her heart hammering, she glanced out the left window and saw the bulky form of John Pickard. With a trench coat stretched over wide shoulders, his face screwed up in a massive scowl, her next-door neighbor looked like an angry football coach.

"You're a fine one," he shouted.

"Please—I'm trying to back out."

He banged on the car again, the sound intimidating.

"You gave them my name, didn't you, bitch? *You gave them my fucking name!*"

Cici stared at him, too frightened to speak.

"Answer me, you tight-assed bitch! You talked to the fucking police, didn't you, blondie? You told them I hit Dustin! You know what I ought to do? I ought to—"

But she didn't wait to hear the threat. She gunned the accelerator so that Pickard had to jump back or be hit. The car shot in reverse down the driveway, narrowly missing her mailbox. In her rearview mirror she could see the man glaring after her, shaking his fist.

It took thirty minutes of driving before she was able to calm down.

What an asshole, she found herself thinking. A child abuser, a jerk . . . almost any name she could think to call him. He was big enough, strong enough, *angry* enough to be the Basher.

But, she supposed, half the men in Detroit were that kind of aggressive. She read about them every day in the *Detroit News*. Wife beaters, party-store robbers, crack fiends, men who shot at drivers on the expressway, off-duty police officers who got into bar fights . . .

It was one of October's pewter-gray days, the sky swollen with raindrops that had already started to spatter down, dotting her windshield. A perfect day for the mood she was in. She had brought a little bag of tapes, and slid one into the player. A Christine Lavin album, *Attainable Love.*

The folk singer's warm voice filled the car, her lyrics full of wry, gentle jokes about New Age love.

Was any love between a man and a woman attainable anymore? Society had grown too complex, too frightening, too violent. Where was honesty? Cici found herself thinking as she passed miles of construction, then Flint and Birch Run, Frankenmuth with its signs for the famous Bronner's Christmas store.

Where was goodness, and kindness, and caring?

THIRTEEN

By the time Cici reached Houghton Lake the rain had turned to snow. Small, icy pellets spackled her windshield like hard dots. Snow in October? It seemed strange. But she remembered that only three hours north of Detroit, the seasons advanced a month earlier.

The village of Clyattville had been built haphazardly on the south shore of Houghton Lake, existing as a tourist stop and supply depot for ice fishermen, snowmobilers, deer hunters, and other sportsmen. From the condition of many of the stores, which had neon letters missing from signs, or peeling paint, it was obviously an eked-out existence.

Cici drove down the main street. Between some of the buildings she glimpsed an expanse of gray, choppy water. Houghton Lake. As a boy Bryan had undoubtedly swum and fished here.

The side streets were lined with old clapboard houses, some turned into bed-and-breakfasts, a few fixed up with aluminum siding and new picture windows. There were two or three small motels with names like Hideawee Inn and Lakeside Motel, and a bowling alley. A small white clapboard church had posted an advertisement for its Sunday sermon: HELL IS REAL.

The hell-and-damnation flavor of the sermon title sent a tremor through her. Was this the church that Junie had attended?

Cici turned around in the driveway of the church and returned to town. She drove through the two shopping blocks and parked in front of a store called Betty Ann's Casuals. A collection of skiwear and wool sweaters hung from pegboards in the window, the sweater arms stretched out straight like a scarecrow's.

Cici shut off her motor and sat for a minute in the car, her breath coming fast.

It suddenly felt as if she had a decision to make. She didn't *have* to go inside. She could go buy some lunch at the Houghton Inn she'd noticed further down the street, and then drive home, back into her own life again, back safely to Bryan.

Involuntarily she glanced down at her left hand, which rested on the steering wheel. The ring gleamed icily in the gray winter light.

Oh, Bryan, she thought as she got out of the car. *Why couldn't our love have been attainable? Why couldn't the romance have been real?*

As Cici entered the shop, bells attached to the door tinkled cheerily.

"May I help you?" A tired-looking woman of about sixty was sorting through a pile of merchandise, and looked up from her work with too-quick eagerness. She wore a pair of beige wool slacks and a beautiful white Aran wool sweater.

"I think so."

"We're having a sale today on all the sweaters on those two tables," the woman added. "Twenty percent off the discounts already marked. It's an excellent buy."

"I'm sure it is." Cici hesitated. "You must be Betty Schwartz, then?"

"Yes."

"I've driven up from Detroit today to talk to you."

Betty Schwartz looked puzzled and a little disappointed. Obviously she had hoped Cici might be a customer. By the look of the empty store, she needed all the customers she could get.

"I'm Cici Davis," Cici explained, feeling awkward. "I'm a friend of Bryan Wyatt's. Actually I'm his fiancée. I've come—that is, I wanted to meet some members of his family."

The shop owner still looked puzzled. "I'm sorry, I don't know anyone by that name."

"Oh!" Cici flushed. "I meant Bryan Wykotsky. He changed his name legally. I . . . I need to talk to you about him."

Betty Schwartz's hands paused in the folding of a green sweater woven with leaping reindeer. Cici could see her fingers clench into the soft wool. "Well, I'm sorry, but I don't think I can help you. I haven't seen or talked with Bryan Wykotsky in years."

"But you knew him when he was a boy, and that's what I'm interested in. Please. I'm engaged to him. I . . . I need to know some things about his background."

"Go to the county offices, then. They have all of those records."

"Mrs. Schwartz . . ."

"I don't want to talk about it," Betty Schwartz said vehemently, walking away from the sale table to stand behind a cash register, as if to put a solid object between her and Cici. "It was twenty years ago—a long time ago. My sister is gone."

"Gone?"

Betty clamped her lips together in a straight line. "I'm sorry. I'm sorry. I really can't talk about it. I really don't think I can help you, Miss Davis."

Then there *was* something. Every agitated movement of Betty Schwartz's told her so. Cici shook her head uneasily, aware that she'd reached a dead end unless she could persuade this woman to talk to her.

"Please! Mrs. Schwartz, I drove three hours up here on the chance you might talk to me. I'm engaged to Bryan. We're going to be married on December 26. Only suddenly there are problems. A . . . a crime committed. I have hired an investigator."

As Betty still looked stubborn, Cici added desperately,

"Please. I have a fourteen-year-old son, Mrs. Schwartz. I can't risk my boy. Suddenly Bryan seems a stranger to me, and I can't marry him until I know."

Bryan's aunt stared at her, blue eyes narrowed. Then slowly her hands relaxed on the cash register and she moved away from it a little. "All right. We could talk some, I guess. But I can't leave the store until my assistant comes in."

A girl wandered into the shop and began browsing among the racks of jeans and slacks, finally walking out without buying anything.

"As you can see, I'm not exactly doing a booming business here," Betty Schwartz explained wearily. "Summers are better, but the winters are a killer. I'm probably going to have to close."

"I'm sorry. It seems like a lovely store to me."

"I've always liked nice things. That's a very pretty diamond you're wearing," Betty added. "You say Bryan gave it to you? He must be doing very well financially."

"Yes."

"Little Boy. That's what *she* called him. The last time I saw him he was about fourteen, I think. It was winter, I remember, and the three of them were at church, that church in town, maybe you saw it. She was praying aloud, getting wild with it, talking in tongues."

The church with the sermon, HELL IS REAL. And June Wykotsky talking in tongues. To Cici's conservative Methodist upbringing it all seemed as alien as an Aztec ritual. Yet she knew such drama was part of worship for millions.

She hesitated, drawn by intense curiosity yet afraid to ask too many questions. She didn't want to spook this woman.

She prompted, "Maybe you could tell me about when Bryan was a little boy."

"Well. You've seen this town. This is it, this is where he grew up. One church, one bowling alley, one movie theater, one blinker light." Betty shrugged as if that explained everything.

"Mrs. Schwartz, I've seen the legal papers that were filed against Bryan's parents. I know about some of the things that happened. Please," Cici begged. "If you could just be frank with me. My whole life is hanging in the balance, and my son's."

There was a long silence while Betty digested this. It seemed she was about to shrug again, and go back to her work. Then she seemed to change her mind.

"All right," she finally said. "But promise me no one will know where the information came from. Will you promise?"

"Of course."

"I mean that." Betty's eyes held Cici's intensely.

"I won't tell anyone," Cici promised, wondering what secrets the woman was about to reveal.

Within half an hour the assistant arrived, a seventy-year-old woman with blue-rinsed hair who was apparently augmenting her Social Security income by working part-time.

"I'll be back in about an hour, Millie," Betty said. She led Cici out the back exit of the shop. In an alley behind the store, an old Blazer was parked. "I'll drop you back at your car later, if that's all right. I hope you don't mind a short ride."

The ten-minute drive took them along the shore of Houghton Lake, past summer cottages jammed on narrow lots, mom and pop motels, campgrounds, and bait shops. The snow had thickened while Cici was in the store and now filled the air with a fine tracery of white.

"The lake must be beautiful in July," Cici remarked to make conversation.

"If you don't mind motorboats. Every year they get worse. I've got two myself," Betty said with the first smile Cici had seen.

They pulled into a long driveway that pierced a cultivated pine woods. The trees grew in die-straight rows, all of them exactly the same size, with an occasional one missing.

"Good Christmas trees," Betty remarked. "I put this woods in. It was the year Bryan and his father moved away. Yes, that year."

The house was made of varnished logs, and built close to the lakefront. Pewter-colored water chopped and smashed on a sandy beach. A wooden dock had been taken out of the water and was stored on the sand under a tarp. A large pontoon and a smaller Chris-Craft were also stored on blocks. Cici could imagine this beach in summer, drenched with sun.

"Did Bryan come swimming here when he was a child?" she asked.

Betty looked at her. "I wanted him to live here but of course it didn't happen. His parents . . . Come into the house, will you? We can talk there. And I have to show you something."

Betty switched on lights as they walked into a comfortable living room furnished with beige couches and a worn but beautiful Chinese rug. The walls were of pine logs, varnished to a golden shine. There were a few oil paintings that looked as if Betty had done them herself.

"This was a deer hunting lodge in the forties, but I fixed it up. Ed helped me—that's Bryan's father. He did most of the work and I paid him. Do you want coffee? All I have is instant, I'm afraid."

"Is he—that is, do you know when he died? Or how?"

Betty, who had been on her way to the kitchen, turned and gazed at Cici over her shoulder, her face bleak. "No, I don't know, and I don't care. I hope he's rotting in hell."

She disappeared into the kitchen, through a pine door that swung back and forth, making a creaking sound. Cici stared after her.

The object that Betty Schwartz wanted to show her was an old photo album, its binding made of embossed leather on which old-fashioned gilt fleur-de-lis had been stamped.

"This album is forty years old," Betty said, holding it. "I started keeping it when I first came here to Clyattville. I was single then. I got married but my husband died in a hunting accident and I just stayed on here to be near my sister, June."

June. The semiliterate author of the diary. "*Whuped him with the hamer,*" June had written.

"Were you close to your sister?" Cici inquired cautiously. Betty had not yet opened the album, her hands resting on its cover, and Cici was dying to see the photos inside—Bryan as a baby and small child.

"When we were girls, yes. But I went to college, Michigan State, and Junie didn't. Our father sent me, and not her. Junie was . . . well, school wasn't for her."

Did that mean that Junie was slightly retarded? Or just emotionally disabled? Intense curiosity filled Cici.

Betty took the album to the dinette table and began turning pages, flipping past old photographs pasted in with triangular photo corners.

"These are just old family pictures . . . my parents' wedding . . . June and me as girls."

Cici looked at a picture of two little girls in checked gingham dresses, their hair in braids. The brunette, Betty, was smiling, her eyes crinkled against the sun, but the blond girl scowled at the camera, her brows pulled together.

"That's Junie," Betty said, pointing. "She hated having her picture taken even then. I don't think I have four pictures of her. And she destroyed most of the ones I did take. She said they were graven images. I did keep another one, though. I'm trying to find it."

"Was she always very religious?"

"Oh, yes." Betty stopped and looked at Cici. "Miss Davis, you and I both know what we are talking about. Junie was a little slow, and she had several mental breakdowns, and was treated at the hospital for them. She wasn't right. It was a terrible home for the boy to grow up in. It wasn't Junie I stayed in Clyattville for, it was little Bryan—Boy, as she called him. But I couldn't help him much. She was too strong. And the judge was partial to a family with strong church connections—he went to their same church. You saw it in town—the hellfire church, I call it."

"I . . . I see."

Betty turned several more album pages. "Oh," she exclaimed. "Here it is. I took this when June wasn't looking and I hid it from her later." She showed Cici another blurred photo, this one of a pretty woman of twenty-five or thirty, with blond hair pulled back at the nape of her neck. In this picture June Wykotsky looked caught in the middle of some swift, agitated movement.

The background of the photo was a wall on which several religious pictures had been hung. In one, a Christ stared ahead with hollow, agonized, Auschwitz eyes.

"Go ahead," June urged. "Look at it closer if you want. This was taken, yes, right after she came home from Ypsilanti State Hospital. A terrible place—the patients yell and scream out the windows at people on the sidewalk. I kept little Bryan for her, and she was angry, said I didn't teach him right, said I'd let him watch television."

Cici studied the picture of June Wykotsky. There was a look to her that seemed familiar, something about the line of her jaw, the shape of her mouth. Then she realized what the familiarity was. If June had been wearing her hair in a modern, 1990s style, she would have somewhat resembled Abby Tighe. Or even herself.

She shivered.

"These pictures are of Ed, Bryan's father," Betty went on, turning another page. Cici looked at photographs of a tall, burly man of about thirty, with light hair and a bristling, biblical beard. The eyes above the beard were piercing. In some of the photos Wykotsky was standing beside a snowmobile. In others, he posed beside an ice-fishing shack displaying a big fish, or on a dock with a string of fish. One shot was of him standing in front of what looked like a small garage.

"That was the shop Ed owned," Betty explained. "They made pine furniture. You know, picnic tables, porch swings, and such."

Cici stared at the photos of Bryan's father, trying to see her fiancé in his father's face. But there wasn't much resemblance. Ed Wykotsky looked like an understudy for a role in a Hollywood biblical epic.

Betty turned the page to pictures of Bryan as a chubby twenty-month-old grinning at the camera, then as a three-year-old standing in front of the same church she had seen in town. The handsome child looked very intense. He squinted into the camera, his home-barbered hair clipped short, the contours of his scalp showing through.

Cici uttered an exclamation and reached for the album, feeling a rush of unexpected feeling. "Oh! Oh, I've never seen baby pictures of Bryan before! He looks so sweet. So . . . I don't know!" The sight of the young Bryan touched her in a way she could not explain. That intense, almost cowed look. He seemed so vulnerable. What had adults done to him?

"He could be very appealing," Betty said shortly, not missing the emotion. "I loved him, too. I saved his life five times. *She* wanted to sacrifice him to God. You have all the papers on that. You know what I'm talking about. She would beat him with a paddle that Ed made in his shop. They both hit him with it, or they used other things. Ed forced him to get out his little wood-burning kit and burn some letters into the side of that paddle."

"What letters?"

"I've told you, my sister had religious delusions. She was—it was why they had to treat her." Then Betty sighed. " 'God's Hammer.' That's what it said. Those were the letters."

God's Hammer. Cici remembered the diary, the word *hamer*.

A picture entered her mind of a huge wooden paddle whizzing downward through the air, crashing into Ann's head.

Oh, no, she thought. *Oh, dear God.* She swayed backward, feeling a wave of sickness.

With a sudden motion Betty snapped shut the cover of the album. "That's it," she said. "Those are all the pictures I have." Her eyes moved down to Cici's ring finger again, and she added slowly, "But there is something more. It's something I've never told anyone, because I never knew for sure, except in my heart. There was nothing I could have done about it anyway because it was too late."

As Cici waited, Betty Schwartz went to an oak rolltop desk and began rummaging through a lower drawer. She finally pulled out two postcards and brought them back to Cici, laying them on the tabletop in front of her.

They were cheap, garish postcards, perhaps fifteen or twenty years old, one depicting a frolicking cocker spaniel, the other a photograph of several kittens in a basket.

"Read them," Betty said.

Puzzled, Cici did so. A brief message was printed on each. *"Living in Royal Oak and have a good house,"* said the first card. It was signed, *"June."* The other card said, *"Went to the Hudson's Thanksgiving parade today. Bryan enjoyed himself, he has got a job delivering the News. June."*

"These were written by June Wykotsky?"

"What do you think?" Betty asked.

Cici felt a twist in her stomach. Would June of the diary have selected such cutesy postcards? She also couldn't spell half this well. She stared at the words, which were printed but did not in any way resemble the angry, erratic printing in the diary.

Cici turned her eyes to June Wykotsky's sister. "No," she said, swallowing. "No, I don't think she wrote them."

"I didn't think so either." Betty paused. "Miss Davis, what I think is too terrible to consider, and yet I have been considering it for nearly twenty years now. I have no proof at all, other than these postcards, but I think my sister is dead. I think Ed Wykotsky killed her. Either that, or she died of natural causes and he concealed the body. *He* wrote the postcards, not her, because he didn't want me to know my sister was gone."

"What!"

Betty Schwartz stared at Cici, her eyes burning. "Miss Davis, I only brought you to my house because I like you. I like your face, and I think you're a decent and sincere person. If I were you, I would break my engagement to Bryan Wyatt, or whatever he calls himself now, as soon as possible. Don't marry him, whatever you do. *Don't marry him.*"

It sounded like a witch's warning. Cici recoiled from Betty.

"There are some people who are different, Miss Davis. They have two sides to them, a good side and a bad side. The black and the white, the good and the evil. Both Junie and Ed were like that, and I'm afraid their son could be, too."

Betty drove Cici back to her car, and numbly Cici unlocked the door of the Cougar, got inside, and started the engine. She felt as if she had gone into mild clinical shock—her skin felt clammy and her heart was hammering in her throat. What Betty had said completely changed her perspective on Bryan.

No longer could she view him as stable, steady, romantic, a "good catch" who made her the envy of other women. Instead there was the whole other hidden background.

"I think my sister is dead. I think Ed Wykotsky killed her. Either that, or she died of natural causes and he concealed the body."

But just as shocking was the paddle that said *God's Hammer*. Was it possible . . . ?

The implications of that hammer boggled her mind, giving her thoughts too terrifying to contemplate.

Cici drove through town, in such a hurry to get out of Clyattville that she almost forgot to stop to get gas at the Shell station near the expressway. The snow had thickened, and the afternoon shadows were turning a deep shade of charcoal.

Her mind seemed in a strange, jumpy, disjointed state, replaying everything Betty had said. *"They have two sides to them, a good side and a bad side . . . Tell me whether you think Ed Wykotsky would willingly turn her body over to the authorities . . ."*

The paddle.

God's Hammer.

She filled the tank herself, hurrying so fast that she nearly dropped the gas nozzle onto the ground. A sudden misery assailed her, sharp and poignant. The Bryan she'd loved hadn't ever existed, had he? He'd only been a surface man, handsome, hard-working, closed to his feelings, unable or unwilling to talk about anything real. She didn't really know him, had clothed the man in her own hopes and fears and never really seen him at all.

She found the entrance to I-75 and entered the ramp, speeding up the car in order to blend with highway traffic. Her hands were shaking, and she had to clench them on the steering wheel to steady them.

Was Bryan the Basher?

God . . . with that kind of background . . . the child abuse, the extreme religiosity . . . being forced to burn the words *God's Hammer* into a paddle . . .

But then, as she began the long drive south to Detroit, good sense swept over her again. It had been frightening to talk to Betty Schwartz, yes, and Betty had a way of sweeping one into her way of thinking. But what did it really mean? Did having a weird family make Bryan guilty of murder?

Suppose Bryan's father *had* killed June or concealed her death. Given the odd family background, Cici thought this was reasonably possible. But it was still his father who had done it, not Bryan. And even if there had been a paddle, it was all more than twenty years ago, when Bryan was a child.

Anyway, Bryan had shown no signs of temper or violence, except for . . . The odd scene weeks ago swept into her head again. Bryan lugging the heavy rug late at night. Hadn't Oleson said the Basher carried his victims away from their homes?

Cici passed a large semi truck, her hands shaking on the steering wheel. The more she thought about it, the more confused and frightening her thoughts became, doubts telescoping into more doubts.

Listen to your hunches, Ann had been fond of saying. *Listen to your body because it's trying to tell you something.*

And she was going to have to make a decision soon. Bryan expected to marry her on December 26. Two months away.

FOURTEEN

It was still snowing as Cici drove south. But after an hour the snow gradually lessened, and the flakes became only an occasional dancing dot in front of her headlight beam. She drove numbly, her mind on automatic pilot. Incredible that she should be having such bizarre thoughts about her fiancé, someone who had been inside her body, as close as a man and a woman ever could get.

Wouldn't a woman know if a man she had let inside her very body was evil? Wouldn't she somehow sense it?

The Birch Run exit was coming up, and Cici pulled off, finding a McDonald's. A busload of senior citizens, on their way back from the huge discount-store mall at the exit, crowded most of the booths, six old women for every man.

Cici stood in line and ordered a cup of coffee. She carried the cup to an empty booth and sat hunched with both hands wrapped around it, as if the steam of the coffee could penetrate the crystalline column of ice in her throat. Was she really going to have to phone Oleson and give him her own fiancé's name?

She would have to do it when she returned home, Cici realized. After all, there *were* connections between Bryan and Ann, Bryan and Abby Tighe. Plus the rug. And now, Bryan's odd and disturbing background, which, most damningly of all, he had concealed from her.

One of the old men got up to return to the bus, laughing and flirting with one of the women. Something about his laugh reminded Cici of John Pickard.

Pickard. Wasn't her neighbor another man who had connections to both Ann and Abby, through the Friday Nighters? He had come on to Ann, was a womanizer, had a violent temper, had beaten his son. He was also massively built, big enough to wreck a house and beat a woman to death.

"Don't worry, honey," said an old woman, passing her booth, her face a wrinkled map of a lifetime. "It can't be that bad. Nothing is."

Cici looked up, startled.

"Honey, I've been divorced once and widowed twice, and I can tell you . . . no man is worth it. Just let 'em go, that's what I say. You don't need 'em."

An hour later, Cici reached the Rochester exit. A few droplets of chilly rain spattered across her windshield, and the wind had picked up, rocking the car slightly as she turned in the direction of home.

Devil's Night—the night before Halloween when pranksters traditionally roam the streets—was tomorrow. Every subdivision was lit up by yard lights and garage floodlights, homeowners attempting to scare away any marauding vandals, who were really their own children. As she drove down her own street, Cici passed a home where several trees had already been toilet-papered. Wind grabbed at the white streamers, ripping them into the night.

Cici pulled into her driveway and flicked the garage door opener. Next door, the Pickard house was lit up, four cars parked in the driveway, the customary pound of heavy-metal rock music drifting out of the windows with a rhythmic throb.

Something drew her to the Pickard house, perhaps the

thought of death. She got out of her car and walked across the grass in the dark. The night air tasted wet, flavored with smoke and dead leaves. Rain seemed to hang in the air, gathering its moisture.

The Pickards' backyard had not been recently mowed, and tufts of tall grass snapped at her feet as she walked. Ahead of her a newly planted spruce tree reached out long, scarecrow arms. Could there be a body buried underneath that tree, the soft earth concealed by the bed created for the tree?

She shuddered. What had the police learned about John Pickard when they questioned him? Had he been cleared? Were they taking action in regard to Dustin and Heather?

Turning to go back, she glanced toward the lit windows. The vertical blinds were open, and framed inside was sixteen-year-old Heather Pickard sprawled on a dinette chair, moodily eating ice cream from the carton.

"What the hell are you doing in my yard?" A hard touch on Cici's shoulders whirled her around. She uttered a small cry. Pickard himself stood before her, wearing a brown leather bomber jacket, the bulky shoulders of the jacket making the man appear even larger and more menacing. He reeked of beer.

"I . . . I'm sorry. I thought I heard a noise," she blurted.

"In my backyard? What kind of noise?" He loomed toward her with the dominating body language of a man who usually gets what he wants through intimidation.

"I wasn't sure." She began to back away.

"Hey, lady, I'm not the Basher, if that's what you're think-ing."

"What?" She felt a throb of fear.

"If that's why you're spying on me, hey? Walking in my yard, looking in my windows. I never hurt a woman in my life."

What was there to say to that? He certainly looked as if he wanted to hurt one now.

"I never hurt anyone," Pickard insisted, following Cici as she started nervously across the verge of grass. "That includes that little shit Dustin. I'll show you, hey? I'll prove it! Come on in my house, I'll show you everything. I'll show you I didn't do anything. The police wanted to look but I told them they had to get a warrant. *You'll* see. No blood. No baseball bats. No bodies."

He followed her into her garage, still protesting his innocence.

Cici stood uneasily with her hand poised over the garage-door button. She could not bring the door downward until Pickard had stepped outside; otherwise she would be enclosing herself in the garage with him.

"John, please leave. I have to close the garage door."

"Hey," he said belligerently. "You sicced them on me, didn't you? That's where I was again tonight. Talking to *them*. The bastards. With all their questions. I'm *not* the Basher, babe. I don't even come close."

She touched the button enough to start the door noisily rolling down several feet. "Get out of my garage. Or I'll call Detective Oleson. I'll tell him you were bothering me."

The man stared at her just long enough to make it clear he would do as *he* pleased, then ducked his head and left.

Relieved, Cici punched the button to lower the door the rest of the way. Pickard was frightening, and he used his body language to control women, a habit she detested. But he had given her an idea. There *were* things in a man's house that he could not hide. Objects—hints. If you looked carefully, if you saw with both your eyes, as Ann might have said.

She stood stock-still, making a decision. She *would* call the police—tonight—but only after she had looked in Bryan's house for herself.

If she found *anything* sinister, anything at all, she could feel justified in phoning Oleson at once. She owed at least that much to Bryan and the love they'd shared. And there would be little risk of her being discovered, since he was still out of town and was not expected back for several more days.

She went into the kitchen. It was dark, and there were no food smells or other evidence that Aaron had "nuked" himself dinner, as he'd promised her he would. In fact, it was obvious that her son hadn't been home in some time, perhaps all day. There was no note on the refrigerator.

Aaron. Another worry.

She sighed, hanging up her coat and turning on lights. She switched on the small portable kitchen TV, just to bring some noise into the house, to make it seem less empty. Channel 4 was running a brief special on the Basher.

Diane Beldine had been one of the earlier Basher victims.

"These are Police Department shots. This is the room where Diane Beldine fought a battle with her attacker, the man police believe to be the Basher. A room that bears the marks of Diane Beldine's bloody and perhaps final struggle."

A photograph showed a room with huge holes in the drywall as if battered there by some massively heavy instrument. Drips and gushes of blood were smeared on the walls, as if the victim had struggled frantically in her own gore.

Cici switched channels and found a movie, *Earth Girls Are Easy*. That damned branch was banging at the window again, sounding like the Gestapo trying to get in. Or a chain-clanking Halloween ghost.

She turned on the burner to make herself some instant coffee and, while it was heating, went to her answering machine to play back her messages. The red light was blinking. Maybe Aaron had called and left a message on the tape.

She rewound the tape and pushed PLAY. There were a couple of hang-ups, then Bryan's voice.

"Hi, honey, hope you're having a nice day."

At the sound of her fiancé's voice, deep, familiar, and sexy, Cici felt a push of blood through her veins. She hung on to the kitchen counter as a rush of memories flooded her. Dancing cheek to cheek, lovemaking, the July evening when Bry had given her the engagement ring frozen into an ice cube.

"I was just thinking about my beautiful Cici and had to let her know. Did you get my flowers?"

Flowers. More of them? Cici felt a spasm of nausea. After this was over, she was going to hate roses, she realized. If . . . but she nervously closed off the rest of the thought.

There was more clicking, a message from her dentist's receptionist about an appointment to get her teeth cleaned, and finally the last message. It was a woman's voice, crisp and professional sounding.

"Mrs. Davis, this is Sergeant Judy Westerman of the Rochester Hills Police. Please call me as soon as possible. We have your son, Aaron, here and we need to ask him some questions. We'd like you to come down right away."

Cici stood frozen. Aaron was in jail.

Maybe this wasn't really real. Maybe this was only an awful nightmare—the entire day—and she would turn over in bed, stretch, yawn, and wake up. Then everything would be fine again, with her storybook wedding to look forward to, the fabulous honeymoon in Hawaii complete with helicopter tour, mai tais on the beach, and a charter fishing trip off Lanai.

Filled with a calm numbness, Cici looked up the phone number of the police station in the phone book. Amazing. She'd lived in the area all her life and never had occasion to go there, or dreamed she ever would.

She phoned Sergeant Westerman, who told her that Aaron, Dustin, Kevin, and Matt had been picked up on suspicion of arson. A neighbor said she had seen four boys who resembled them near Bryan's garage on the night of the fire.

"Arson?" she repeated numbly. "My son is being charged with arson?"

"Not being charged, just questioned."

"But . . . he's only fourteen," she protested, knowing how stupid it sounded.

The officer sounded tired. "We've had them as young as eight. We've already talked to the three others and sent them home with their parents. You were the only one we couldn't reach."

"And? What conclusions have you drawn?"

"All the boys deny it."

Cici left immediately for the station. Fighting her panic and alarm, she barely was aware of making the drive. Arson! That sounded *so* serious. Obviously the boys weren't talking, but Cici knew that her son had at least been at the scene of the fire. God . . . should she call a lawyer?

At the police station, she waited half an hour before a tall, attractive brunette in blue uniform emerged from a warren of offices and spoke her name.

"Mrs. Davis?"

"Yes . . . may I see my son alone first? Before you talk to him, I mean? I want to make sure he's all right."

She was shown to a small, cluttered office. Inside, like a bad boy in the principal's office, her son sat hunched in a chair. His hands fiddled with an empty cardboard Pepsi cup, methodically ripping it into strips. He glanced up as she entered the room, then looked down at the floor.

"Aaron," she choked.

"Mom . . ." Aaron started to sob, the sounds rending.

Cici hardened her heart. "Just stop your crying and wait until I find out how to release you. We've got to have a lawyer present before they question you."

"I-I can't talk," Aaron gulped.

"Why not? Aar—"

"I did it. I lit the match, Mom. We all set the fire. But I can't talk." Aaron's voice dissolved in tears. "It's Dustin, Mom. His dad'll kill him. His dad *hits* him, Mom!"

Cici swayed, feeling as if she had received punch after punch in her gut.

"I'm sorry, I'm sorry," Aaron choked. "I—I just hate Bryan so much. He's such a j-jerk, Mom, and you wouldn't listen, you wouldn't listen because I'm just a *kid,*" her son accused bitterly.

It took her another half hour to free her son, after making arrangements for him to come in with an attorney present. As they were leaving, Sergeant Westerman stopped Cici in the hall.

"Mrs. Davis, however this comes out—and I personally believe these four boys did set that fire—I just want you to know one thing. Arson is a heck of a lot more than just a boyish prank. Gasoline is very dangerous stuff. We've had cases where the arsonist himself ends up getting burned in the fire—sometimes fatally."

The cold words and even colder look raked across Cici's heart. The officer had no idea that Aaron was a good boy, a nice boy, from a good home. She assumed her son was trash—the dregs. Careless and stupid.

Aaron followed her out of the station, silently getting into the passenger seat of her Cougar. Although it was cold, he wore no jacket and shivered as a gust of wind swirled through the parking lot. Rain had started, chilly droplets that would keep Devil's Nighters indoors. Why hadn't it rained the night of Bryan's garage fire? Cici thought bitterly. Then this wouldn't have happened.

"Where's your jacket?" she asked.

"They didn't let me get it."

"My God, they should have—it's forty-five degrees out."

"They didn't let me," her son repeated in a muffled voice.

Cici started up the motor, anger causing her to gun the motor too loudly. She turned north on Livernois, starting toward home.

"I know you're concerned about Dustin," she finally said tightly. "And that's fine. I know his father does hit him because I saw it. But you boys broke the law—you could have killed yourselves or someone else. Burned them up in a terrible fire."

Aaron's voice quavered. "Mom . . ."

"I just can't believe you, Aaron. And this isn't the first vandalism you've done, is it? It's only the first one you got caught at. You and your friends have been tearing through the neighborhood like a dose of salts through a sick rabbit." It was a phrase Cici's father had used, and it popped effortlessly out of her mouth now.

"Mom!" Aaron gave a horrible giggle, sliding down into his seat, sinking his chin onto his chest. His mouth worked, and she could see he was close to sobbing.

"I don't *ever* want this to happen again, Aaron," she snapped.

They drove a mile or two in silence. But as they were slowing for the light at the intersection of Livernois and Avon, near the banquet hall where she had first met Bryan, Aaron suddenly reached for the door handle.

"I'm getting out," he announced.

"Out? Do you mean out of the *car*? Aaron, don't be ridic—"

"I don't want to ride with you. I'm going to walk home."

"Aaron! Aar, you don't even have a jacket!" But to her frustration and dismay, her son had already shoved open the car door and jumped out. He began trudging north along the right shoulder of Livernois, an absurdly vulnerable and quixotic figure.

"Aaron!" she shouted from the car window, flooded with helpless love, feeling like a mothering, screaming shrew. "Aaron, I want you to come straight home. Straight home, do you hear me!"

Her words were swept away by the wind as Aaron continued to walk.

Cici didn't know whether to follow along in her car or to drive on home, but another car was tailgating her, impatient to get moving, so she accelerated and drove the remaining mile and a half home. It wasn't that long a walk, and maybe Aaron needed to be alone for a while with his thoughts. Maybe he even needed to cry. God knew she did.

She reached home for the second time this evening. Incredible, the day she'd had. Pulling again into the garage, she shut the large door and sat in the car. She leaned her head over the steering wheel, folded her arms, and wept, her body shaking.

One little cancer had created all this, hadn't it? Oh, yes!

By creating the need, the void she'd tried to fill with Bryan. From there it had all been downhill. She hated the cancer, and she hated Bryan, and she hated herself for alienating her son.

She sobbed and sobbed, the tears burning. Finally the worst of the energy was spent, and she sat trembling and drained.

Feeling as if she were about ninety years old, she opened the car door and went back into the kitchen, where the lights still burned and the TV still played—she'd forgotten to turn it off. Glancing at the clock she saw to her shock that only an hour and twenty minutes had passed. And she still needed to find out about Bryan.

She made a telephone call to an attorney, a man she had gone to college with, who promised to see her and Aaron tomorrow. Then she changed her clothes again, putting on black jeans and a navy sweatshirt, adding a pair of black walking shoes that she found at the back of her closet. She didn't want to wear anything white, anything that would attract notice, because she didn't plan to drive over to Bryan's. She would walk, blending into the darkness that stretched between the suburban homes. That way she wouldn't leave her car parked outside Bryan's house and advertise her presence there.

Tonight was the only chance she might have to get into Bryan's house when he wasn't there, and she couldn't afford to waste it.

The phone rang and she snatched it up, thinking that it must be Aaron calling for a ride.

"Cici, hello." It was Bryan. "Just thought I'd call before I went out to a dinner meeting. I left a message before. You weren't home. In fact, I phoned a couple of times. I called at work and they said you took the day off."

So Bryan was the source of the hang-ups she'd found earlier on her machine. She felt a spasm of guilt mixed with fear.

"I had a doctor appointment and some errands to run," she explained carefully. "You know, a Pap smear, and then I wanted to pick up something for my mother's birthday—it's next week, next Tuesday."

Her mother's birthday was in February, but it was all she could think of on short notice.

"What did you get her?"

"A blouse at Mitzelfeld's," Cici blurted, improvising. "And a matching skirt. It was on sale. Lined wool. The fabric was very rich looking, very nice, and my mother likes wool."

She must have sounded convincing, for Bryan changed the subject. "Are you going out tonight?"

Cici's mind struggled to recall her normal calendar, to remember what day this was. Her daily life seemed very far away and irrelevant, almost a joke. "Oh, just to my aerobics class," she said. "What about you, Bry? When do you think you'll be home?"

"Not for a couple of days. They've really got me loaded

down. Meetings all day tomorrow, and then another dinner with suppliers."

She was deeply relieved. "Well, I'll be looking forward to seeing you," she said woodenly. Their conversation was suddenly sounding very, very stilted. She wondered if Bryan could see through her, if he could know what she was planning to do.

But how could he? Anyway, he was in Cincinnati. He could not possibly arrive home in the next hour, so she'd be perfectly safe even if he decided to get a cab and go to the airport right now.

"You're my beautiful Cici," he told her softly.

"I . . . I love you, Bry," she forced herself to say. And knew as she said it that she was telling the truth. She *did* still love Bryan, which somehow made everything else more painful. After you had hired an investigator for your fiancé, wasn't the relationship over with anyway? Because the trust had already died.

"Good," he said. "Good. Well, I'd better get going, hon. I've got to meet them down in the lobby. We've made reservations for nine."

"Okay."

"Think of me, Cici. Always love me. I want you to love me forever. Will you?" Bryan often said things like this, and Cici had loved the romantic expression of feelings, but now she felt deadened, as if he were speaking to someone else, not her.

"I do love you," she managed to say.

"Forever," Bryan insisted.

"Forever," she promised, feeling her body tremble all over.

She decided to wait to leave until Aaron arrived home. She wanted to be sure he was safely under their roof before she ventured out. Not that she expected anything to happen—it wouldn't. Still, she would feel much better if she could tell Aaron where she was going.

She turned up the TV volume and switched to VH-1, watching a new Bonnie Raitt video. Then Bette Midler came on, singing "The Rose," which had been Ann's favorite song, and Cici nervously flicked the dial to yet another channel.

Her longing for her best friend was sharp. She felt she would explode with her need to talk to Ann. She'd even settle for talking into Ann's answering tape, if only her friend would be there at the other end to answer it.

The back door slammed.

"Aaron?"

"Hi." Her son slouched into the kitchen, his eyes puffy and wind-reddened. He was shivering. She could see the tremble of his mouth that he was trying to hide. He wanted this to be over, she knew; he wanted her comfort, her love, and didn't know how to ask. He was, after all, only fourteen, and he'd gotten himself into more trouble than he could handle.

"Feel better?" she asked gently.

He nodded. "Have we got any hot cocoa? And some microwave lasagna? I'm hungry."

"Help yourself. I just bought two or three packages of lasagna." She took a deep breath. "I think we ought to talk to a lawyer, find out what your legal situation is. I called Mort Reidell, and we're going to see him tomorrow."

"Are you going to call Dad?"

"Do you want me to call him?"

"No," he sighed. "Anyway, he doesn't care that much. He doesn't want me to bother him. I'm going to pay it back—why should he care? I'll pay for the garage."

Cici nodded, touched by his bravado. A garage cost thousands of dollars, which Aaron knew because he had participated in the remodeling of their own garage last year. "We'll work it out, Aar. Maybe Bryan's insurance company will accept restitution. I don't know."

Aaron was bent over, peering into the refrigerator, poking around among the grapes, apples, containers of yogurt, and various leftovers. The back of his neck, with its vulnerability, its fuzz of light hair, seemed unbearably touching to Cici. She went to her son and put her arms around him.

"I love you, Aar. I'll always love you. Because you're my son, but also because you're *you* and I know what a good person you are inside, how good and loving you are. We'll get through this, son. We'll get our lives back to normal, I promise."

As she spoke he relaxed his muscles a little, accepting her embrace. Cici held him, feeling the love go from her arms into him. Thank God, he still needed her.

Finally, reluctantly, she pulled away. "I'm going out for a walk, Aaron. I—I have to go."

"Okay."

"I said a walk," she repeated. "To Bryan's."

"Okay, okay."

Cici reached for the dark, lined denim jacket she had chosen. "I'll be back in a little while," she promised.

Aaron went to the window and watched as Cici cut across the front lawn and crossed the street in the direction of Bryan's. She seemed to disappear into the darkness, sucked up into the light rain.

Aaron watched until Cici was gone. Although he had tried to keep a poker face when his mother hugged him, her words of love had shaken him up.

He didn't deserve them.

Jail. All four of them huddled together in a cell, trying to look as tough and cool as they could. The sights and sounds in the other cells, a guy throwing up into a toilet in plain sight of sixteen other people, a black man yelling *"fuck fuck fuck,"* over and over. A big guy with Harley-Davidson tattoos all over his meaty forearms.

Aaron felt the guilty shivers go through him again, making him feel sick. Why had he let Dustin push his arm toward the gasoline? He didn't have to let that happen, but he hadn't resisted. Maybe because he wanted to see the fire, too.

And he'd loved looking at the blaze. The exciting feeling of knowing *he'd* helped cause it, that he'd gotten even—

Except it didn't feel so good anymore; it felt terrible. He felt lost, like he didn't want to be by himself, couldn't. And now his mother was on her way for a "walk," which anyone, even a stupid person, had to know meant she was on her way to Bryan's house to get all lovey-dovey.

Aaron pictured his mother kissing Bryan Wyatt. He gave a sigh of disgust that turned into a little, squeaky gulp. He went to the refrigerator and took out a package of lunch meat, two pieces of bread, and several packages of microwave lasagna.

FIFTEEN

Nervousness made Cici walk quickly, her feet moving silently on the wet pavement. God—Aaron's life seemed about to fall apart, too. She had to settle this, get them both back to normal.

The neighborhood seemed caught in a misty spell, like a village in a Dean Koontz horror novel. A damp fog rose up off the pavement, blending with the rain to create whitish halos around yard lights and house lamps. Several cars passed her, tires slapping wetly. A large dog barked as she passed a yard, the sound hollow and baying.

Once, she thought she heard footsteps behind her, but each time she turned, there was no one and the sounds faded. Cici decided it was her imagination. She felt guilty and anxious, and was projecting this on her environment. How many times did a "thirty-something" woman resort to what amounted to breaking and entering?

By the time she reached Bryan's house, the rain had turned into a steady drizzle, soaking her jacket and forming cold droplets on her hair and eyelashes. Two lights glowed from the house, lamps that Bryan kept on timers. The tree under which she had stood that September evening more than six weeks ago dripped pearls of water.

Cici paused under its laden branches, remembering that night when she had stood, watching Bryan unload the rolled-up rug from his van.

Standing here, the sight seemed to replay itself, the way Bryan had to reach, lift, and haul in order to carry the rolled cylinder. Thinking back, she realized how heavy it must have been to make him strain like that. Once he had even dropped it, then picked it up again. What could have been inside it? The rug was one thing she'd look for in the house, she decided.

She started across the cul-de-sac. The damaged garage had been torn down by a wrecking company and carried away, leaving the cement slab. She was relieved to see that no car or van was parked in the driveway or on the street. Bryan wasn't there.

Still, a panicky thought stabbed her. What if a neighbor looked out his window, saw her, called the police?

She nervously eyed the house. Bryan had never given her a key, and once she broke the window glass, she would be officially committing an illegal act.

I'm crazy, she thought, listening to the swishing sounds her leather shoes made in the grass as she walked to the front door.

Do I really want to do this?

But if she didn't do it, she would never know for sure, would she? Because there could be things in Bryan's house that the police would never see, that would look suspicious only to someone who knew him well.

She stood breathing in the fine, misty droplets of rain. This was really the moment of choice, wasn't it? She could turn around, walk home in the rain, and telephone Detective Oleson. Start the official wheels rolling that would either put Bryan in jail or free him of any suspicion.

But if she gave his name to the police, the newspapers could print his name as an "alleged suspect." Bryan's name, even his picture, could be plastered over the entire state. Being innocent wouldn't matter. He could still lose his job and reputation.

No, she owed him something. If she went through the house and found nothing . . .

And then she snorted to herself, the sound bitter. Who did she think she was? Was she vain enough to think that *she* would be able to interpret any clues she found?

Her hesitation seemed to stretch on for endless seconds. And then she pressed her lips together and pulled a small tack hammer out of her pocket, along with the roll of masking tape she'd stuffed there. If she didn't do this she would never learn the truth about Bryan . . . or about herself.

She had to learn what kind of man she herself had chosen, what she had set in motion.

Being a burglar was ridiculously easy, Cici thought again, especially in suburbia where lots were large and neighbors stayed inside their houses on a rainy night. She easily deactivated the security device. She had committed the code, her former house number, to memory. Then she broke the window, reached inside, and flipped open the dead bolt and lock.

However, as she stepped into Bryan's foyer, a wild, rabid barking filled the air. A dog!

Cici gasped in terror before realizing that it was Bryan's electronic dog making the noise. She rushed toward the socket where he had plugged in the "dog" and yanked the cord out of the socket. The ruckus stopped in midbark.

She stood shaking, raindrops dripping off her. What if one of the neighbors had heard?

Her heartbeat slamming in her ears, she stood waiting for some kind of sound—a door slamming, maybe, or a siren. But there were only the normal noises of the house—the tick-tock of the numerous clocks and the pop of something expanding inside the joists.

She gazed around. The living room and foyer, lit by one lamp on a timer, seemed full of sinister shadows. A large drawing on the nearby wall depicted a clock opened to reveal its mechanical parts. The lines were stiff, rigid, harshly drawn. Ann had believed Bryan's pictures revealed him psychologically.

Thinking of Ann steadied her a little. Sensible, cynical,

humorous, loving Ann. Her heartbeat gradually slowed to a rhythm approaching normal.

Still Cici hesitated. She'd never done anything like this before—where should she even start? What did television detectives do? Her laugh to herself seemed ragged, on the verge of hysteria. Then she thought of Bryan's study/den, where he kept his personal papers in a pigeonhole desk amazingly neat and orderly.

That would be as good a spot as any, she decided. Personal papers were revealing, and perhaps there would be notes, jotted phone numbers, even a journal.

The den was dark, pooled with shadows, several of the clocks ticking at counterpoint to each other. Why had she never realized how odd it was for a man to own so many clocks? The house echoed with their ticking and deep, guttural tocks.

Cici padded into the room, pulling out the small penlight she'd brought for the purpose. It cast a dainty, narrow beam. She shone the light toward the desk, a beautiful, genuine antique in distressed oak.

The lid rolled upward easily. She shone the beam inside, where stacks of papers and folders had been arranged in tidy piles. Leafing through them she saw catalogs from antique dealers, programs from estate auctions, even a publication from Sotheby's. Nothing sinister in that. She pulled open a drawer and discovered file folders neatly arranged, utility bills filed by month.

Curious, she pulled out a folder labeled *Telephone, 1990.* It contained Michigan Bell telephone bills for amounts like eighty-nine and seventy-four dollars. The long-distance bills, she saw, were mostly to Cincinnati and Minneapolis, cities to which Bryan regularly traveled. Even the numbers ended in zeros, like those of legitimate businesses. The listing of phone calls to other exchanges in the area also seemed unremarkable. Bryan had only made a few. Maybe she should copy down the numbers, call them, and see who answered.

Then, hastily, she shoved the phone bills back into their folder. She didn't have time to copy them. Anyway, she felt sure that what she was looking for would be more obvious than that, jumping right up at her with unmistakable meaning. God . . . she felt so jittery. She was getting an uncomfortable urge to run.

Another folder said *Detroit Edison,* and she briefly opened it, seeing a bill for $310.

Three hundred and ten dollars? For a month's utility bill? Perhaps there had been a mistake. She was just shuffling through the other bills when she heard a bonging noise. She jumped violently; then the bongs intensified, became a cacophony of rich strikes. It was the hour—all the clocks had been timed to strike together.

Bongbongbongbong, the sounds feeding upon each other.

Cici wiped perspiration from her upper lip, fighting another strong urge to flee. *Whoa,* she told herself. *They're only clocks.*

She had just turned to the folder again when she felt a crawly sensation, a premonitory ripple of the skin on the back of her neck.

She froze, slowly turning.

"Cici," Bryan said. His face was a granite mask of anger. "Cici. What are you doing here?"

She stared at him, speechless with fright. He wore an expensive Burberry trench coat dotted with rain, his glossy blond hair darkened by moisture. His features were distorted, nostrils flaring in a way she found very frightening. Oh, God, where had he come from? Had he somehow followed her over here? Had his been the footsteps she'd thought she heard?

"What are you doing in my house?" he repeated, glancing down at the incriminating penlight.

She fought her fright.

"I . . . I would have called you if you'd been in town," she blurted, her mind rapidly searching for a plausible explanation—anything to explain her illegal presence here. "But I thought you were in Cincinnati and I needed . . . that is, I think I left something here. My driver's license."

"Your what?"

The story seemed far-fetched, but now she was stuck with it.

God, why hadn't she prepared a better lie? She'd been such a fool to come here! When he'd called her earlier he couldn't have been in Cincinnati at all.

"My d-driver's license. I was too embarrassed to tell you. I had it out the other day to check to see whether it had expired. I must have put it down on a table—maybe your desk—I was just looking for it."

Chilly blue eyes probed hers. "So you decided to break into my house? Spy on me? Go through my things? Where have you been in my house? Where?"

"Nowhere. Just here. Bryan—"

"You were spying!" Bryan's voice sounded tight, taut, she heard with fascination and fear. He was furious. And she could not blame him. How would she feel if the situation were reversed, if he had broken into her house? She'd be just as furious.

She fumbled on, making up the story as she went along. "I wasn't spying. I just wanted my license, because I had to go to the police station today and they asked for it. I was going to pay for the door, Bryan—I was going to call a glass service tomorrow and have them fix it."

Another lie. She hadn't thought that far ahead. She felt another wave of the nausea that often struck her in tense situations.

"Oh, a glass service! Oh, excellent! That would make it all right, wouldn't it? Just repayment for the destruction of an antique piece of glass. I think you're lying, Cici." Bryan's eyes were as cold as December sleet.

"I'm not lying!" Thank God she'd left her purse at home so he couldn't check and find her license still in her wallet. She moistened her lips, thinking with despair that it was all over, wasn't it? The pretense.

"I left Cincinnati this afternoon, Cici, after I called and couldn't get you. Where were you today? Why weren't you at the Job Center?"

"I told you, I had a doctor's appointment and then I did some shopping." She faltered.

Bryan's eyes held hers for several more excruciatingly long seconds, and finally he looked away, rubbing his temple as if it had begun to throb with a piercing headache. "All right," he said shortly. "I'll accept your offer to pay a glass company to fix my door. Meanwhile I'll repair it with plywood. But there is one more thing."

The way he said it, so angry. "Yes?"

"The wedding. We're stepping up the date. I think we'll fly to Honolulu tomorrow and be married there."

She stared at him, stunned, unable to believe what she had heard. "The wedding, Bryan? *Tomorrow?*"

"We can get a license in Honolulu."

A steel cable seemed to pull inside her stomach, forming a knotted mass. *Marriage tomorrow?* After what she had just done?

"But Bryan . . . this all sounds so—so sudden. I have a son, a job. I can't just go to the airport and fly out of Detroit on a whim. What's wrong with our original date?"

"It needs to be advanced," he told her shortly. "There have been phone calls—a man asking questions. You hired him, didn't you, Cici?"

"Bry . . . no, I didn't."

"Don't lie! I'm not stupid, you know. And I know your mother's birthday isn't this month because you told me once that she was born in February. You forgot you did that, didn't you? And now you are going to prove yourself to me. You're going to marry me tomorrow and put an end to this . . . this hell."

This hell.

More and more Cici began to feel as if she'd stepped into some bizarre drama with a script she had not read. Bryan had known all along about McVey—or at least been suspicious. He hadn't trusted her any more than she'd trusted him. Their relationship had come unraveled like a loose ball of thread, revealing there was nothing at the center.

Bryan took her arm and pulled her into the kitchen. Rather than struggle with him, Cici went. The huge kitchen seemed a vast, cold expanse of white counters, white Formica and floor, more like a coroner's office than a real kitchen. In the adjoining mudroom area, a sponge mop leaned against one wall as if recently used.

Why had she never noticed how obsessively *clinical* everything was, she thought wildly. Ann had been right . . . so right! That was why Bryan had hated her. Because she'd seen him clearly.

She took an experimental step toward the door. "I'll go home and get my checkbook, Bryan, and write you a check for the door. I'm sorry I broke in. I guess it was a pretty stupid idea, wasn't it?" She forced a laugh. "I can't believe I was stupid enough to leave my license—"

"Didn't you hear me?" The words cut across her sentence. "We're leaving for Hawaii tomorrow. I bought you some luggage as a surprise, the kind with wheels on them. I've got the set downstairs."

"Luggage? Bryan, I don't want any luggage. I already have a set." Her laugh was high, brittle, nervous. "Bry—don't you see, we have to face this. We have to talk. Maybe we should . . ."

A smell was emanating from him, sharp, pungent. The sweat of fear? *Was he afraid of her? But why?*

"Gucci," Bryan remarked stiffly. "I bought you Gucci. It's very nice, the best. There's a store at Somerset Mall that handles it. And tomorrow I will have roses for you before we board the plane."

He sounded like a computer reciting love poems, Cici thought with a spurt of revulsion. The trappings. Oh, she'd had all that—the roses, the gifts, the beautiful clothes, brooches, the fancy restaurant meals—but there had never been any substance, had there? And she'd accepted that for herself. Sold herself short, all because of her mastectomy, her fear of being alone and unwanted.

Numbly she shook her head. "Bryan . . . I don't want to marry you. I—I can't. We're strangers, really. We don't know each other. And now I . . . I really should be going home. We'll talk again in the—"

His hand closed on her forearm. *"No,* Cici. You're going to come with me now. To see the luggage."

Luggage. When her doubts were foaming up like some corrosive chemical, burning the synapses of her thoughts.

"No. Bryan . . ."

"Oh, yes. Yes you are. Yes you are going to look at my gift for you, my dear, darling fiancée." The words lashed her. *"My dear. My darling."*

She struggled furiously, but he had already pushed her to the top of the stairwell, his face contorted with the first real emotion she had seen in him—an anger so virulent that it horrified her.

"No!" she shouted, unable to believe this was really happening. "No! Bryan, please! I don't want to go in the basement! Bryan!"

He had already forced her down four or five steps, and she discovered it was impossible to fight someone who stood several steps above her. When she tried, Bryan's heel swung out and struck her a blow on her shoulder.

Cici stumbled backward, nearly falling on the next lower step.

"Down," Bryan commanded. "Go on down, go in there, Cici. In the hobby room to wait. Otherwise, I'll push you."

He would push her? The man who had declared undying love for her? There was no choice, nowhere to go but down. Within seconds, she reached the bottom landing. Bryan came down beside her and pushed open the hobby-room door, shoving her inside and turning the lock.

It was like being thrown into the bottom of a cardboard box. Only a small amount of ambient light relieved the heavy, smothering darkness, which, like the upstairs, was alive with clocks ticking and a sort of rhythmic, low-grade hum.

"Bryan!" Cici screamed. She pounded on the door with her fists, then kicked it. The toes of her walking shoes weren't intended for such punishment, and her big toe hurt through the leather. "Bryan! This is ridiculous! Let me out of here! Bryan! *Dammit! Damn you!"*

Through the door she heard sounds of Bryan's footsteps returning upstairs, and then there was the slam of the door at the top of the staircase. She felt a wave of stunned, angry disbelief.

He had closed it on her—he had locked her down here like a bad child.

"Bryan! Bryan!" she cried again, then heard the tearing panic in her voice and rubbed her fist across her mouth, silencing herself. She had to stop screaming, she knew. Her screams would feed him somehow, make him worse.

God—it was nearly pitch black in here.

The darkness was as smothering as a black velvet pillow. She'd always had a terror of being locked up, and now she fought a shudder of claustrophobia. Her heart was hammering urgently.

She had to get out of here—now.

A clock behind her suddenly pinged out the quarter hour, out of step with the others. Cici jumped, clapping her hand over her mouth to keep back another shriek. Now she could hear creaking sounds on the ceiling above her, which was, of course, the floor upstairs. Bryan was walking across the house. What was he doing up there? Gloating over the fact that he had her locked up?

No. She heard his voice, although she couldn't distinguish any words. He must be talking on the phone.

She fought the panic and disorientation.

She mustn't scream. If she screamed, he'd hear her . . . he'd revel in her fear. He was punishing her. The darkness in here . . . so intense.

She realized that her thoughts had become thready, laced with hysteria. She had to get hold of herself, start thinking clearly again.

Her hand, brushing down the wall near the door, touched something sharp and plastic. The light switch. With relief, she flicked it upward.

Light flooded into the hobby room, so brightly yellow, so wonderfully normal that her eyes ached. She realized that she was staring at one of Bryan's drawings, hung on the wall next to the door. It showed a banjo clock with a face drawn on its front. She'd seen the picture several times before, but never this close. She stared at the human face he'd drawn on it. It showed an old man with a flowing, luxuriant beard and a frowning, Jehovah-like countenance. That beard was like Ed Wykotsky's in the photograph album.

Yet she felt sure the picture represented God. More hell-and-brimstone religiosity. *Why? What did it all mean? Why had he locked her in the basement? What was he going to do with her? Surely he didn't really intend to marry her tomorrow in Hawaii. It made no sense at all.*

She backed away from the picture and into the center of the room. Floorboards again creaked overhead as Bryan's voice stopped and he moved about again.

Cici forced herself to walk the full length of the long room. Little had changed since the evening Bryan had brought her, Ann, and Larry down here at Ann's insistence. There were still the same long hobby tables shoved against the walls, and shelves fixed by brackets to one wall, displaying cast-iron banks, clocks, and other items waiting for repair. Cupboards on the opposite wall offered more storage space than most homeowners ever dreamed of.

The expensive, gleaming parquet floor looked more as if it belonged in a Bloomfield Hills mansion than in a workroom.

Of course there was no "surprise" luggage. Had she really expected there would be? He'd just dumped her down here. If there was a telephone extension . . .

But her hope quickly died. There was a phone jack, but no telephone. And the windows were filled in with thick glass bricks, too small to crawl out of even if she managed to break one without attracting attention.

"Bryan!" Cici called through the door, hoping he could hear her. "Bryan . . . please. I know you're angry because I broke into your house. I—I guess it was pretty stupid, wasn't it? I needed my driver's license and I thought I could just pay you for the broken glass . . ."

No response. The creaking of the floor treads continued, as if Bryan were pacing back and forth, unable to settle.

"Bryan! Bryan . . . we'll talk about getting married tomor-row. We really do have to talk. Bry . . . we can't talk when I'm locked down here."

Silence.

"I just want to talk to you. *Please.* Would you let me come upstairs? Would you unlock the door?"

But Bryan—if he heard at all—refused to answer, and after a few more minutes of calling and pleading, Cici stopped, pressing her hands to her face. Tears of frustration rolled down her cheeks.

Calm, she thought. *Calm yourself. He hasn't hurt you yet. Maybe he won't. He is just angry and trying to punish you. If you wait a while, he'll calm down.*

Or would he?

There was a stool by one of the hobby tables, and Cici sank onto it, realizing the gravity of the situation.

Bryan had her locked up down here like a prisoner. When was he going to let her out? And even more importantly . . . what was he going to do to her?

SIXTEEN

Aaron microwaved a package of lasagna and made himself a lunch-meat sandwich, stuffing it with the crunchy bread-and-butter pickles he loved. He loaded his plate and carried it into the family room, setting it on the coffee table. He returned to the kitchen, poured himself a cherry-flavored Pepsi and brought it back.

He found the remote and tuned in MTV, which was playing a rap video by L.L. Kool J. The funky, knee-jerk beat filled the room, taking away some of the emptiness.

But midway through the square of lasagna, Aaron's appetite died. He got up and began to pace about uneasily, struck by a restlessness he could not really explain. He kept going to the window, gazing out through glass streaked with raindrops. Beyond that was the misty night, saturated with black.

Jeez. He hated rain. And he *hated* being alone in the house. Being alone was the creepiest, the worst thing of all.

He went to the phone and dialed Dustin's number. The phone rang twice and then he heard his friend's voice.

"H'lo?" Dustin sounded scratchy and hoarse—about as bad as Aaron himself felt.

"Dustin? Dust?"

"Yeah . . ."

"What happened, man? You know, with your dad?"

There was a silence. "Shit, what do you think? I told him I didn't do it, but the fucking bastard didn't care. He said he was going to give it to me—I have to wait. Man, this time it'll be a lot more than just a plain whipping."

"Oh," Aaron said, unable to think of anything more comforting. He felt another wave of guilt. He hadn't talked—yet—but he'd be talking tomorrow to a lawyer. Would the lawyer make him tell? No, lawyers weren't like that. Aaron knew from watching TV they could be as crooked as anyone.

"Shit," Dustin went on, his voice thready. "I'm out of here, man . . . just as soon as I get my driver's license. I hate him, man. I'm goin' to California." A pause. "I got the cable on. What're you watching?"

"Thirteen," Aaron said, naming the MTV channel.

"Yeah, me too."

A black girl with full buttocks straining at a tiny spandex skirt was now gyrating on the screen, her eyes slitted with desire. Except for the videos, Aaron had never seen a girl make such frank, humping movements. They discussed the issue of how fat a girl's ass ought to be. Would Aaron screw a black chick like the one on the screen, if she wanted him?

"Sure," Aaron said, thinking that he would never get the chance. He would probably be twenty before any chick wanted him. He stayed on the phone with Dustin for an hour, watching MTV with him from their separate houses, while eating his sandwich. Then Dustin's voice suddenly changed.

"He's back. He went out to get his usual twelve-pack of beer—he's gonna get plastered. He looks in a real shitty mood, man. I gotta go."

"Dus—"

But his friend had hung up.

Aaron slowly replaced the receiver in its cradle, feeling the loneliness sweep over him again as he realized that his mother had not yet returned from her walk. Thinking of what she'd say if she found dishes scattered all over the coffee table, he carried his plate and glass out to the kitchen and dumped it in the sink.

He carefully scraped off all the lasagna gunk and loaded his plate in the dishwasher. Yeah, sometimes he was a slob but tonight—after being in jail, after becoming a juvenile delinquent—now was not the time. He knew his mother. She could take the big stuff, but one little thing like dirty plates might push her over the edge. He didn't want to get screamed at tonight. No way.

Returning to the family room, Aaron threw himself on the couch again. A Janet Jackson video was playing now—a crazy, funky, dancing Janet, with a whole row of dancers behind her. He thought Janet was only medium sexy. Paula Abdul was better.

He focussed on the screen, his gaze trancelike as he unconsciously rubbed at his eyes.

An hour had passed.

Cici spent the time alternately slumped on the stool and pacing the basement workroom, unable to believe that she had really gotten herself into this predicament. She could hear the occasional creak of floorboards and knew that Bryan was still in the house, standing guard overhead.

How long was he going to keep her imprisoned down here? But at least he hadn't been violent, except for their struggle on the stairs. He hadn't actually *hit* her . . . yet. Maybe he wouldn't. Maybe this was just his way of punishing her.

Maybe, she speculated, this was what Junie had done to him when he was a little boy, locked him in a closet. So now he did it to women, to show his power over them, his domination. Repeating what had been done to him.

Oh, what shit, she said to herself angrily.

Who cared why he had done it? Amateur psychoanalysis wasn't going to help her now. She was locked in here and Bryan showed no signs of relenting and letting her out.

Had any of the Basher's victims been locked up? She struggled to recall the TV specials and newspaper articles. She didn't think they had. But wasn't it a fact that the police seldom released all the information they really had about a case? So she didn't really know *all* the things the Basher did to his victims. No one knew that. No one who was still alive, anyway.

With effort, Cici wrenched away the image. If she kept up those kinds of thoughts, she'd fall apart, become a helpless jelly of terror. Her imagination was her own worst enemy, she knew.

It was eleven o'clock. The clocks went through their hourly *bongbong,* some of them in the basement, others echoing through the floorboards from upstairs. Heavy grandfather bongs; lighter, more delicate shelf and wall-clock pings.

Eerie.

Creepy.

God, she was never going to allow a *bonging* clock in her house again.

The sound of the clocks died away, and only a faint background humming noise was left. Cici got up and began another round of pacing. Odd, that humming noise. Wasn't it much stronger down here in the hobby room? Maybe Bryan kept some sort of running appliance down here.

She began looking around now, searching for the source of the noise, the act giving her something to do besides think, brood and worry. There was a gray fuse box fastened to the wall over one of the worktables, and she went there first, thinking it might be the source of the noise. Next to it was a thermostat with a timer that probably regulated the heat in the basement. But neither of these devices seemed to be particularly noisy.

Cici continued around the room, stopping to examine some of the clocks, thinking perhaps one of them had some unusual workings that might produce the extra noise. But all seemed ordinary to her . . . nothing unusual that she could see, from the slight knowledge she had gleaned about clocks from talking to Bryan.

Another creak overhead stopped her search. She stood stockstill, her heart slamming. Bryan was again walking across the house. Was he coming downstairs to let her out? But then she heard the flush of a toilet, and knew that he wasn't coming down here at all. Thinking about the toilet, she realized she could use one herself.

At the end of the long room was a small bathroom with vanity and shower, and several pairs of clean white work coveralls hanging on a hook. Cici used the toilet, thankful that at least there was water. She had a sudden flash of herself grown thin and anorexic like Karen Carpenter, crawling across the beautiful, golden parquet floor, dying of starvation.

What would she do, really do, if Bryan did not relent in an hour or so?

Aaron, at home, absorbed in his stereo or MTV, might not notice her extended absence. Why should he? Bryan *was* her fiancé. He might even assume she'd be spending the night, although she had never done that. Cici knew her son would never bring himself to telephone her at Bryan's.

She continued to roam the hobby room, drawn now by the row of deep, floor-to-ceiling cupboard doors running along the right wall of the room. Examining one at the far end of the row, trying the handle, she saw that there was a small, neat lock set into the luxurious paneling so that it was barely visible.

There was a sudden sound, like that of a refrigerator motor starting up. Cici bent her head closer to the door. Was the electrical humming sound coming from within the cupboard?

Why would Bryan keep a refrigerator inside a cupboard?

Cici drew a couple of deep breaths, angrily thinking that she was already being punished for breaking in—so why not compound her crime? What did she have to lose now? He'd done this unspeakable thing to her . . . she owed him nothing now.

Striding over to one of the worktables, she poked among the few small tools hung neatly from clip fasteners on the wall until she found a long, thin metal file.

It took a major effort to pry open the door, but finally Cici was able to manage it. She had taken a woodworking course in high school, and had helped her father remodel a deck. The physical effort felt good, draining away some of her adrenaline. She also enjoyed the act of ruining the beautiful finish of the door. Dammit! Bryan deserved this. What in these cupboards could be so important that it had to be locked up?

She pulled the full-length door open wide and stared inside. The enclosure was about six feet by six, its entire bottom half occupied by a white chest-type Montgomery Ward freezer. Pasted on the freezer lid was another of the carefully typed labels, like the one on the Clyattville box. This label read *May 2, 1980*. Odd. Cici took a step backward, startled.

She'd expected to see valuable antiques, more old letters and diaries, maybe a collection of 45 RPM records—anything but the plain white freezer. What could be more middle-American, more utilitarian than this?

The freezer motor hummed slightly. Cici opened the double doors to their widest, then lifted the freezer lid, curious to see just what foodstuffs Bryan considered important enough to lock away.

A tray of supermarket foods occupied the top basket: Bird's Eye frozen peas, containers of Kool-Whip, Mountain Top pies. Most of the pies were cherry, except for one blackberry.

All those calories. When did Bryan eat such pies? She had never seen him eat sweets. In fact, several times he had commented negatively on her love of chocolate ice cream.

Frowning, Cici pushed the cupboard doors shut again and walked to the identical cupboard next to it. It, too, was locked. A mechanical hum seemed to emanate from that cupboard, too. An appliance-motor sound.

Something caught in Cici's throat and seemed to stick there. The beautifully paneled door seemed so blank . . . too blank, as if it held some kind of secret. She took the file out of her pocket and moved it toward the lock.

What the heck. If she had broken open one door, she might as well open two.

A second white freezer occupied the next cupboard. This one bore the Sears Kenmore brand name, its white porcelain unscratched and fresh. The label on its lid read *February 10, 1970.*

Two freezers? Cici shook her head, wondering if Bryan was

one of those people who thought they had to squirrel away a lot of food in case Russia dropped atomic bombs on Detroit.

More curious than ever, she pulled up its cover and saw another array of foodstuffs, frozen vegetables and beef and pork roasts, some nearly covered in white rime.

More food. Definitely strange. She saw that the plastic wrap around one of the roasts had torn apart, and that the meat inside was white and freezer burned. A price tag hung from one corner, and Cici turned the roast around to glance at it.

Sixty-eight cents per pound. $3.40 for the whole roast.

Cici couldn't even remember when meat had been sixty-eight cents a pound. A chill went through her, a shiver that was not caused by the cold air drifting up from the freezer but by an apprehension far more basic.

How old was that meat? Why had Bryan saved it all these years?

She glanced along the wall, counting six doors in all. Was there a freezer in every one of them? Dated and organized? By the mechanical humming that had always filled the house, and filled the room now, she now realized that there could be. Maybe that was why the electric bill she'd found had been so high.

Incredible. She couldn't believe this. She closed the Kenmore's lid and moved down the row. She knew, with a sick, twisting sensation in the pit of her stomach, that she was going to have to lift the top basket of one of the freezers and look underneath.

The rain was pounding down harder now, sluicing down the window glass, blurring it wet.

Aaron was getting restless, tired of the videos that he had heard and seen so many times he could dance along with them and repeat all the lyrics. He picked up the remote and began zapping down the channels, catching bits and pieces of a nature program about whales and a clip from a channel he particularly liked called "The 90s."

He stopped to watch a man talking about his business selling condoms from vending machines. Then a strange 1960s commercial about atom bombs, a cartoon turtle telling kids to "duck and hide" when the bomb came. *When* the bomb came.

Aaron shivered, flicking the channel button back to the videos. God. The whole world could explode around him someday. He glanced at his watch uneasily, wondering if his mother was still out walking in the rain.

Who was he kidding? She was at Bryan's by now, probably in bed with him . . . Aaron knew that was what his mother and Bryan did when they were alone. He knew his father did it with Tara, so why not his mother with Bryan?

He picked up the phone again, dialing Matt's number, but Matt's mother answered the phone, telling him in a crabby voice that Matt was grounded and would be allowed no phone calls for two weeks.

"Yeah, um, okay," he mumbled, hanging up.

He dialed Kevin, but got the family's answering machine and finally hung up, feeling more despondent than ever. A little boil of hurt was beginning to fester inside him. Of all nights for his mother to go over to Bryan's.

With every passing second he was feeling more deserted, more abandoned. No one cared about him, did they? His father didn't even know he'd been arrested. Maybe he should call and tell him.

Yeah, tell him he had a J.D. arsonist for a son.

Aaron dialed.

His dad had a new tape. *"Hey, we're not home. Don't be shy, just wait until the—"*

He slammed down the phone, angry at himself for his weakness. Dumb! Stupid! That's what he was. He could picture his dad now, telling him what a dork he was, what a juvenile delinquent.

Where *was* his mother? Sighing, Aaron decided to go to his bedroom and turn on his stereo. And maybe he'd take a nap, yeah.

Going to jail made a person tired.

Cici went back to the stool and sat down, planting her elbows on the work surface of the table. The hardness of the wood on her skin brought her back to reality. She rubbed her hands tiredly over her eyes. Six freezer units, all of them the chest type, had been hidden inside the six deep cupboards she had pried open. One was a Hotpoint, two were Montgomery Ward, one Sears Kenmore, the others Amana. It was as if he'd purchased them from more than one store so that a nosy sales-clerk wouldn't get curious.

Six freezers, some with more than one date label pasted to them.

Bizarre!

She couldn't think of *any* good reason why a bachelor like Bryan who seldom cooked would have six of them hidden in his basement. Even a big farm family that raised, grew, killed, and froze everything they ate might not own so many. Why? Why would it be so important to him to have not one, but six freezers? Her unconscious mind answered the question.

A sentence she'd seen in the diary popped into her head, Junie's jagged, psychotic script jumping out at her.

"God don't want no disturb of her bones."

What if . . .

Cici shook her head violently, a shudder running through her entire body. Oh, God . . . now she *was* really getting para-noid, wasn't she? One hour spent cooped up in Bryan's creepy basement, listening to the clocks and to him creaking the floor-boards overhead, had turned her into Stephen King, her thoughts full of the grisly and the unspeakable.

She did *not* want to get up and look inside those freezers. No way did she want to do that.

She sat there shaking, angry at herself for being such a coward. In books or on TV, the woman detective bravely breezed into deadly situations, handling them with finesse and even wit. But she wasn't some scriptwriter's fantasy; she'd already gotten herself way in over her head and she didn't like it one bit.

She had closed the cupboard doors to conceal the evidence of her break-in, but she knew that Bryan was the fussy type, the kind of man who noticed everything. When he eventually came down here he was going to see the pry marks. Even if she didn't look inside the freezers, he'd think she had.

So she might as well. Because if she didn't look, she'd never know what or who Bryan was, would she? Wasn't that why she had come here in the first place, because she wanted to face it head on, see what sort of man she'd let herself fall for?

Slowly she got up and crossed the room, choosing at random the next-to-last cupboard she had opened.

With a sense of opening Pandora's box, Cici lifted out the large freezer tray, setting it on the parquet floor beside her.

So ordinary, the pies and plastic containers of Kool-Whip, the frozen peas and corn. A happy Suzy Homemaker assortment of goodies.

However, as soon as she lifted the tray out, the illusion ended. Instead of food, underneath the tray were heavy folds of pastel-blue cloth. Cici stared down with a thrill of fright. It was a down comforter, covered with specks of frost.

A comforter, in a freezer?

Cici felt a little wave of nausea, but swallowed it back hastily. Slowly she reached forward and touched the cloth. It felt icy, almost oily from the cold, like something dragged from a grave.

She snatched away her hand, uttering a small cry of distaste.

But she forced herself to keep unwrapping, until she had unearthed a black plastic leaf bag, tightly taped at the neck. It was identical to the bags homeowners put out at the curb for the trash pickup, that even tonight were lined up at curbs everywhere in the subdivision. So common, so ordinary.

But there was nothing ordinary about this bag. Inside it she could see a mounded shape . . . a shape very, very familiar.

A sour spew of bile forced its way up the back of Cici's throat and threatened to overwhelm her. God! Could it really be what she thought it was, feared it was?

Her breath was shallow as she jabbed the file into the plastic, creating a long rip. With cold, shaking hands she pulled the rip farther apart. Stiffly, the plastic parted.

Cici pulled back with a strangled scream.

Inside the leaf bag lay curled the frozen, perfectly preserved body of a woman. Bent in a fetal position like a child sleeping, she wore a blood-soaked white sweatshirt that said DETROIT PIS-TONS, and a pair of stonewashed denim jeans. She looked about twenty-five years old, slim, tiny.

Cici breathed deeply through her mouth, trying not to faint.

Was this Abby Tighe?

She forced herself to look. Dishwater-blond hair tangled back from a small face that had been so badly battered there was nothing now but a crusted, blackish-red mass where the nose had been. The hair was badly matted with more blackish clumps, and one eye socket was entirely filled with frozen blood, on which crystals of ice had formed a white patina. The other eye, covered with frost, stared unseeingly.

Wooziness overtook Cici in waves, along with a choking nausea.

The Basher . . . The Basher had done this.

Was Bryan the Basher? Oh, God, what other explanation could there possibly be?

SEVENTEEN

Cici reeled from one freezer to the next, uncovering two more women, each wrapped in plastic and shielded by comforters.

Their faces were so beaten and shattered that shards of bone and pieces of teeth protruded from the mouth of one poor woman. Their blood had frozen to a blackish color, and frost had disfigured them even further, giving them the look of Hollywood special-effects horrors.

More than one label decorated four of the six freezers. Perhaps more bodies were hidden under these women, crammed two or even three into a freezer, but Cici, ignited with horror, sobbing and hyperventilating, could not bring herself to look.

Was Ann down here in Bryan's basement? Was Ann one of these pathetic, horrible, beaten, frost-covered bodies?

She went back to the first freezer, the one labeled February 10, 1970. It contained food that seemed decades old, so thickly coated with ice and rime that the brand names could not be read. Cici, crying, pulled away the top freezer tray. Inside was a human form loosely wrapped in an old, shabby, handstitched quilt done in an ironic "lover's knot" pattern.

"No," she sobbed. "No, no."

Heart pounding, she tugged at one corner, pulling away the folds.

There was no garbage bag for this corpse. This one had been left virtually open to the ravages of the freezer. She was in her forties, her face and body so badly affected by freezer burn that she looked more like a mummy than an actual woman. The clothes the body wore seemed old, from the late sixties or early seventies. The blond hair, too, had been done in a style from that same era.

Cici thought of a photograph. A blond woman scowling at the camera.

Junie. June Wykotsky. Bryan's mother!

And visible just beneath her shoulder was something furry—a dog's matted coat. The dog June had written about in the diary, the pet who had died and been put in the freezer instead of being buried.

Cici backed into the center of the room, gasping and panting, clammy sweat pouring down her face as waves of nausea began to flood her. But she brought the spasms under control and staggered to the most recent freezer, the only one without a label, as if Bryan had somehow lost heart.

Ann was inside. Or rather something that resembled Ann. A strange Ann, her skin purplish-pale, not yet freezer damaged, but covered with runnels and splashes of dark red, frozen blood. An Ann whose eyes—

Cici could look no more. She broke away and ran to the small bathroom, where she was violently sick, spewing up the contents of her stomach into the commode.

Ann, Ann, Ann, she wept, sobbing as quietly as she could, terrified now that Bryan would hear her and come down to the basement.

She sank to the floor and sat huddled near the bathroom door. Her hands were frozen from handling the freezers, and the insides of her finger bones ached. She sobbed silently, her mouth wide, head shaking in agony.

Why? Why? Why had he done it? How could he have killed someone as wonderful as Ann, a woman who had done nothing to him? My God . . . he *was* psychotic . . . She twisted from side to side, pounding the floor with her fist.

Finally her sobs became shudders, then died away. Bryan was the Basher, of course. The earliest victim had probably been Bryan's mother, June Wykotsky, the other victims arranged in grotesque chronological order, with Abby Tighe next to the last and Ann the most recent. All stored away in chilly order, like the work of some mad coroner.

"There are some people who are different, Miss Davis," Betty Schwartz, Bryan's aunt, had told her. *"They have two sides to them, a good side and a bad side. The black and the white, the good and the evil. Both Junie and Ed were like that, and I'm afraid their son could be, too."*

She pictured Bryan as a young boy, physically abused by his psychotic parents, forced to burn the words *God's Hammer* into a heavy, hardwood paddle Ed Wykotsky made in his furniture shop.

Then perhaps one day the hot-tempered Ed beat his wife too severely, maybe before the very eyes of their fourteen-year-old son. June died of her injuries. Not believing in autopsies, Ed concealed the death from the authorities, putting June's body in the family freezer.

It was probably at that point that the family moved away from Clyattville, Cici figured. After all, too many neighbors and church parishioners would notice that June was missing. Ed and his son moved to the Detroit area, where Ed sent the bogus postcards to Betty Schwartz and others June had known. They took the freezer with them . . . with the dead woman inside it, wrapped in the "lover's knot" quilt.

Cici took deep breaths, fighting the faintness that seemed to suck all the air from her lungs. From her psychology course, she knew that youngsters who are abused often grow up repeating the same vicious circle of violence on their own children—or on others.

What if Bryan had grown up and begun to imitate what his father had done? Killing women in fits of violent anger with the same kind of club used on him, then "preserving" them in the freezers . . .

No! Cici thought wildly. *This isn't happening!*

Drawing deep breaths, Cici brought her head down to her knees, applying the same fainting remedy she'd been taught in high school. She concentrated on sucking in huge gulps of air, forcing the blackness away.

Then she sat up again, her mind grimly going over the clues that had been there all along—if she'd only seen them. The humming appliance sound always in the house, which Bryan had masked with his collection of tick-tocking clocks. Bryan's paranoia about vandals and burglars, which was created by a fear that someone might get into the house and find the freezers and their grisly contents.

His ownership of a generator in case the power went out—a disaster that would thaw the bodies. No wonder he had been hysterical the night of the garage fire when the power *had* been temporarily out.

Even the electronic dog! Most people that fearful of burglars would keep a dog to warn off intruders, but Bryan was afraid to have a real dog, *because a real animal might smell the corpses.*

Oh, God . . . oh, God . . . She realized that her thoughts had segued off into horror again. Anyway, it didn't matter about the hows and wherefores anymore, did it? There were much more immediate things to think about.

There was another creak of a floorboard from upstairs, and a muffled voice as if Bryan were talking on the phone again. Although she couldn't hear the words, his voice sounded tense, frightened.

Cici stiffened, her heart slamming violently. He must be thinking about her right now, deciding how to kill her. Was he even now placing a phone order with Montgomery Ward for a freezer to put her body in? A wild laugh took possession of her, and she clamped her teeth down hard on her lower lip, silencing it. What was she going to do? How long did she have until he decided to come down here?

She wasn't going to give up without a fight, she told herself grimly. But how? What could she fight him with? He was a big man, and muscular, and although she worked out regularly, she weighed 125 pounds to his 185.

Aaron, she thought in agony. Her son would assume—rightly—that she was at Bryan's, and since Bryan was her fiancé, the man she was *supposed* to be with, why would her boy think she was in any danger? Worse, Aaron could wake up the next morning and assume she had already returned home and left again for work, so it could be twenty-four hours or more before her son realized she was missing.

Oh, God, what if Bryan killed her?

Aaron would be so devastated. He'd never get over it. He'd be forced to live with Tom, who didn't really want him. He'd end up with psychological problems that would ruin his life . . .

She pushed away the wave of debilitating sorrow. *No.* Bryan wasn't going to kill her because she wasn't going to let him. She was a bright woman—a survivor. She had survived cancer, hadn't she? Faced a woman's most terrifying nightmare and won. After that, anything else had to be easy.

She gazed toward the end of the room where the door, now locked from the other side, led to the stairs. It was there that Bryan would enter. He'd probably be carrying a club, wouldn't he?

The club called God's Hammer, meant to terrify, to turn its victims into quivering, terrorized jelly.

What if she wouldn't quiver?

What if she attacked him first, caught him off guard?

Shaking, she regarded the plan, wondering if she really had the guts to carry it out. She wasn't the violent type, had never even played team sports in high school. But the thought of her son crying at her funeral fueled a burst of adrenaline in her. Dammit! What did she have to lose? She'd be damned if she'd become one of those poor women with a Sears freezer for her grave.

She walked around the room gathering a small supply of weapons from the tools hung on the wall. A screwdriver, a small hammer, the file that she already had tucked in her pocket. There were no knives or axes—nothing really sharp, she noticed. These were probably locked up in a multidrawered cabinet set next to one of the worktables. She decided to pry it open, and was just starting to work away at the edge of the door with the file when a noise from upstairs froze her.

Footsteps . . .

The branch kept knocking against the window, ruining Aaron's attempts to take a nap.

Bang. Bang.

Then a slow, drawing *scraaaape* that sounded like Freddy Kruger's fingernails. Aaron grabbed the sheets he'd pulled tightly around his face, yanking them even higher.

Scraaaaape . . . bang! Bangbangbang!

The noise was driving Aaron crazy. How many times had Cici asked him to get the ladder and climb up and trim that branch? About a dozen, Aaron would bet. But he'd been lazy, a procrastinator, it hadn't sounded like a fun thing to do, and he'd pretended he'd forgotten.

Now he squirmed under the covers, drawing his knees up, then shivering because the sheets felt cold against his bare skin. Worries jabbed his mind like tiny bits of glass. What was going to happen to Dustin if he talked? Were they going to have to pay money to rebuild the garage? Glumly Aaron remembered there'd been a van, too—worth thousands of dollars. It'd take them years of working at McDonald's to repay that kind of money.

He tossed aside the sheet and leaped out of bed, going over to his stereo and cranking it up to full volume. Yeah . . . Paula Abdul again. Just what he needed, Paula's sweet, creamy voice to make him feel better.

He climbed back under the covers and lay on his back, arms folded under his head, staring up at the ceiling. He was still feeling very tense. An occasional shadow cast by a car would leapfrog across the darkness, stretch itself thin and be gone. Paula was singing his favorite, "Opposites Attract." He thought about the video, her dancing with a big, floppy cartoon cat. The dial on his digital radio-alarm clock said one-thirty.

One-thirty A.M. And where was Cici? Still at Bryan's?

Aaron shifted his position restlessly, thinking that his

mother always was home by midnight—well, nearly always, because she wanted to make sure *he* was home. She'd even told him so once. *"Mothers have curfews, too, Aar. All adults do, only we set them for ourselves."*

Funny, that he'd think of that . . . and now she was breaking her own curfew. Uneasily he twisted again, stretching out and doing a big stretch until his tendons popped.

The phone interrupted him in midstretch. He slid out of bed and searched through the mess on the floor, rummaging under a pile of old shirts until he found the telephone.

"Yeah?" he said, picking it up.

"Hey," Dustin said.

Aaron felt a spasm of disappointment that it wasn't his mother and then immediately swallowed it back, angry at himself for being a baby. A crybaby afraid of the fucking dark, afraid of a banging branch. Worried because his mama wasn't home to coddle him.

He said, "What's up? Your old man . . . well, you know?"

"He went out again, man—took a six-pack with him. Drinking and driving. Hey, I'd like to see him get a ticket, man. Pulled over by a fucking police officer." Dustin's laugh was bitter. "Hey, Heather's here. She says we can use her car, man. Go out and rip off a few mailboxes, do a few lawns. Make the homeowners mad."

Aaron held tightly to the phone. He didn't want to be alone—no way did he want that. But somehow he didn't feel like ripping off mailboxes, either. And after being in jail . . . "I don't know."

"Man, it's practically Devil's Night. We gotta get out on Devil's Night. I got some firecrackers left over from the Fourth of July, Aar . . . some good old smoke bombs."

"Smoke bombs?"

"And some other good stuff." In the background Aaron heard a feminine giggle. "Hey, Heather said she wants you, she wants your body. She loves your body, she—" Sounds of giggles and hitting and laughter.

Aaron gripped the phone, thinking that Dustin was so lucky

to have sisters and brothers, people around. He never had to be alone, did he? "I don't know, man."

"Hey, don't be such a *pussy*. I already got Matt coming over, and I called Kevin, he's gonna sneak out of the house, too. And Heather, man, she wants you. I can tell, I can look at her face and see she's all hot with desire . . . mad for you, crazy wild for you, man . . ."

More wild laughter, then the sound of the phone bonging onto the floor as brother and sister teased and fought.

"Dustin? Dust?" Balancing the phone, Aaron reached for his shirt. "Dust? Dustin! Hey, pick up the phone! Hey, man, yeah . . . I'll be right over."

Cici crouched on the other side of the basement door, the sharp file poised to pound on Bryan's face as soon as he entered the room. Her heart was hammering so thickly in her throat that it seemed to block out the oxygen.

But he wasn't coming.

He'd stopped halfway down the stairs.

God, she'd been so sure she'd heard him cross the house to the kitchen, and then his steps descending the stairs, but there'd only been six steps, then it stopped. Was he standing on the staircase trying to work up his nerve to murder her?

Her hand was beginning to shake, and after a moment, Cici lowered the file. She stretched a little, trying to relax the knotted kinks in her back and arm. Her mouth was as dry as a dish towel. Her fear had dried up all her saliva.

A minute passed.

Two minutes.

Three.

Then ten. She heard the clocks upstairs *bong* out the quarter hour and suppressed a scream. She couldn't stop herself from shaking. This was like the Chinese water torture. *Why didn't he come downstairs and get it over with?*

Then she heard it—another footstep.

Her heart tripped as if given an electrical shock. He *was* coming down!

Tensely she waited as Bryan descended the remaining steps,

each one seeming to take a millennium. She tried to count, but her mind refused, and then there was silence again and she realized he must have reached the bottom. She could feel his presence, only inches away from her. Standing there, hating her.

She waited for him to open the door.

But he didn't open it. Was he afraid, too? Afraid of what he might do to her? Trying to work up his courage to kill her? But she'd always thought of the Basher as being fierce and violent, not afraid.

"B-Bryan?" she whispered, readying the file.

He said nothing, but there was a scraping noise as he shifted his feet on the parquet floor of the foyer area.

"*Bryan.* Do we have to do this?" she pleaded desperately. "Bry, I . . . I loved you, part of me will always love you. Please, don't do this to us. Please, open the door and we can talk . . . as friends."

Friends! a small voice in her mind cried. Bryan had never been her friend, actually. He'd only fulfilled a role.

He did not reply to her plea. She could sense his presence, brooding, silent, angry. She shook her head, feeling her skin crawl with tension. The Basher killed in the heat of passion. Why hadn't Bryan opened the door and attacked her yet? What was he waiting for? Was he waiting for the killing urge to strike him so he could beat her to death?

"Bryan," she whispered. "Oh, God, don't keep me in suspense like this. I never hurt you. I never wanted to do anything to hurt you . . . Could we please talk? Could we please be friends?"

Another long, excruciating silence. Finally he spoke. His voice was hollow. "I heard you."

I heard you. What did he mean? Panic spurted through her. Had he only heard her speak, or had he heard her jimmying open the cupboard doors? Did he suspect she'd opened the freezers? Or was that why he'd locked her down here in the first place, so that she *would* do exactly that?

"I was just waiting for you to let me out," she said vaguely.

"I heard noises. I want to know what you've been doing. What you've seen . . ."

"I . . . I've seen nothing."

"You lie!" he cried hoarsely. "You lie, Cici! You've always lied! You've never loved me. You've only used me, haven't you? As all wicked women do, using me for sex and for your own godless purposes."

"What?" She gasped. The injustice of it was stunning. "Bry! I was engaged to you. We were going to be married. I never . . ."

Then she stopped. Bryan was . . . in another dimension, wasn't he? He was psychotic, thinking thoughts that had no basis in reality.

"Oh, Bry," she pleaded. "Just let me out of here so we can talk face to face. Let me go home to my son. I never hurt you, Bryan. I only wanted to love you."

"No one loves me! Only God loves me. And he . . . *he*—" Even from behind the door she could hear the harsh swallow as Bryan choked back whatever he had been going to say.

A long, long silence followed. She, crouched on one side of the door, he on the other, the pause stretching out so long that she could hear a car speed past the house, horn blasting. Maybe Bryan needed to talk to her like this, with a wooden door between them, like a confessional. Maybe she could draw him out, calm him down. It was worth a try.

"Bryan? You can talk to me. I'll listen. I promise I'll listen and I won't make judgments."

More silence so heavy, so fraught with danger and evil that Cici felt the nausea again, the sharp, sour taste of stomach bile.

"*Him,*" Bryan finally said in a hollow voice.

"Who? Bryan, please, it's safe to talk."

A monotone. "*He is the One, he shows me the way of the Lord Jehovah, and what we must do to please Him. And I . . . and I . . . I have to hide it, because the bones must be saved, the bones and flesh.*"

Cici felt a primal shudder rack her body. Bryan sounded uncannily like Junie's diary.

"Bryan, tell me about . . . about God's Hammer," she improvised.

"It was wood. *He* made it on the lathe. I burned the name in it. Burned it with my kit. *He* made me, he forced me."

"He? Do you mean your father, Bryan? He made you burn the letters?"

"Yes . . . yes . . ." Then something unintelligible that Cici didn't hear. ". . . and then hit me with it. Over and over and over and over," Bryan said monotonously. "He said it was God's punishing rod, and he—he used it on her."

On her.

The picture leaped into Cici's mind, Ed Wykotsky beating Junie, all of it juxtaposed with an image of the dead woman in the freezer.

"Your . . . your father used the wooden paddle, God's Hammer, on your mother?"

"On June . . . Junie . . . on her." There was the sound of harsh weeping. "But it was me . . . he made me pick it up . . . he made me hit her too. Over and over! Over and over! *Over and over and OVER AND OVER AND OVER."*

Cici sagged backward, stunned.

He was telling her that his father had forced him to help kill his mother.

"Bryan," she choked, wild sympathy and fear mingling in her. "Oh, Bry, Bryan. You were only a child—you couldn't help what he made you do. It wasn't your fault."

"I beat her with God's Hammer until her teeth fell out and her nose was bloody and there was a hole in her skull. Then we put her away, we preserved her bones for God, and I . . . and I . . ."

More spasms of weeping—racking, agonized. Real emotion this time so harsh that it tortured.

"I did what he wanted, I did everything he wanted," Bryan sobbed. *"I did it all, Cici. I am weak, do you hear me? I am weak but God is strong and he . . . he is even stronger."*

She swallowed back her terror. Who was the person Bryan called "he," who was even stronger than God? His father? A voice, perhaps, that spoke in Bryan's mind? She had to keep him talking through this episode until he calmed down, reached some semblance of normality. If Bryan really was psychotic, then perhaps he had been treated for it. Maybe someone else knew of his problem . . .

"Bryan," she began cautiously, "are you on some kind of medication? Is there any medicine you should be taking right now to make you feel better? Or someone you want to call? A counselor maybe?"

"No medicine," he said flatly. "And no . . ." The words trailed away.

In the background Cici heard a new sound.

More footsteps.

Footsteps that were not Bryan's.

The wave of hope and gladness she felt was so intense that she swayed with it, her pulse skyrocketing. Someone must be coming to rescue her! Oh, she wasn't going to die after all because now someone else was here and they'd help her, they'd talk to Bryan long enough for her to get up the stairs . . .

"*No,*" Bryan said. His voice suddenly rose into the upper registers of a fear so gut-wrenching that Cici, too, behind the door, felt it rack her.

"*NO,*" Bryan sobbed. "*NO. NOT ANOTHER ONE. PLEASE . . . NO—I WON'T DO IT AGAIN—I CAN'T, I CAN'T, I CAN'T!*"

There was a crashing sound.

Then the door burst open.

EIGHTEEN

Rain had turned the subdivision road into a black, wet, shiny surface on which the headlights of Heather's old Bobcat reflected like lasers. Aerosmith blasted from the car radio, filling the air with hard, supercharged sex.

Heather had brought two six-packs of beer and they all grabbed for the cans, swigging great drafts of the metallic-tasting liquid.

"Man," Dustin kept saying. "Man! Let's find us some mailboxes, huh? Or maybe a house! Yeah, we'll run the car right up on the grass, blast down the garage! That'll show 'em!"

"Not with *my* car," Heather cried. She had on her black leather jacket again, the shoulders sewn with long, jiggly fringes. "I don't want to wreck my car!"

"You won't wreck it, man. It's already wrecked. You got a front end that looks like it ran into a damn semi truck! And your . back end is heavy duty, man." The four boys giggled and sniggered and pushed each other.

Aaron, wedged between Heather and Matt over the gear

shift, laughed with the others. But, man, he felt tight tonight, his nerves taut as wires. A funny feeling was growing inside him, an ugly one he couldn't quite name.

He sucked on the beer can, taking enormous gulps, hoping that the beer might make him drunk enough to forget that he was a J.D., and his father didn't even really care, and he had to decide whether to tell.

"Hey!" he called, tossing the emptied can to the floor. "We got any more of these? I wanta get *high!*"

Someone handed him another can and Aaron popped the top, foam spurting all over his jeans. He lifted the can and chugged it.

"Hey," cried Heather possessively. "Don't drink so fast. You'll drink it all down and there won't be none for the rest of us. There's only twelve cans, you know."

"Hey, I'm thirsty," Aaron told her defiantly, crumpling the empty and tossing it after the other one. But he didn't reach in the backseat for another. The beer wasn't making him feel any better.

They careened through the neighborhood. Tomorrow was trash pickup day, and homeowners had dragged garbage cans and plastic bags out to the curbs. Since it was leaf-raking time, many of the homes had fifteen or more big leaf bags lined up in front. One home had more than thirty.

"Shit," Dustin crowed. "All those fucking leaf bags, a whole army of 'em! Come on, Heather, let's get us some leaves!"

"No," the girl protested.

"Do 'em, do 'em, do 'em," Dustin urged, leaning forward from the backseat to grab his sister's right hand on the steering wheel.

Heather uttered a shriek, and they careened up on the grass, running over the row of bags. Leaves and plastic flew, scattering past the side windows like confetti.

"Man, excellent!" Dustin yelled.

"Excellent!" the boys echoed, including Aaron.

"Hey, what about old man Petterman?" Kevin demanded. DeWayne Petterman was the assistant principal at school, a tall man with a potbelly and a deep dislike of kids. He had twice expelled Kevin.

"Petterman? Naw, we did him two or three times. He knows it might be us," Matt protested.

"Yeah, let's do him again—really trash him this time. We'll drive right into his picture window. Ram the bumper right in his living room."

"Not in *my* car!" cried Heather. "Hey, you guys, you're stupid! You put that last dent in it—stupid ass Dustin and the rest of you guys. You're not going to get *my* car any more wrecked."

"Your car, your car, your car," taunted Dustin. From the backseat he reached forward and gave his sister a hard punch on the arm. "Old Leather Heather! Round heels! Beaver pussy!" he taunted. "Heather *is* a beaver! Beavery beaver!"

"Shut up!" Heather screamed. "Shut up, shut up, shut up!"

"Beaver. Beaver Cleaver."

"Shut up, shut UP!"

They took a corner with a squeal, the wheels running up over the curve with a jolt that slammed Aaron back against nothing, wrenching his neck. A woman jogger wearing silly-looking shorts over sweatpants was running along the sidewalk and stopped to stare at them.

Great, Aaron thought. Heather was so angry she wasn't looking where she was going. In a minute someone would call the cops and they'd be back in jail again. Hard-core J.D.'s.

"Bryan Wyatt," he said. The words emerged from his mouth as if they'd been floating around inside him for hours, a part of the tension that consumed him. "Man, let's go see the garage, see what damage we did, huh?"

Heather made a U-turn at an intersection and squealed the car back the way they had come. Aaron felt a gnawing, ugly curiosity. What would the burned-out garage look like now? An old, dead, blackened, wrecked hulk, he figured.

But when they cruised past, yelling and shouting and squirting beer at each other, Aaron saw that the garage had been hauled away, leaving nothing but the slab of cement it had been built on. Next to it Bryan's house was wreathed in a mist that had drifted up from Paint Creek. Several windows had dim lights burning, like lamps set on low.

Aaron narrowed his eyes.

Something was strange. He didn't see any car parked in the driveway or in front of the house, no sign of Bryan at all. So how could his mother be there if Bryan wasn't?

Sliding his eyes over the house, he noticed that Bryan, too, had left out eight or ten leaf bags for the trash pickup. There was also an object that looked like another flattened appliance box. SEARS, the lettering said. CHEST-TYPE FREEZER. THIS SIDE UP. DO NOT STACK.

Just like last week, Aaron remembered as they drove on past. Another jolt of unease caused the beer inside his stomach to churn. Bryan was a busy guy, huh? Buying appliances left and right.

Definitely weird. Especially for a guy who never cooked for himself—always ate out in restaurants or let someone else do the cooking. And weirder still was the fact that only last week there had been another freezer box out there at the curb.

Kevin was spraying more beer on Heather. Spatters of foam hung in her hair like raindrops and ran down her neck, the fringed jacket, and even the steering wheel.

"Dammit!" she screeched, rubbing her face. "Dammit! I hate you! I hate all you guys! I must be crazy to take you out in my car! You jerks! You jerk-offs! You turds!"

Aaron leaned toward her, helping her to brush the wetness off her jacket. A thought had occurred to him. An ugly thought, a strange one, needling at the back of his mind.

Weird, more than weird. Bryan Wyatt and the whole setup of his house, the whole thing. And his mother was in that house.

"Heather . . . Heath. Turn the car around," he heard himself say.

"What?" She glared at him, classifying him with the others. "I hate you, I said! I really, really hate you! As soon as I stop this car I'm going to spray beer on *you* guys. You're going to get it right up your stupid noses. I'll pour it right up your face!"

"Please, Heather," he begged. God, why didn't he have his own license? "Hey, just turn around in a driveway, okay? Drive past the guy's house again. I want to see that freezer box. Please?"

"Box, who cares about a stupid box?" Heather scoffed, still angry about the beer. But giving Aaron a sidelong glance, she obediently pulled the Bobcat into a driveway and made the turn.

Aaron stared at her, a new sensation fighting with the unease in his stomach. Heather was doing it—doing what he said. And suddenly he knew with a deep, wrenching feeling that she really did like him. Yeah, man, that's why she rode around in the car with them all the time. Not because of her brother, but because of him.

They cruised back toward Wyatt's house.

And then he saw something even stranger.

A man came stumbling out of Bryan's front door. He dashed onto the driveway and toward the empty cement slab of the garage. He stopped with a loose, lurching movement, looking behind him as if something bad, really bad, were chasing him.

It was Bryan Wyatt.

The door exploded open with such violent force that it knocked Cici backward and sent her spinning onto the floor. The file skittered out of her grip as she landed on her right hip.

Even as she was landing she was already twisting around, trying to get her feet under her, to squirm away from the man lunging through the doorway, huge paddle raised in the air.

The Basher!

And it wasn't Bryan, it was someone else.

A taller man, with wider shoulders and a heavy-slabbed, bull-like look to him, with—horribly—a pair of panty hose pulled over his face so that his features were mashed down, unrecognizable.

WHACK!

WHACK!

WHACK!

Frantically she twisted away from the violence of the blows that would have killed her if they'd landed.

"Please, God . . ." She didn't even know she was pleading

as she half ran, half stumbled across the room, her hip banging with another painful blow against the edge of one of the hobby tables.

CRASH! Another blow swung after her, landing on the table with such force it collapsed one support leg. An old cast-iron bank was near one edge, and Cici fumbled frantically for it, grabbing it with hands that were sweaty, rank with fear.

CRASH! Another blow, only inches from her!

Cici whirled and tried to throw the bank at her attacker, but desperation made her aim too fast. The bank crashed harmlessly to the floor near the Basher's feet . . . which were wearing a pair of dirty Reeboks that looked suddenly familiar.

She crawled away from her attacker, cowering under the shelter of the tabletop. Blows rained down on its surface as if swung by some malevolent giant. CRASH! SMASH! BANG! God, the paddle must be made of some incredibly hard wood—it was like hammered steel. And the Basher wielded it like Paul Bunyan.

SMASH! The second table leg went and the front side of the tabletop crashed down to the floor, crushing her backward toward the wall. Objects rolled to the floor—an old Regulator clock, a glass jar full of bolts. The glass shattered, exploding bolts everywhere.

"Please!" Cici screamed, huddling down in the shelter formed by the overhang of the large, heavy, laminated-wood slab. She could see the Basher's feet, in muddy, battered running shoes, tensing with prehensile strength for another of the massive blows. *"Please, please!"*

It was like pleading with the Terminator. Maybe he didn't even hear. Maybe he was deaf inside his own psychosis, buttons permanently set on kill.

CRASH! The club battered down on the table.

SMASHBANGCRASH. More blows hit the table, each one with enough force to crush bones. Cici uttered a panicky sob. Her terror was just what he wanted, she knew . . . he wanted her sick, ill with fright, a slave to his mercy. He was getting off on it!

Yes . . . she could hear him grunting, and the sounds were

almost sexual in nature—a man masturbating, driving toward climax.

She felt a wave of violent revulsion.

Another blow landed, and the entire table quivered from its force. What kind of man would be that strong? She had to pull herself out of this passivity, this helplessness. If she could somehow dart out of one of the open ends of the table, reach the antique bank, maybe, use it as a weapon . . .

She wriggled to the end of the triangular enclosure that was farthest away from where she calculated the Basher was. The cast-iron bank lay just beyond it, and beyond that was the table she'd gone to before, near the thermostat and fuse box.

The fuse box!

Darkness! Pitch darkness! She remembered her terror when Bryan had thrown her down here. Because of the small, high windows fitted with thick glass squares, the basement room held very little ambient light. If she could only switch off the lights. Then *he* would be as blind as she was—a heavy, angry beast nuzzling around in darkness, unable to find its victim.

SMASH! Another killing blow, reverberating on the wood over her head so violently that Cici knew it would have crushed her skull. It *would* crush her skull, or another blow like it . . .

Oh, God, God! *Who the hell was he?* He wasn't Bryan, she knew that much. She'd slept with Bryan, knew his body well; she would recognize him even with a panty-hose mask pulled over his face. This man was definitely taller, thicker, burlier.

Cautiously she peered out behind the end of the table slab again. The fuse box looked impossibly far away, about twenty feet. Could she possibly get that far before he killed her?

On hands and knees she crawled toward the opening, darting her eyes in the direction of the Basher. Only his shoes were visible, his legs clad in jeans. He took a massive step backward, and she saw how wide his shoes were, the fleshy feet spreading at the leather.

Football player's feet.

And then she knew.

John Pickard. Those were his feet—she'd seen them dozens of times as he worked in his yard, pushing a lawn mower, planting trees, doing all the neighborly yard things. But it made no sense. Why would he be over here at Bryan's? If Pickard was the Basher, then why were the bodies in Bryan's hobby room?

She heard a grunt from beyond the wood, a deep, animal-like, sexual grunt. And then the huge shoes came in her direction, and she heard the loud, ringing crash of yet another blow.

SMASH! The blow shook the wood and sent sharp splinters flying, only millimeters away from where she had planned to exit.

Like a cat tormenting its victim, he knew she'd try to escape. He'd been prepared for her all along.

He was going to beat her to death.

Soon.

"Hey, man," Dustin said, his voice squeaking. "Who the hell is *that?*"

"It's dickhead," Aaron whispered.

They stopped their arguing and stared as Bryan Wyatt walked past the car, his movements stiff, automatic. He looked like some movie clone, some android, Aaron realized with a sinking sensation. Bryan's eyes stared straight ahead as if he didn't see Heather's old Bobcat and didn't care. He kept wiping his hands against the sides of the trench coat he wore, wiping and wiping as if there was dirt he couldn't get out.

"Spaced out," Heather whispered. "Hey, he's definitely dorked on something."

"Hey, what's he on? Some good dope?" Dustin laughed nervously. His hair looked very white, but shadows had fallen along his jawline, giving him a stark yet oddly familiar look, like someone else Aaron knew.

And then Aaron saw the resemblance, and an eerie, sickening twist spiraled up through his stomach into his throat. How could that be? Something was very, very weird.

Because he knew who Dustin looked like.

Dustin looked like Bryan Wyatt.

And there went Bryan now, dork-walking along the sidewalk like someone had just given him a lobotomy, still rubbing his hands along his coat like they were all covered in something very, very dirty.

His mom, in Bryan's house.

That freezer box by the curb.

Why would a man who lived alone and never cooked need *two* freezers? Unless he wanted to put something big in them? Something weird and horrible and . . . and dead.

All the oxygen seemed to leave Aaron's throat. He opened his mouth to take in another breath, but the air he pulled in didn't seem to have any substance.

"My mom," he said, realizing that the unease he'd felt all night had had to do with her, and Bryan, and ugliness, and evil . . . God, his mom!

"My mom's in Bryan's house . . . oh, God!" And suddenly he was crying, clutching at Dustin's arm and pulling at his sleeve and crying some more, yanking at him with urgency.

"We gotta go in there, Dust! We gotta! It's my mom! My mom! She's in there!"

CRASH!

Splinters flew as the massive paddle pulverized the corner of the wood tabletop. A tiny needle of wood stabbed the skin of Cici's cheek. She jerked away, her heart pounding so fast that she wondered if she was going to have a heart attack.

She tried to still her panic, tried to think. She was trapped here under the table—at his mercy. Just where he wanted her, of course. He got off on terrorizing women, sucking up their fright and horror. But she felt sure that within seconds, he would tire of the game and drag her out.

Yet the space under the tabletop was still relatively safe and she couldn't bring herself to leave it, not until she saw an opening, a space to run through. Otherwise she'd be a rat racing out of one trap into another.

How many blows of that huge paddle—God's Hammer—would it take to kill her? If he got in a good solid blow, only one.

CRASH! SMACK! She would see Pickard's shoes move first toward her, then away, his feet flexing under the force of the blows he repeatedly delivered. Didn't the effort tire him out?

Repeated blows, all of them punctuated by the Basher's heavy orgasmic breathing and words growled low in his throat.

She couldn't hear what the words were . . . something about God, and worshiping, and hellfire.

She felt her skin crawl.

God. Hellfire. Damnation. All the stuff in the diary— psychotic religious stuff, the exact same religiosity spouted by Junie. But how could that be? This was her neighbor, John Pickard. It was almost as if . . .

Then as she crept close to the wall to huddle out of the way of the Basher's blows, Cici felt the hair on her skin rise.

A good side and a bad side.

The black and the white, the good and the evil. Both Junie and Ed were like that.

Junie and Ed . . .

Ed . . .

John Pickard. Who she once noticed had an eerie physical resemblance to Bryan, and whose son, Dustin, also looked some- what like Bryan. The same blondness and square-jawed good looks!

What if Pickard wasn't his real name at all?

What if his real name was Ed Wykotsky?

The beard in the album photographs, the Jehovah beard, could have been shaved off. Add twenty years and more weight to the man's frame, let him gradually become 1990s hip . . . Hysteria grabbed her and for a second she felt her emotional defenses crumble, her thoughts fly apart into disordered, terri- fied fragments.

Oh, yes! Horribly, so horribly, it all fit. Ed Wykotsky had been the woodworker, the womanizer, the violent man who pleasured in beating women to death. Ed did kill Junie, forcing his son, Bryan, to help him, making him an accessory in the murder. Then he forced the fourteen-year-old boy to move with him to Detroit, where he later changed his name and appear- ance, becoming John Pickard. He took a job as a wood model- maker at G.M.

Later, when Bryan went to the University of Michigan and

entered the adult world, Pickard remarried a woman with children, had a son of his own, Dustin . . . and continued to kill.

Oh, God, was Pickard's ex-wife one of the bodies in the freezers?

But always there was Bryan, a young man ruined by his repressive, severe upbringing, still in thrall to his father, believing that Ed was "stronger than God." Secretly living in the same subdivision, within phone contact of Ed, at his father's beck and call.

God is strong, but HE is even stronger, Bryan had sobbed.

All of Ann's speculations had been right. Bryan *was* a rigid, wooden type who harbored a lot of anger, a man who believed himself guilty of murdering his mother. When religion was used as a club, how easy to force him to store away the bodies in his big, empty house, or even help transport them.

Or occasionally participate in killing them?

Cici felt a sudden, hot wave of nausea.

The Basher had taken several steps backward, the blows temporarily pausing. Suddenly she heard a wrenching sound. Metal scraping violently against wood.

She stiffened, rigid with terror. He was pulling away the hinges that held the table slab to the wall! Within seconds, she would be exposed like a trapped rat, open and vulnerable to the terrible paddle.

NINETEEN

*N*o, *dammit!* Cici thought grimly. *He's not going to kill me. I won't let him. I don't care how big he is, how horrible . . . I'm going to stay alive.*

Her eyes darted, searching for a way to delay the moment when the Basher's massive hardwood club would crash down on her skull. The iron bank, shaped like a grinning monkey, lay on the floor several feet away in a scatter of spilled bolts.

Could she throw it at him? Then run past him, somehow get to the door and run out?

But instantaneously her mind rejected the idea. He was blocking her exit. He was a big man pumped up on adrenaline and the club gave him a three-foot-longer reach. Besides, she had crouched under the table so long that her legs were cramping—what if she stumbled?

Unless . . .

She remembered the fuse box above the table only feet away. Could she race that far, madly dashing? If she could just get *on* the table. When Bryan had pushed her down the stairs, he'd been above her, the position one of power and domination. She'd been at a tremendous disadvantage. Couldn't she turn that against the Basher? *On top* of the table she'd be at an awkward angle for the blows, might be able to dodge them, and certainly would be able to kick and throw objects down from the shelf above.

And there was also the fuse box. If she could douse the lights in the room, they'd both be blind and she'd have even more of an advantage.

"Aaaah," cried the Basher gutturally, wrenching at the tabletop. "BITCH! CUNT! GOD PUNISHES . . ."

God has nothing to do with you, bastard, Cici thought, waiting tensely. He had to set himself off balance. This would happen when he actually lifted the tabletop away. There was no way he could both move that heavy piece of wood laminate and maintain the club in killing position. She could gain a few seconds.

She waited. She could feel his anxiety growing. Did he sense it, too, that one moment of vulnerability that would give her a fighting chance?

Then it happened. The table was lifted away from her with both the Basher's hands on it, giving her a few seconds' chance. Cici felt an instant's horrified, panicky exposure before throwing herself out from under. Thank God for her aerobics. She couldn't believe the desperate strength in her legs as she sprinted for the other hobby table.

Three running steps.

A near-disastrous skid on the slippery, scattered bolts.

She threw herself toward the table, but her jump was too short, and she hit the table edge with her stomach, the blow jabbing into her solar plexus with punishing force.

She shrieked with pain and terror and scrambled desperately upward.

With a heave of muscles and wrenches of pain in places she hadn't known could feel pain, she was on the table. She sprang from a crouch to her feet. A wild, atavistic triumph filled her and she almost yelled out. She could look down on him now! She had some power!

He'd ripped off the panty-hose mask, revealing a face reddened and contorted, lips drawn back, eyes rolling with a wild, righteous fervor like a TV preacher's. But it was definitely John Pickard, his dyed yellow hair shining in the light.

"AAAAH!" he yelled, readying for another swing.

"No! No way!" she yelled back. She watched him bring Fury's Hammer back like a golf club, readying it for the powerful swing. A swing, she knew, had a set trajectory and usually ended with some kind of follow-through. But there could be no follow-through here because the paddle would land flat on the tabletop . . . or on her.

"AAAHGH! GOD!" With a shout he swung.

Cici jumped away before he could topple her. Her balance, honed not only by aerobics but by years of childhood ballet and acrobatics, was superb. She felt another boost of that wild adrenaline, an odd kind of joy.

"You're not going to kill me!" she screamed, dancing above him. Her hand touched the fuse box and she whirled and yanked its cover open.

Two rows of black levers controlled the lighting in the entire house—but she had no idea which was for the basement and didn't have time to find out. She simply used both palms and snapped each row in the opposite direction.

Instantly the lights doused.

A smothering darkness dropped across the hobby room.

The kids saw the lights go out in the house.

One second the house was lit by two or three lights, a typical suburban dwelling similar to all the others in the neighborhood. Then—blackness.

"Man," Aaron muttered, pulling in his breath. Eerie! Especially when they'd seen Bryan Wyatt walk past them, disappearing into heavy shadows at the intersection, a fleeing, guilty figure. What had he done in that house? The way he kept turning to look behind him, as if someone might be pursuing him. Or *something* . . .

Aaron's anxiety had grown so quickly that it seemed a solid mass stuck in his throat, choking off his breathing.

Dumb! he thought angrily.

He was so incredibly, incredibly dumb! He'd lain in his room, listening to his stereo and sleeping a little, while his mother was out walking in the dark, in the damn, fucking wet *rain,* and he knew deep in his soul what kind of jerk Bryan Wyatt was, he'd known from the beginning, and he still let her go off into the night.

"She's inside," Aaron insisted urgently, yanking at Dustin's arm. "She's in there! He's a jerk, a jerk! What if he hurt her? Dustin . . . Hey, man, we got to go up to the door and find her. Dustin—Dust!"

Dustin was turning his face from side to side, nostrils flaring uneasily, as if he sensed something the rest of them hadn't perceived yet. "I don't know, man."

"I've gotta. I've gotta go see."

Aaron didn't have time to argue. He simply crawled across Kevin, pushed open the car door, and jumped out.

He ran up the walk, taking the front steps in one jump.

"Aaron, Aar . . . hey, wait up." Turning, he saw that Dustin was behind him. And Heather, too, her black jacket almost making her disappear in the darkness except for the sweet paleness of her face and the whites of her eyes.

They reached the front door with its beautiful, Victorian etched-glass pane, now inexplicably shattered. Aaron skidded to a stop, unsure what to do next. But if the lights had gone *out,* and Bryan Wyatt wasn't even *in* the house . . .

His mother *was* in the house. It had to mean something terrible.

"We've got to go in," he gasped.

"Hey," Dustin began.

"We can't," Heather said, her voice high and scared. "Aaron, this is wrong, we can't—"

Then they heard it, coming from inside the house, faint but high-pitched, angry and desperate.

Cici's scream.

"Aar!" Dustin's face was white, pinched looking. "Aar! Who is that? Is that your mother?"

"Yes, dammit!"

Aaron yanked open the door, which Bryan had left un-locked. Bits of glass shook loose and fell inside the house, and the screaming became louder, unmistakably his mother's voice.

"Go on," Aaron snapped, giving Heather a push. "Go on—take the car. Go and call the police, okay?"

"The—"

"Go on, go call them, it's nine-one-one, Heather, dial nine-one-one!"

Sobbing, she broke away and ran back to the car, where Matt and Kevin were still seated inside, bewildered, staring out the windows.

Aaron ran inside the house. "Come on, come on, come on, come on," he repeated, his voice squeaking high.

He heard his friend behind him as he rushed into the dark living room. Pitch black, scary black, ten times blacker than the worst nightmare Aaron had ever had.

"Mom!" Aaron shouted hoarsely. "Mom!"

A pounding crash answered him, sounding far away, like a battle going on in a distant room.

"Mom!" Aaron screamed, trying to orient himself in the dark pool of blackness that saturated the house.

"I can't see, I can't see, I can't see," Dustin yelled behind him. "I'm gonna trip!"

"You won't trip. Come on, Dust!" Aaron called.

But Dustin was right. Hardly any light came from outside. Furniture created large, dark blobs, and there was a glitter of light reflecting off some shiny metal surface. Aaron had only been in Bryan's house twice, and he'd hated it, hadn't looked around much. Shit! They might as well be blindfolded.

There were more crashes—muffled, as if from a distance. Another scream.

A male shout.

"Shit, shit!" Aaron cried as they struggled through the room. Behind him he heard Dustin swear. Something fell on the floor in a tinkle of broken glass. Maybe one of the dumb clocks that Bryan had not let him touch.

Aaron crashed into something else, another table, then a

wall. He was crying as he ran his hand wildly up and down the smooth plaster, searching for a light switch.

He found one. But when he frantically flicked it, nothing happened. The electricity was out.

Dammit, dammit, dammit! The screams were getting louder, and the crashes sounded terrible. Now he could tell they were coming from beneath his feet—from the basement hobby room, that big room where Bryan had all his worktables.

But where were the basement stairs?

He charged in the direction of what he thought was the kitchen and something solid came up to hit him in the face, knocking him backward with the force of a car hitting him.

Another wall, slamming him in the face. A stabbing, incredible pain knifed all the way up his nose into his head. Then a wave of nausea bent him double.

Struggling with it, he heard Dustin behind him, moaning in pain, too. "Aar, I fell. I fell back there, I twisted my ankle. I twisted it good, maybe broke it."

"Then wait here," Aaron snapped, swallowing bile and blood and starting toward the kitchen.

The darkness was as smothering as roof pitch, and just as thick.

"BITCH! CUNT!" screamed the Basher, lunging forward.

From her position on the table Cici twisted behind her, groping upward with both hands to the four-foot-long wooden shelf that hung over the table, positioned on metal brackets. It was, she knew, laden with rows of clocks, more banks, ships in jars—antique junk Bryan had collected or was fixing. She yanked at the shelf, pulling it away.

Objects fell wildly, scattering to the tabletop, something hitting Cici's left foot with a sharp jab of agony.

"YOU FUCKING CUNT!" screamed her attacker, in surprise and pain. Evidently something had hit him, too.

But Cici already had the shelf board gripped in both frantic hands. It was too thick and wide to be swung easily over her shoulder like a golf club, but by gripping hard and bracing her feet she could move it side to side. It was big, heavy, and would more than do the job.

She readied it, lips pulled back from her teeth, breath pulling dryly through her throat.

The damned dark. So black, like the inside of death. Where was he? How would she know when to swing, what part of him would she hit? She realized she could not mess around with this. She might get only one chance, and if she missed he could snatch the board away from her, even use it against her. Then she would be worse off than before, because he'd surely kill her, and fast.

"Come on, come on, come on," she heard herself cry, taunting him. *"Come on, Ed . . . Ed Wykotsky!"*

"GODLESS BITCH!"

"Come on!" she screamed again, bracing, readying herself. Her hands were slippery with sweat and terror. *"Come on, Basher! Hit me! Go ahead, hit me like you hit Ann!"*

The long shelf board swung hard, awkwardly, the end wobbling. Cici despaired, thinking she'd missed, and then there was the muffled impact of wood hitting something giving, like flesh.

There was a deep, gut grunt. The board sank deep into that softness.

She'd hit him! God! She'd hit him bad!

"Oh!" Cici screamed and pushed the board again, shoving the end outward as hard as she could. Into him again!

The effort wrenched her back agonizingly. She was rewarded by the sound of another painful grunt. Then a clatter. Had he dropped the Hammer? Had she hurt him? The damned darkness made it impossible to see!

But at least she'd thrown him off balance and maybe hurt him badly, and there wasn't time to fuss. This was her chance. Still clutching the board, she jumped down from the table. To jump off in the dark was terrifying, and she landed awkwardly, the impact stinging upward through the balls of her feet.

She swung the board again in another wild, wobbling arc, but it didn't hit anything, just went around emptily, and then she dropped it and staggered across the hobby room, racing blindly for the door.

The door . . . an impossible goal. The darkness of the basement was like heavy funeral cloth, choking, smothering, total. Darkness . . . nearly gagging her with its thickness. Behind her the Basher cried out his rage, not dead, maybe not even badly hurt, floundering around just as she was, trying to find her and kill her.

Two terrified people battling in the dark. One of them huge, male, and insane.

Cici ran two frantic steps before her right shoe skidded on the scattered bolts. She crashed down, landing flat on her stomach on top of something hard. One of the damned banks. Its bulk was like a rabbit punch to her solar plexus, knocking out all her air.

She lay there downed and gasping. She couldn't move, couldn't breathe. Was this it? Was this the end? And then he was on her, a wide, sweating body that somehow covered all of her, crushing her beneath its weight, and she knew she was going to die.

As she felt the hands close around her throat, Cici managed one last, frantic scream.

The high-pitched scream electrified the air.

"Mom, Mom, Mom!" Aaron shrieked.

He no longer felt the pain in his nose or even remembered hitting it at all. He careened through the kitchen, slamming against walls and counters toward the basement stairs that he remembered were off the pantry area. Or maybe the shouts were only in his head. He was crying again, sobbing with rage and fear.

He'd already forgotten about Dustin, crumpled somewhere in the dining room clutching at his ankle.

He yelled, *"Mom, I'm coming, I'm coming!"*

Somehow he had reached the pantry area. Something brushed his hand as he went past—a broom or mop handle. He grabbed it as he went by. From the clacking metallic sound it made he guessed it was one of those sponge mops with the water-squeezer device at the end. Yeah, he'd used one of those at home on the kitchen floor; he knew how it worked. It had a hard, cutting edge.

He raced into the ink-black stairwell, which was like throwing himself off a dark cliff. Dragging the mop behind him, letting it clatter on the steps, he leaped down the stairs. God—like killing himself, rushing into black.

He was flung forward by momentum, stumbling downward, trapped on some death-defying ride at Cedar Point, totally out of control. But suddenly he was on flat floor again, and he knew where he was. In the little hallway area that opened to the furnace room and the big hobby room.

Pitch black.

Which door was which? Where was he? The blackness made him dizzy.

"Mom!" he shouted in despair.

A choked, gagging scream came from his left. Suddenly the whole layout seemed to click into place in his brain, and he remembered coming down here before, old Bryan bitching at him for touching the clocks, the room with its row of cupboard doors on one side, the other side lined with worktables.

He lifted the scrubber mop and pushed it ahead of him like a long blind-man's cane, stepping into the room.

"Mom!" he yelled into the impenetrable black. *"Scream again so I'll know where you are."*

Blackness and an incredible pressure around her neck.

She lay splayed on her stomach, her fingers clutching desperately at the strangling hands around her neck, trying to dig at the thick fingers, pry them away. If she could just bend one back—but the fingers were thickened from years of hard physical labor and would not bend.

Already her mind seemed to segue in and out of balls of white, exploding light. His hands were too strong to pry away and she didn't have any air left in her struggling lungs.

This was death, wasn't it? A horrible, sucking struggle to breathe.

Elbow, a little voice said in her brain, and she made the

colossal effort to let go of his hands and bring back her elbow. She smashed it upward and backward as hard as she could.

A smash! Hitting something with a sinewy feel to it! His throat? God! She hoped it was his throat. She wanted the Adam's apple. Darkness and lights exploding in her head, she smashed him again.

And suddenly there was air. He let go, and she might have heard him crying out something; her ears didn't seem to work properly. Cici gasped in a huge gulp of air, bucking upward like someone in a seizure.

She could smell his fear and fury, his stink. She felt him scrabble on the floor beside her and knew what he was searching for—Fury's Hammer again, the club. If he found it, he'd batter her to death in seconds.

"Mom! Mom! Mom!" Dimly she realized that Aaron was screaming something, had been yelling for several seconds.

Aaron was here in the basement, and when the Basher finished killing her, he would murder her boy, too, her innocent, loving fourteen-year-old. They'd both be on the eleven o'clock news, victims whose story was depicted on TV.

Cici could feel hatred bloom in the interstices of her brain as she heard something swing through the air with a metallic sound to it. Aaron had something—was swinging it. But it wasn't any match for the Basher's weapon—a matchstick to the paddle called God's Hammer.

She had to prevent the Basher from getting to the Hammer.

She began kicking, forcing all her life energy into the kicks, nearly wrenching her legs out of their sockets. Her kicks landed on the hard-softness of another human body. Knees, testicles, belly . . . She drew upon an inner craziness she discovered in herself, a force in her that had nothing to do with love, or honor, or goodness.

A force that simply wanted to *kill*, and would kill, because if she failed, *she* would be dead and there wouldn't be any more anything, and right now she wanted to live more than she had ever believed she could want anything.

"Mom! Mom!" screamed Aaron.

Cici didn't hear. She used her toes as weapons, didn't care anymore, really wanted to kill and maim and destroy.

She didn't hear the sirens until there were voices, too—the voices of police officers breaking into the basement.

EPILOGUE

The hospital waiting room was crowded with teenagers and their parents, following a multiple-car pileup on Opdyke Road. Policemen stationed outside the door were keeping back the crowds of TV cameramen and newspaper reporters, who were in a frenzy of excitement because the Basher had been caught.

Aaron sat huddled near Cici, waiting his turn to have his nose set. By the looks of the crowd ahead of them, it was going to be a while.

"Hold on," Cici said, patting her son's hand. "It shouldn't be much longer now."

Aaron looked like the victim of a street fight, his nose crooked, blue and yellow streaks already blossoming under both his eyes. Cici knew she herself didn't look much better. It was the first black eye she'd ever had.

"Aar . . . you were wonderful. Coming down there with that mop—without you we wouldn't have made it, son."

"Without you, you mean." Aaron gazed at her with the incredulous look of a child who discovers that his parent is a hero. "I can't believe you, Mom . . . you really beat him up. You knocked the tar out of him. You turned him to jelly."

"But not so jellylike that he can't go to prison for a very, very long time," she said hoarsely. "And Bryan, too . . . for years and years."

Her relief that she had not killed the Basher was profound. No one, not the police, or Aaron, or any other friend, would ever know the brief insanity she'd had to force upon herself in order to survive.

For a few minutes she'd been every bit as crazy as the Basher, and she knew it, and would always have to live with that incredible knowledge.

"It's so weird," her son went on. "Dustin's father. Dustin's father was the Basher!"

"Ed Wykotsky," she said. "His name was really Ed Wykotsky. But there were two Bashers, son."

"Two?"

"Bryan, also. The killing was . . . a part of both. They both had the same psychosis, Aar. They shared it. Maybe sometime you'll know what I mean."

Cici swallowed, her throat still painful from the crushing fingers. There was so much more. In a while she would tell it all to Detective Oleson—tell him about Ed and Junie Wykotsky, the diary, Fury's Hammer. The little boy who had been beaten and changed and emotionally flattened, who had been forced to fit into his father's evil.

But it could wait now. The violence had already begun to fade in her mind. Merciful amnesia, a montage of receding pain. She had tried to kill, had gone into her own insanity, temporary but in a way, briefly, like theirs. She would dream about it for months.

A man was looking at her from across the room—one of the teenagers' fathers. Cici averted her eyes. Someday she knew she'd find someone again . . . someone who could be her best friend as well as her lover and husband. But that would not be for a long time.

"Aaron Davis," called out a nurse who had come into the waiting room.

"That's you, Aar." She nudged her son.

"I'm going in by myself. You don't have to come in, Mom," he said, standing up. He started across the waiting room toward the door the nurse held open, a good-looking and clean-cut boy whose face already showed new lines of pride. He had risked his life to try to save her, had injured his nose on her behalf, and had not once complained of pain. He would grow up fine now, she felt. Somehow, they would settle the affair of the burned garage. And get help for Dustin. Aaron would become a good and fine man.

Cici felt a rush of love so surging and strong that it brought tears to her eyes.

I love you, Aar, she said silently as her son went to have his nose set.